Liberated Ladies

Unconventional heiresses...full of big ambitions!

Friends Verity, Jane, Prue, Melissa and Lucy are unconventional ladies with scandalous yearnings and big ambitions—to be writers, painters, musicians—but the only safe sanctuary to exercise their talents is in one of their family's turrets!

They have no wish to conform and be drawn into society's marriage mart, unless they can find gentlemen who value and cherish them for who they truly are...and *not* the size of their dowries!

Read about Verity's story in
Least Likely to Marry a Duke

Jane's tale in
The Earl's Marriage Bargain

Prue's journey in
A Marquis in Want of a Wife

Lucy's romance in
The Earl's Reluctant Proposal

All available now

And look for Melissa's story

Coming soon

Author Note

Lucy, the fourth of my Liberated Ladies, was more than happy to stay single. But then her music was snatched from her and, it seemed, so was all the joy and magic in life. I wondered how she was ever going to get it back, but then Max arrived—too perfect, too cold, too aristocratic for her—and he knew how.

Reluctantly, it seemed, Max found himself giving Lucy the magic back and, in the process, shattering the ice that had imprisoned him for years. What happened then surprised them both...

I hope you enjoy following Lucy and Max's journey together as much as I did writing it.

LOUISE ALLEN

The Earl's
Reluctant Proposal

HARLEQUIN
HISTORICAL

HARLEQUIN®
HISTORICAL™

Recycling programs
for this product may
not exist in your area.

ISBN-13: 978-1-335-50605-4

The Earl's Reluctant Proposal

Copyright © 2021 by Melanie Hilton

This edition published by arrangement with Harlequin Books S.A.

For questions and comments about the quality of this book,
please contact us at CustomerService@Harlequin.com.

Harlequin Enterprises ULC
22 Adelaide St. West, 40th Floor
Toronto, Ontario M5H 4E3, Canada
www.Harlequin.com

Printed in U.S.A.

Louise Allen has been immersing herself in history for as long as she can remember, finding that landscapes and places evoke powerful images of the past. Venice, Burgundy and the Greek islands are favorites. Louise lives on the Norfolk coast and spends her spare time gardening, researching family history or traveling. Please visit Louise's website, www.louiseallenregency.com, her blog, www.janeaustenslondon.com, or find her on Twitter @louiseregency and on Facebook.

Books by Louise Allen

Harlequin Historical

Marrying His Cinderella Countess
The Earl's Practical Marriage
A Lady in Need of an Heir
Convenient Christmas Brides
"The Viscount's Yuletide Betrothal"
Contracted as His Countess

Liberated Ladies

Least Likely to Marry a Duke
The Earl's Marriage Bargain
A Marquis in Want of a Wife
The Earl's Reluctant Proposal

Lords of Disgrace

His Housekeeper's Christmas Wish
His Christmas Countess
The Many Sins of Cris de Feaux
The Unexpected Marriage of Gabriel Stone

Visit the Author Profile page
at Harlequin.com for more titles.

For the Quayistas for restoring
lockdown sanity via Zoom.

Chapter One

July 19th, 1815—London

*T*hump.

Lucy woke with the scream lodged in her throat, yet, when she looked down at her hands cradled defensively against her chest, there was no pain, no blood. A dream? But the sound had been real, she realised when it came again. This time she recognised it for what it was: a fist hitting the door panels, not a keyboard cover slamming down on her unwary fingers.

She scrambled off the sofa, confused and oddly dizzy. Where was she? It came back as she stumbled to the door, turned the key. Lady Sophia's piano lesson... That was what she was here for, she recalled as the door opened and she backed unsteadily away.

'Sophia, what the devil do you think you're about, locking yourself in here for half the day?' The speaker stopped dead, three strides into the room. 'Who are you and where is my sister?'

'Lucy Lambert and I do not know.' Lucy sat down

with an inelegant bump on the sofa and stared at the man. *What is wrong with me?*

'She said, um… She said she had received an urgent message to go to her old governess. She said she would return in two or three hours and that I should make myself comfortable, take refreshments, read a book. It was ten o'clock when she left.'

The clock on the mantelshelf chimed four thin notes. 'But that's impossible.' Lucy blinked it into focus and as she did so the louder, deeper, strokes of the hall clock echoed the time. 'We spoke for a moment or two. Lady Sophia was in great haste, but she pointed out the refreshments on the table and showed me the bookcase for entertainment. Then she left. That way.' She pointed to the second door. 'I was thirsty, so I drank a glass of lemonade and sat down to go over my notes for the lesson and… That is all I recall.'

The man stooped and picked up something from the carpet. 'Yours?'

'Yes.' She reached out and took the little notebook, her thoughts coming into focus as her vision cleared. 'The lemonade. That is why I feel so strange. She drugged me.' Then, indignant as it sank in, '*Drugged* me!'

The man went to the table, picked up her glass, sniffed it, then poured some liquid from the jug and sipped. 'You drank this?'

'It wasn't very nice.' Rather bitter, she remembered. 'But I was thirsty. It is hot outside. I did not like to ring and disturb the staff.'

'Who are you?'

Lucy could guess who *he* was because she had looked up Lady Sophia Harker in the *Peerage* before accepting the invitation to come to her home. Single women with any sense did not enter the private homes of complete strangers, not without taking some basic precautions. Lady Sophia Harker lived in Cavendish Square with her stepbrother, Lord Burnham, the son of her mother's second husband.

'Miss Lambert, music teacher.' She produced one of her newly printed cards from her reticule. 'My lord,' she added as an afterthought.

He took it, and Lucy got the better of her indignation, nagging headache and confusion and looked at him properly for the first time. Max Fenton was what her friend Melissa—never bashful—would describe as a fine example of his sex, she supposed. Not a massive specimen thankfully, because being of only medium height herself she disliked being loomed over. Even so, he had more than enough presence to fill the room and was possessed of an aura of chilly authority that, as he was clearly displeased, was uncomfortable.

Another friend, Jane, Lady Kendall, who was an artist, might not want to draw him, Lucy decided. He was too predictable—tidily just under six foot, she guessed. Lean and fit, but not overly muscular. Regular features—strong, straight nose, firm jaw, dark grey eyes and modishly cut light brown hair that looked as though it might bleach blonder if exposed to the sun.

Thirty, possibly. No scars, freckles, imperfections and just the hint of a dip in his chin that he would no doubt hate to have called a dimple. Yes, Jane would dismiss him as not interesting enough to be a challenge for a portraitist.

'Will you be able to describe me adequately later,

do you think?' he enquired, and Lucy realised she had been staring.

'Yes, I think so. When confronted by an angry male it is always prudent to be able to describe him afterwards to the authorities,' she said and had the satisfaction of seeing him blink.

Mousy, skinny, brown-haired music teachers did not normally bite back when sneered at by earls, but recently Lucy had found her teeth and something that was not so much courage as a sense of frustrated irritation with the ways of the world. It was, she had discovered, a perfectly good substitute for bravery.

'You think I might become violent?' He spoke as he walked away from her to throw open the other door, the one his stepsister had left by.

'I have no way of telling, my lord. You appear to be labouring under a strong emotion and I have noted that some gentlemen, in the absence of the real cause of their anger, will lash out at whoever is nearest. Verbally or otherwise.'

He opened the door, looked through, sighed, closed it again and walked back. 'I do not *lash out* at women, children, servants or animals, Miss Lambert. You are quite safe.'

However, you, My Lordship, are very much on edge, despite your veneer of calm.

'Excellent. I am much reassured that all those you consider your inferiors are safe from your ire.' She stood up and looked around for her bonnet. 'In that case, if you will be so good as to pay me, I will be on my way.'

'Pay you? For what?' Lord Burnham enquired. His eyebrows had drawn together into a straight line that echoed the lips that had tightened when she had answered back.

'For the waste of a day. I was engaged to give Lady Sophia a morning's lesson in the pianoforte, not to be drugged and rendered unconscious for the best part of six hours. In addition to which I will have the expense of a hackney to return home from this wasted journey. I certainly have no intention of walking, not after this experience.'

'How much are you owed?'

Lucy did a rapid calculation, added in the cab fare, a weighting for the effects of the lemonade and five shillings for aggravation by the earl and told him the result.

The eyebrows did not relax, the vertical line between them growing a little deeper.

'The labourer is worthy of her hire, my lord.'

'Of course. But before I do pay you and you leave, Miss Lambert, tell me exactly what happened today. My sister, you see, does not have a governess, retired or otherwise, closer than Northumberland.'

That explained his grim expression, at least. 'You think she has eloped?'

'I *think* I would like to know what happened.' She was not quite certain, but she thought he grew tenser at her suggestion.

This was definitely a man used to getting his own way without an argument. 'I was recommended to Lady Sophia by a friend of mine, the Duchess of Aylsham.'

There, that's given you pause, my lord.

Lucy did not give him time to express any doubts about a duchess being the friend of a spinster who earned her living as a humble music teacher. 'Lady Sophia wrote to me expressing an interest in learning the pianoforte and engaged me to come and give her a preliminary lesson for two hours this morning. You appear surprised, my lord.'

'Exceedingly. Sophia has been proficient on the pianoforte and the harp since childhood.'

'She implied she was a complete beginner which, I must admit, struck me as unusual for a young lady of her background. I suppose I thought she had struggled with it as a child.'

Lied to and *drugged. I would like a word with you, my lady.*

Lucy refrained from saying what she felt and continued to report as concisely as possible. The man had some excuse for both anger and concern, she could understand that.

'I arrived as requested at half past nine and Lady Sophia told the butler that she did not wish us to be disturbed. But that cannot be right—if he was expecting me to be teaching her to play, why was he not concerned when there was no music and no one emerged for hours?'

'Because when I came in just now he informed me that my stepsister was engaged all day with a teacher of French and that as she found the language so difficult—another untruth, I regret to say—she needed to immerse herself without distraction. Hence the refreshments to cover luncheon. As this is her sitting room and that door leads to her dressing room and bedchamber, there would be no need for either of you to emerge to use the…facilities.'

'And there is a back stair to the ground floor, I suppose?' Lady Sophia appeared to be an excellent strategist as well as an accomplished liar.

'A branch of the servants' stairs, yes.' The Earl had the air of a man concentrating on not grinding his teeth. 'You arrived. Then what happened?'

'I was shown in, but Lady Sophia immediately put on her bonnet—I had not even untied the ribbons of mine—and said, in an agitated manner, that she had received an urgent message and that she must go to her frail governess, but would return in a while. She begged me to stay so that we could begin her lesson when she returned, promised to pay me extra for my trouble and pointed out the refreshments. She also locked the door and left the key so that I would feel secure, being in a strange house, so she said. Then she rushed out that way.'

The headache was clearing now and she could remember more. 'It was peculiar, now I reflect upon it. She appeared animated, but not upset. More excited, I would say.'

'I have no doubt of that.' At least Lord Burnham no longer sounded as though she was a dishonest housemaid about to be sacked for stealing the silver. He was clearly more exasperated with his stepsister than with her.

'So it *is* an elopement?'

To her surprise Lord Burnham stopped pacing and sat down opposite her. 'Not yet,' he said cryptically. 'Or so I hope.' He raked his fingers through his hair, looking considerably more human. 'You say you are a friend of Aylsham's wife?'

'We have been friends for years, since before Verity married Will.' She ignored the way his expression changed when she used their first names. Lucy reminded herself that antagonising members of the aristocracy was not the way to begin a successful career teaching their families. 'I choose to make my own living, but that does not make me unfit for polite society,' she added mildly.

'No, it does not,' Lord Burnham said slowly. Those cold grey eyes were surveying her much as he might have sized up a horse he was being offered for sale, one he suspected of being unsound in some way he could not quite detect. 'But have you the gowns for it?'

Lucy knew she was gaping and closed her mouth with a snap. 'What has my wardrobe to do with anything, my lord?'

'Humour me, Miss Lambert.'

He did not *appear* to be completely deranged. Lucy decided to indulge him. 'My wardrobe is adequate for dining with a duke, attending a garden party or dancing in select company, yes.' She did not add that it had been considerably boosted by gifts from her married friends discarding their pre-wedding gowns for outfits more suitable to married ladies of rank.

'Mmm.' The Earl, elbows on the arms of his chair, steepled his fingers and began thoughtfully tapping them against his lips. Lucy waited patiently for him to finish whatever the thought was. 'You say Sophia left almost immediately after you arrived, before you had the chance to remove your bonnet. Had you raised your veil?'

Lucy eyed the door, rapidly revising her assessment of Lord Burnham's mental stability. It was closed, but not locked. If she scooped up reticule and bonnet and ran—

'Well? Had you?'

She walked her fingers along the sofa to her right,

hooked the cord of her reticule and began to pull. It
hurt, but she was becoming used to the strain on the
injured tendons now. The cord slid over her wrist and
she stretched to pick up the bonnet as though prompted
by his question. 'The veil?' She folded it back. 'Let me
think. I was just lifting it, then I let it drop, I think—she
took me by surprise—and then she had gone.'

'In that case,' said Lord Burnham, 'what would you
charge for an entire week?'

'An entire week of what?' Lucy relaxed a little.
'Music lessons?'

'Your time, Miss Lambert. I wish to hire you for a
week to attend a house party.'

'You… You *libertine*.' She found she was on her
feet and halfway to the door. No, not deranged at all,
merely a rake. Poor Lady Sophia, having to live with
a stepbrother like this!

'Really, Miss Lambert, I am asking to pay for your
time and your assistance, not your bod—your *person*.'
He was on his feet, too. 'Hear me out.'

The old Lucy, before her injury, would either have
hardly noticed an improper suggestion or would have
been cast into confusion at having to deal with it. She
realised just how much she had changed when she
found herself sliding the long hatpin from her bonnet and holding it beneath the veil as she stopped and
turned back, one step from the door.

'Very well. But I should warn you, Lord Burnham,
that so far I have formed the impression that you are
either a rake or unhinged. Possibly both.'

'*You* would be unhinged if you found yourself responsible for a pretty, well-dowered eighteen-year-old
with as much common sense as a bank vole, the town

bronze of a cloistered nun and a disposition for parties, shopping and romance. Especially *romance*,' he added bitterly.

When she stayed where she was he walked away to the window seat at the far end of the room. 'Please, sit again. Move that small chair to the door, if you must. You can always hit me with it if I become a ravening beast and sticking that hatpin into me does not stop me in my tracks.'

There was nothing wrong with his eyesight, however unstable he might be in either mind or morals. 'I am listening.' Lucy perched on the arm of the sofa, the hatpin still in her hand.

'A little family history may help. My mother died when I was ten and my father remarried late in life, for companionship, I believe. His choice was Amanda Harker, the Earl of Longdale's widow. She had a daughter—Sophia—who was ten years old at that time. I was twenty by then, so the arrival of a stepsister who was a mere child hardly impinged on my life.

'When my father died four years ago I gave my stepmother the full use of all the family homes. I am unmarried, so I had no reason to unseat her and she had her own social circle. Then three years ago she became ill—or fancied herself so. She installed a distant cousin as a chaperon for Sophia and took herself off to Bath where she has fallen under the influence of some quack healer. She alternates between sending Sophia ridiculous tracts on inner healing, inappropriately large sums of money and letters expressing a fervent desire that she marry.'

'And the cousin is an inadequate chaperon?'

'Miss Hathaway is a *romantic*.' His tone might have been appropriate for pronouncing her to be a dead rat.

'Replace her.' It seemed an obvious solution. 'There are any number of single ladies of excellent breeding, firm will and much reduced circumstances who would be delighted with the position.'

'She is employed by my stepmother. I am, as head of the family, Sophia's guardian. I do my best to influence her, protect her, but I can hardly compel her into prudent behaviour by force.'

In the absence of anything more constructive to say than *Oh, dear,* Lucy made encouraging noises.

'Her godmother has invited her to a house party, I refused to provide her either maid or carriage—it appears she has found a way around that and has set out on her own. I encountered Miss Hathaway returning from the pharmacist as I came in.'

'Her godmother is not a suitable hostess for an unmarried girl? That seems… Whereabouts does she live?'

'Staning Waterless in Dorset. Her name is— '

'Ah, it must be Lady Hopewell.'

'You know her?'

'I spent some time in Great Staning, which is ten miles away.' Lucy had grown up near there, to be more accurate, and had left only three weeks ago, just as soon as her hands were healed sufficiently to manage with just the help of a seventeen-year-old maid-of-all-work promoted to personal maid.

Her friends had wanted her to stay with them, of course, but that was too much like running away from home. She had left—on her own terms—although she was not so proud, or so foolish, as to refuse the help of her friends the Duchess of Aylsham, the Countess of Kendall and the Marchioness of Cranford in finding respectable lodgings and making introductions to potential clients. She wanted to make a success of her new life, not have to pocket her pride and go crawling back home a failure.

'I have never met Lady Hopewell,' she added. 'But surely, if all Lady Sophia has done is to run away to her godmother, then it will be a simple matter to go after her and bring her back.'

Her own family was perfectly respectable gentry and they did not mix in aristocratic circles. But she had heard her mother and the other more upright members of the congregation holding forth on the sins of the widow in a way that was decidedly uncharitable, given that she merely appeared to be highly sociable and fond of parties. But obeying the outward rules was what her parents were obsessed with. Apparently, bitchy gossip about the sinful was not covered by the dictates of godly behaviour. Lucy had thought that the frivolous widow had sounded rather fun.

'There is no reason why she should not visit Lady Hopewell, if it were not for the fact that she was so very anxious to do so and that her interest did not seem usual. When I suggested that we accept a different invitation to a house party in Northamptonshire she became so upset that I was suspicious.

'I believe the silly chit fancies herself in love and her urgent desire to attend the house party is driven more by the wish to be with this wretched man than it is by the desire to gratify her godmother.'

'Who is he?' Lucy asked, not expecting to be told.

Lord Burnham did not tell her, although not for the

reason she had been expecting—discretion. 'I have no idea, Miss Lambert. He could be some callow youth or a hardened rake for all I know. All I do know is that one of her more sensible friends was concerned enough to speak to Miss Hathaway about hints that Sophia had dropped. Then Miss Hathaway told me.

'I have nothing to go on other than the belief that a man who an eighteen-year-old girl cannot admit to knowing is no fit suitor. Which, to come to the point, is why, if I cannot keep her away from him and she will not confide in me, I need to find out who he is.'

He paused and Lucy found herself trying to read the expression in grey eyes that seemed all too effective at hiding his thoughts.

'I can arrive at Waterless Manor and expect a warm welcome from Dorothea Hopewell and glares and sulks from Sophia—but she is far too cunning to be easily caught with the object of her affections or be tricked by me into revealing his name. But another young lady should be able to observe unsuspected, discover who he is and inform me.'

'You want me to spy on your stepsister? But that is—'

'In her best interests,' Lord Burnham interrupted impatiently. 'She is innocent, wealthy and impetuous. Do you wish to see her ruined or, at best, making some utterly inappropriate match because you are too nice to watch her?'

'It is not my business to watch her,' Lucy said indignantly. But his words had hit home. Her friend Prudence had fallen for an unscrupulous rake, lost her virginity to him and, as a consequence, had to make a very hasty marriage to another man. The fact that it had turned into a love match was the purest good luck. 'But I do understand your concern...'

'I will pay you five guineas a day for however long this takes. You will travel in comfort and be entertained lavishly. I believe Lady Hopewell has a very fine new pianoforte, one of concert standard.'

And he thinks that is an inducement? It would be torture. Lucy doubted she'd be able to stay in the same room with it.

'I no longer play, my lord. I cannot.'

'How so? You teach.'

She stood up, held out her hands in their thin black kid gloves so he could see the twisted fingers on her left hand, the shortened middle finger on the right. 'I can demonstrate, with discomfort, enough to guide a pupil. I cannot play.'

'What happened?' Lord Burnham got up and moved closer.

'The keyboard lid slammed down and I was not fast enough to move my hands away. It is not something I choose to discuss, my lord.'

Not something she could bear to.

Chapter Two

Max looked at the long-fingered hands. A keyboard cover might fall, but would that be heavy enough to inflict broken bones, to crush a fingertip? *Slammed down*, she said. A person had done this to her, deliberately.

The thought that Miss Lambert was someone who had attracted violence made him uneasy, but on the other hand, if she was a friend of the Duchess of Aylsham—wife of the man known as the Perfect Duke—then he could be certain she had not been at fault.

He could have a word with Aylsham before they left... No, no time for that. He must take the risk. This would not be like last time. This time he would save an innocent, however much she resented it.

Max shrugged. There was no reason to make Miss Lambert any more uncomfortable than she already was by speculating aloud about her injury. 'A great pity,' he said. 'Now, what do you have to say to my proposition?'

'You wish to employ me as a spy?'

'I wish to employ you to assist me in protecting my

stepsister,' Max said. 'I realise that as a single lady you may not be fully aware of the dangers Sophia may encounter if she puts her trust in a man of unsteady character—'

'Yes, I am,' Miss Lambert said without a blush for such a shocking admission.

Really, for such an insignificant drab of a female she was remarkably self-assured. Nothing to look at, of course, which made him decide that, however she had acquired her knowledge of the dangers to young ladies, it was not by personal experience. Libertines had far prettier and richer prey to pick from.

Miss Lambert had soft brown hair, no figure to speak of, nondescript features and brown eyes, possibly her best feature, narrowed now in what looked remarkably like irritation.

Being lured here under false pretences and then drugged would be sufficient reason for anyone to be annoyed, but young ladies were trained from birth to be sweet and accommodating. Something else was adding acid to Miss Lambert's tongue and he wondered suddenly if she was still in pain from her injured fingers.

'Your hands—do they hurt you?'

She raised her eyebrows at the sudden personal question, but answered readily enough. 'Not particularly, until I stretch my fingers or try to grip hard. Or knock them. It has been eight weeks since it happened.'

He watched her as she spoke, but the anger he sensed in her did not appear to be related to the injury. Not directly, at any rate.

It was not that he was particularly interested in the workings of Miss Lambert's mind, but he wanted to be certain that whoever he employed for a task was fit for it. Inefficiency was unacceptable, but it was his responsibility to choose wisely in the first place and the threat to Sophia made his usually iron-hard stomach churn.

'Five guineas a day including today and my expenses?' Miss Lambert said.

'Yes,' Max said, impatient now. He would have paid double that. He knew that if he turned up on Dorothea's doorstep and began to probe into Sophia's behaviour, his infuriating stepsister would become a pattern card of virtue and the man dangling after her would go to ground.

'In that case I would like ten guineas now.' He was not sure what had shown in his expression, but she said, 'I presume you have never had to pay rent in advance to secure your rooms, or worried that you would not have sufficient funds to continue to employ the maid on whom your respectability depends.'

'No,' Max admitted. To be honest, he had never given the finances of the genteelly poor a second thought. 'Here.' He handed over the coins. 'I will collect you at six tomorrow morning from the address on your card. Please bring with you everything appropriate for two weeks.'

There was no point in setting out now. Sophia, the little wretch, had too long a start on him and it occurred to him that stopping her en route would give him no chance of identifying the man involved.

'Thank you, Lord Burnham. I will be ready.' Miss Lambert put the money in her reticule, her bonnet on her head and let herself out of the door before Max had a chance to say anything else.

He had a momentary qualm, almost a feeling of foreboding. This ordinary young woman was unimportant, useful only as a way of protecting Sophia, so why did he feel as though he had started something in motion? He had a sudden mental image of a huge boulder rolling unchecked down a hillside, flattening everything in its path, and gave himself a sharp mental shake. *Nonsense.*

A long and doubtlessly tedious journey down to Dorset is all that lies ahead, he told himself.

He wondered just where his wretched sister had found the money to hire a post chaise, because headstrong she might be, but Sophia liked her comforts. He was not going to find that she had endured hours on the common stage, thank heavens.

The anger that had sustained him for the past half-hour ebbed like a retreating wave and he sat down abruptly, all too aware that underlying his show of irritation at Sophia had been a fear that cut like acid on raw skin.

Julia. Laughing blue eyes closed for ever. Long dark lashes sticking to wet skin as pale as porcelain, the lush black hair she had been so vain about tangled with the foul water that made her sodden shift cling to every revealing curve of her young body...

No.

He was not seventeen and powerless now and he would not let the nightmare have power over him. Besides, the heedless young woman he was anxious for today was as cunning as a basketful of monkeys. He would find his cash box empty, he had no doubt, and her ladyship would have hired a chaise and four and two postilions to see her safely to her godmother. It was once inside that house that she would be in danger.

He, on the other hand, had the prospect of ten hours

with the prickly Miss Lambert. Or perhaps not… Max tugged the bell pull. Time to make preparations for the morning.

Early rising was a matter of habit for Lucy. Mama and Papa considered lounging in bed—which meant staying there a moment beyond six-thirty—virtually a sin, so breakfast had always been at seven-thirty sharp.

Lucy had risen at five, having decided at three o'clock that she would definitely go with Lord Burnham. The money was just too tempting. The prospect of possibly as much as seventy guineas, as well as two weeks with no expenses for her, or for Amy, her maid, would give her a very comfortable reserve to live on until she had established her business on firmer foundations.

At the moment she had a bank account with fifty pounds in it—a legacy from her grandmother—and just over ten pounds split between her reticule and her corsets.

She had left home just as soon as she was sure she could manage to travel to her friends in London and, when her parents had flatly forbidden her departure, she had told them that if they did not pay her legacy and her quarter's allowance, then she would tell the entire parish what had caused her injuries.

'It was an accident!' her father had spluttered. 'And caused by your own outrageous behaviour on the Sabbath.' When she had simply waited, silent, he had narrowed his eyes. 'You can prove nothing.'

'Do you wish to risk the gossip and speculation?' Lucy had asked and had received her money. Then she had been told that she was a disobedient and immoral disgrace, shown the door, and warned never to darken it again.

At least I am not pregnant and it wasn't snowing.

With the help of her friends she now had a very pleasant, though modest, lodging, a wide-eyed maid and a talent that could earn her a living without risking her virtue. At least, she hoped so. Lord Burnham had behaved in a most gentlemanly manner so far. Although that could just be his low cunning, of course. She had no experience of rakes, or of many men either, come to that. Her friend Prue had fallen for a cold-hearted seducer and it was only outstanding good fortune that had saved her from utter disgrace.

She stared critically at her reflection as Amy—much better with a needle than the curling tongs—rather inexpertly twisted up her mistress's hair and pinned it, something she could no longer manage easily herself.

Or it could be that Lord Burnham *was* a libertine, but that plain music teachers were of no interest to handsome, eligible earls. He doubtless had a beautiful mistress who possessed sophisticated erotic skills, whatever they might be, and any number of eager and pretty young ladies hoping for a proposal of marriage: she couldn't be safer.

Lucy and Amy were waiting on the pavement in Little Windmill Street, wrapped up against the cool morning air, when not one, but two sleek black travelling carriages drew up, both with the same crest on the door panels. A groom jumped down and took their modest luggage—a small trunk and two valises between them—and loaded it on to the back of the second carriage as Lord Burnham descended from the first vehicle.

'Good morning, Miss Lambert.' He raised his hat and gestured to the carriage with their luggage. 'I trust you will be comfortable in here. Grenley will look after you and there is a refreshment hamper.'

'Good morning, Lord—'

But he was already getting back into his coach and the groom was standing with the door held open. Lucy climbed in with a tight smile for the man, Amy scrambling behind her. The only other occupant was a young woman in a plain black travelling dress and bonnet sitting with her back to the driver. A maid, she guessed.

'Good morning, miss.' The young woman half rose and bobbed as much of a curtsy as was possible in the space. 'I'm Grenley, miss. Lady Sophia's maid.'

'Miss—' What had Lord Burnham told the maid about her? Had he given her name or not? She feigned a stumble, muttered something and then added more clearly as she sat down, 'This is my maid, A—Pringle.' She remembered just in time that, for the sake of both her own status and Amy's within the household they were visiting, calling a servant by her first name would be considered very bourgeois.

Grenley moved to one side to make room for Amy and then sat silently looking down at her hands.

Naturally shy—or does Lady Sophia insist on her being a meek dogsbody, I wonder?

'You did not travel with Lady Sophia, then?'

'No, miss.' She shifted uncomfortably. 'I packed for her and then I overheard Lord Burnham telling her that she was not to go, so I started to unpack and she said to leave everything because she would make him change his mind. That was the day before yesterday. Yesterday she gave me the whole day off and when I got back she had gone and His Lordship was not best pleased, I can tell you.'

'And Lady Sophia's chaperon? Miss Hemmingway, was it?'

'Hathaway. His Lordship dismissed her and gave her the money to go down to Lady Sophia's mama in Bath. She was in floods of tears, but he'd gone all icy. Ever so polite and no shouting, but— You know?'

'Fortunately not.' Although she could imagine all too well. 'Poor lady. I do not imagine she had much control over Lady Sophia's actions.'

'No, miss. But she was a bit of a wet duck, if you know what I mean. Always drooping about and reading novels and sighing.' She seemed to realise that these revelations, which were fascinating Lucy, were indiscreet and subsided into awkward silence.

The carriage moved off and Lucy smiled at her own maid who was staring round at the passing scene with eager curiosity. No one could accuse Amy of being either silent or a dogsbody. She must remember to warn her not to discuss her mistress's business when they arrived.

A sudden thought had her sitting up with a jerk. Her reticule landed on the floor of the carriage and the maids bumped heads as they both scrabbled to retrieve it. Of all the things that had run through her agitated brain last night, this, the most important, had been absent.

What was Lord Burnham going to tell Lady Hopewell about her? Who would he say that this uninvited guest was? He could hardly introduce her as a music teacher brought along to spy on his sister and a single gentleman could have no respectable reason to be escorting a young lady who was completely unrelated to him. There was only one conclusion that their hostess could come to—even someone as inexperienced as Lucy was perfectly aware of that.

And what if it was the correct conclusion? What if the Earl had lured her to this house party on completely false pretences and had every intention of seducing her? Was there even a house party? It might all be a cunning plot to abduct her.

Then she looked at her own reflection in the glass and common sense reasserted itself. A handsome, eligible, rich, humourless, domineering earl did not need to go around seducing boring and irritable music teachers by means of elaborate deceptions. He only had to lift a finger and women threw themselves at him, she was sure of that.

But even so, she could hardly arrive with Lord Burnham and offer no explanation, nor could she use her own name. Lambert was not at all unusual, but her parents lived quite close to Lady Hopewell's house, even if they never mingled in such circles. Someone— staff or guests—might know of a local Lambert family. She must ask Lord Burnham what they were to do about it at the first change of horses.

The two maids were looking out of the windows. Lucy did the same. This was going to be a long journey and she hadn't thought to bring a book or a travelling chess set. Before, on a lengthy carriage ride, she had just allowed the music in her head to sweep through her. Her friend Miranda had told her that her fingers would be in constant motion, playing the notes.

Now the music was still there, of course: she could hardly forget it. But she could not play it and the loss made her want to weep. When she was able to play, it would flood through her, taking over her body, flowing from her fingers. Now, listening to the music in her head was like having someone describe a scent or a colour rather than being able to smell or see it for herself.

It had taken her several weeks to understand. At first there had been pain and shock, then the void where the music had been was filled with the world and all the people and things in it that she had always been able to ignore before, all clamouring for her attention. There was no escape from it now and, somehow, she had to learn to live like this, totally focused on the here and now, on other people.

Her friends were different and always had been. They were all creative, tolerant and supportive. They had never minded her abstraction. She loved them dearly, but only now was she coming to understand how tolerant they had been, how willing to accept her as she was—only half attending, not quite engaging. It had been selfish, she acknowledged with new-found insight.

But accepting that was no real help in dealing with a world that she had to learn to navigate, tolerate, conform to—not when her music had been torn from her. A butterfly without its wings was just another creeping insect.

She was feeling sorry for herself again, she realised. No wonder she was so irritable. There was this whole intrusive, half-strange world to deal with and the knowledge that she should be managing better. She should be thankful that her injuries had not been worse, that she had good friends and a skill that should enable her to earn her own living.

Somehow she had to learn how to be less abrasive, more accepting, without becoming just another meek little mouse of a spinster.

And that is quite enough self-examination and good resolutions, Lucy thought as the carriage began to slow. If this was a stop to change horses she would tackle Lord Burnham now.

'My lord!'

Now what? The confounded female was making her way across the cobbled yard towards him with the air of a brig going into battle against the entire French fleet. Max had provided her with a comfortable carriage, refreshments *and* she had two maids to chaperon her. On top of which he was paying her a great deal of money.

'Miss Lambert?'

'We have not discussed how my presence is to be explained to Lady Hopewell and the other guests.'

Which was true. Max had intended to puzzle out that tricky point somewhere between London and Staning Waterless and inspiration had yet to strike. 'There is no need to worry about that.'

'Of course there is. And do not stand there looking so ineffably superior—I can assure you that it does not fill me with confidence.'

As Max had been aiming at projecting reassurance stemming from trustworthy masculine superiority, this was not the response he was hoping for. He fixed her with the look that normally reduced people to uneasy silence. 'Tell me, Miss Lambert, are you always so irritable?'

'If you had as much to be annoyed about as I have, Lord Burnham, I can assure you that you, too, would be irritable.' She glared at him from under a plain coffee-coloured bonnet that ought to have been drab, but somehow managed to set off those indignant brown eyes and the colour in her cheeks. It suited her, that flush of annoyance. In fact, a state of irritation seemed to bring out the best in her looks.

Which is not saying much, Max thought regretfully.

Feminine beauty was a constant source of pleasure that he was as happy to admire from a distance as he was to enjoy intimately: he did not have to possess it to enjoy it. Although all his mistresses had been very lovely, naturally. He felt a passing pang of regret for Hortense, the latest. Not that he missed her throwing Meissen figurines when provoked, but still...

'We have to think of something, otherwise everyone will assume I am your mistress,' Miss Lambert said flatly, erasing the fleeting memory of Hortense's delicious skills at making up a quarrel.

'I very much doubt it,' Max retorted without choosing his words.

Miss Lambert's chin jerked up, the flattering colour vanishing from her cheeks. 'I am quite well aware that I am plain, Lord Burnham. A gentleman would refrain from pointing it out quite so bluntly.'

Protesting that she was not plain was futile—the woman had a mirror, he was sure. Max had the presence of mind not to make things worse. 'That is not what I meant. Anyone who knows me would be aware that I would not dream of bringing a...a partner of an irregular kind to a gathering where ladies would be present.' Which made it sound as though wild bachelor parties were another matter altogether, he realised, as Miss Lambert curled a lip.

'A very fitting guardian for a young sister, I am sure. Discretion coupled with hypocrisy. Even so, however convinced your acquaintance may be of that discretion, we still need a reason for you to be escorting me.'

'And I told you, I will think of one. Now, the fresh horses are harnessed, so if you will take your place we can be off.'

'In a moment.'

The provoking female turned on her heel and marched into the inn, presumably in search of the privy. Ladies were supposed to slink discreetly out of the carriage and slip inside, not make it quite clear what they were about while leaving a gentleman to kick his heels.

Max signalled to the coachmen to wait and began to pace, wondering if he had suffered a brainstorm the day before when he suggested this scheme. He could hardly get in his own carriage, let alone drive off leaving Miss Lambert to make her own way back across a crowded inn yard.

She emerged five minutes later, characteristically unappreciative of his chivalry. 'There is no need to march up and down, I was as quick as I could be.'

Max closed the carriage door behind her and strode back to his own vehicle. He had thought her gently reared—now he was beginning to wonder. *As quick as I could be*, indeed! Had the female no shame?

Max sank back against the squabs with a muttered curse that made Hobson, his valet, jump and applied his mind to the question of finding a plausible and respectable reason why he was turning up at the house party uninvited and with the addition of an unknown female. At least it gave him some relief from brooding on Sophia.

But he had definitely experienced a brainstorm the day before.

Chapter Three

$Miss$ Lambert refrained from pestering him for two more stages and, by the time they arrived at The Ship in Farnborough, Max had what he thought was a convincing explanation for both his own arrival on Dorothea Hopewell's doorstep—and hers.

'Would you care to take a stroll, Miss Lambert?'

He held out a hand to steady her as she stepped out and, to his surprise, she took it. He remembered in time not to put any pressure on it for fear of hurting her.

'Thank you.' She sounded subdued, which was a relief, of course, given that he had no plate armour to protect him from any further prickliness, but she removed her hand the moment she was on the ground.

They walked to where a patch of rather worn turf and an old apple tree gave shelter to a pair of benches, but Miss Lambert ignored them, apparently preferring to pace up and down.

'I shall tell Lady Hopewell that I was concerned to see that Sophia had arrived safely,' Max said. 'She knows how headstrong my stepsister is, so it will come as no surprise that she took herself off without wait-

ing for me to organise transport and an escort. Sophia
will not have told her she did not have my permission.'

'But what about me?'

'You, Miss Lambert, are the daughter of an acquaintance who finds himself in difficulties—which
I will be far too discreet to tell anyone about and Lady
Hopewell will not ask. I discovered that your father was
not in London to meet you from Harrogate—'

'Harrogate?'

'Where you had been companion to an elderly relative. We need you to have arrived in London expecting to be met and with nowhere to go when you were
not. I was in receipt of an urgent message from your
father and went to the inn where the stage had depos-
ited you. I racked my brains for a solution to finding
respectable accommodation for you and then discovered that Sophia has gone rushing off without me. Solution: cast myself on the mercy of my dear friend
Dorothea Hopewell.'

Silence. Max braced himself for a list of criticisms,
but Miss Lambert was merely considering his suggestion.

'Excellent, provided one has no objection to telling
falsehoods—under the circumstances, I cannot see how
we can avoid them. But there is one problem.'

Max, who had relaxed, tensed again.

'I will have to change my name or your sister will
recognise it.' She looked around, clearly in search of
inspiration.

Max followed the direction of her gaze to a shop
front across the road. 'Rumpole and Marsh: Cabinet
Makers, Undertakers and Funeral Furnishers?'

'Miss Rumpole sounds most strange, but Marsh will

do nicely. I will retain my first name. At the next stop I will remove my maid from the carriage and instruct her on all of this. I assume you do not wish your stepsister's maid to know our purpose?'

'Absolutely not.' Max did not know whether Grenley would obey him if he told her to be silent about his plan. In any case, he was not at all certain he wanted someone in his employ who would be disloyal to Sophia. 'Very well, Miss Marsh. Shall we proceed?'

Lucy had not given Amy any reason for the journey down to Dorset. At the next change of horses she asked the maid to accompany her as she stretched her legs around the yard while Grenley hopped down and scuttled off into the inn, presumably in search of the necessary.

'Amy, can you be very discreet? Good. I am helping Lord Burnham because he is concerned that Lady Sophia, his stepsister, may have made an undesirable acquaintance.'

'A man, you mean, Miss Lambert?'

'Yes, and I am to try to discover who he is. Now, we must be as careful as possible—poor Lady Sophia is quite under the influence of this person and there is no saying what indiscretion she may commit if she discovers my purpose. No one can know who I am, so I am using a different name and I am not telling anyone I teach music. You must call me Miss Marsh.'

Amy listened wide-eyed to the story of how Miss Marsh had found herself stranded in London. 'I've been to Harrogate, Miss L—Miss Marsh. My auntie keeps a boarding house up there and I helped out for a month when her daughter had her baby. So if anyone asks, I

can sound as though I know what I'm talking about.
Miss Marsh,' she repeated, nodding firmly. 'I'll keep
saying it, then it will stick.'

'Thank you, Amy, that is very helpful. And I must
get used to calling you by your surname so you do not
feel out of place with all the other ladies' maids.'

Lucy wished she could afford to pay the girl more—
she was clearly bright and loyal. Then she realised that,
with Lord Burnham's fee, she could.

They took their seats again and Lucy discovered
she was feeling better than she had for weeks. This
was an adventure quite outside her experience, and
now she felt more secure about her disguise as Miss
Marsh, she was almost relaxed. Even the infuriatingly
superior Lord Burnham was proving to be reasonable.

Of course, when they arrived at Lady Hopewell's
house there could be any manner of snares awaiting her. She had to hope there was no one from the
neighbourhood who might recognise her—her parents
lived only ten miles away. Then, in addition to that and
watching for clues as to Lady Sophia's love, she had
to remember her supposed reason for being there *and*
make conversation.

Lucy had always sailed quietly through life, her
head full of music and her abstraction from everything and everybody explained as shyness. Now she
had to be sociable, which was worrying.

Still, she consoled herself, she would be a very insignificant guest among far more prominent people.
She could be a quiet wallflower, make herself agree-
able to Lady Sophia if possible, and watch and listen.
She felt a little unease about spying, but surely, if the
man intriguing with Lady Sophia had good intentions,

he would be open about his feelings and seek Lord
Burnham's permission to court her.

No, with this secrecy he would prove to be a rake: ei
ther a subtle rogue or a seemingly well-meaning suitor
like the wretch who had seduced her friend Prue. He
would certainly not be some humble but worthy swain
daring to aspire to a lady, because otherwise he would
hardly be a guest at an aristocratic house party.

Thinking of Prue was reassuring. Yes, this was the
right thing to do and, by some miracle, it was the prof-
itable thing as well. Her cynical friend Melissa would
say that anything too good to be true probably was just
that, but on the other hand, this adventure also con-
tained Lord Burnham's chilly presence and the prospect of small talk, so that dire warning probably did
not apply, the negative aspects being already obvious.

Lucy sat back, closed her eyes and set about invent-
ing a plausible elderly relative in Harrogate, a father
who had been called away on urgent family business
and a thoroughly dull personal existence that no one
would want to bother to quiz her about. She exercised
her fingers as she plotted, stretching and curling them
as Dr Horncastle had instructed her, trying to ignore
the ache and the pull, the occasional sharp twinge when
her fingers cramped without warning. They were not
getting much better now, but at least she might stop
them becoming worse.

It was past five o'clock when the carriages finally
pulled up outside Waterless Manor. At least the name
of the place was a possible talking point, Lucy thought,
adding it to her painfully short list of safe topics of
polite conversation.

Footmen came out, a black-suited butler descended
the front steps and bowed gravely to Lord Burnham
and went back inside. By the time a footman was handing her down from the carriage a short, plump lady
with a startlingly high crown of blond curls on her
head was surging down the steps.

'Burnham! What a delightful surprise! Dear Sophia
never mentioned that you were coming—such a *pretty*
head full of fashions and flirtations and no common
sense, the sweet child. No, no, never apologise for arriving unannounced, you are always welcome under
this roof. Now, who might this be?' She turned beady
blue eyes on Lucy and smiled, which was a relief.

'Miss Marsh, the daughter of an old friend of mine.
She found herself stranded in London and I am hoping we can cast ourselves upon your mercy.' He bent
to murmur something in Lady Hopewell's ear and she
nodded, patted his arm and turned to her butler.

'Formby, I believe the Rose Bedchamber is free.'

'My lady.'

'Then please see that Miss Marsh's luggage is taken
up and her maid is accommodated. I hope to get to
know you better when you have refreshed yourself,
my dear. We are gathering in the drawing room before
dinner,' she added kindly.

The bedchamber proved to be small but charming,
although exceedingly pink, and the butler informed
Amy that he would have hot water sent up immediately.
'Come to the Hall when you have finished, Pringle, and
you will be directed to your room.'

'It's all very nice, Miss… Miss Marsh. I just hope
the servants' hall isn't too stuffy,' Amy observed, peering into cupboards once Formby had left. 'Oh, here's

the dressing room, miss. I'll lay your things out for when the water arrives. Which gown for this evening?'

Thank heavens for Verity and Jane's kindness, Lucy thought, mentally reviewing the gowns they had insisted she accept.

'The cream silk with the amber ribbons and the brown and gold Paisley shawl and my amber set,' she decided. The amber necklace and earrings were, with Grandmama's pearls, virtually all her good jewellery. Mr and Mrs Lambert were firmly of the opinion that all a young lady required in the way of adornment was her own pristine virtue. Clearly she was not virtuous enough, Lucy decided as she studied her reflection in the mirror, because she certainly felt her appearance *would* be helped by additional adornment.

She peeled off her gloves while Amy took the hot ewer from the maid at the door and then sighed with relief as she plunged her hands into the warmth. The scars stood out starkly across her knuckles, but at least the missing fingertip had healed now. If it was not for those ugly red lines she might have risked leaving off her gloves during the day, but for evening they were, in any case, *de rigueur*.

Had Lady Hopewell accepted Lord Burnham's explanations? She had seemed a pleasant person and, of course, it would be highly insulting to doubt a gentleman's word. The thought gave her pause: Lord Burnham was telling untruths on her behalf, which was not honourable behaviour.

But was it? She pondered the point as Amy tightened her corset strings. He was attempting to safeguard his stepsister which was definitely what a gentleman should do and to do so he needed Lucy's help and he could not compromise her—so, logically, not telling the truth was the correct thing to do.

She was making excuses for him, Lucy realised, and wondered if that was because it would make her feel safer if she believed that he was a man who would take care not to damage her reputation by carelessness. Or action, she thought with a renewed qualm.

'Are you cold, Miss Marsh?' Amy almost spoilt the effect by grinning with triumph at remembering the right name to use. 'You shivered.'

'No, just a little tired, I expect.' Even so, she was glad of the soft folds of the Paisley shawl and resisted the urge to wrap it round herself to cover her modest neckline. Lord Burnham was not a rake—he had behaved impeccably.

Objectionably as well, she added, as she pulled on her cream silk evening gloves and took the reticule that Amy handed her. Frosty, emotionless and always right. Still, that was better than being all hands...

With that somewhat unnerving image on her mind, Lucy ventured out and found that she could locate the main staircase easily enough. The footman on duty in the hall escorted her to a pair of tall double doors which stood ajar, allowing a loud buzz of conversation to escape. He opened them fully for her and, taking a deep breath and straightening her back, Lucy ventured into the room full of strangers.

Lady Hopewell, thankfully, was an attentive hostess and came over immediately. 'Now come along in, Miss Marsh. I trust you found your room to be comfortable? Yes? Excellent. Now, let me see.' She raised an eyeglass on a stick and scanned the room through it. 'Who shall I introduce you to first? Ah, yes, Miss

Thomas and Miss Moss, this is Miss Marsh who is all alone, so I am relying on you to make her feel quite at home.' She beamed and swept off to greet a middle-aged couple who appeared in the doorway.

Lucy smiled. The two young ladies, both she guessed about nineteen, a few years younger than she was, smiled back politely. They did not have quite the experience to survey her without it being obvious, Lucy thought with inward amusement. Probably they were confused by the excellence of her gown and shawl contrasting with the simplicity of her jewellery and hairstyle. She sensed a certain relief that she was not a rival to their prettiness.

'You are from Dorset, Miss Marsh?' That was Miss Moss, a petite brunette with very pink lips, a pointed chin and a very good set of pearls.

'I have been in Harrogate for some time as companion to an elderly relative,' Lucy said. 'But I have visited Dorset before. Are you and Miss Thomas from the locality?'

She rather doubted it, because she did not recognise the names.

'Hampshire, both of us,' Miss Thomas said, then her gaze shifted towards the door. 'Oh, who is that gentleman?'

'Lord Burnham,' Lucy said without thinking. Then she realised that she would have to admit to some acquaintance with the Earl, otherwise, if she had been seen alighting from one of his carriages, it would seem most strange.

'He escorted me here when I found myself in difficulties, stranded in London. My father had been called away and there was a misunderstanding over dates—a

complete muddle, in fact. I arrived on the stage from
Harrogate to find the house was shut up, Papa somewhere between London and Brussels and no one to turn
to. Fortunately, Papa was able to contact Lord Burnham, who rescued me.'

The story was flowing now—she just had to recall
all the details for the next time someone asked. 'He
very kindly secured an invitation for me to attend the
house party and gave me the loan of one of his carriages for myself and my maid,' she concluded, slightly
breathless.

'Oh.' Miss Thomas looked disappointed. 'So you
and he are not…' Her voice trailed away suggestively.

The old Lucy, the one with her head full of music,
would never have noticed that tone of voice, nor the
avid look in Miss Thomas's eyes. This Lucy most certainly did.

'Whatever can you mean, Miss Thomas? Not what,
exactly?'

The girl backed down immediately. 'Oh, betrothed,
of course. Goodness, what else might I have meant?'

'No, I am not betrothed to Lord Burnham,' Lucy
said decisively. 'Nor anything else that you might imagine. His Lordship, although infinitely obliging in this
matter, is also authoritarian, arrogant, cold and ruthless. One cannot imagine anyone less amiable to be…'
She realised, far too late, what had caused the wide-
eyed expressions on the faces of the two young woman
as they looked past her.

There was a moment of sheer panic as she heard in
her mind just what she had said. It took only a second
to reach a decision: she would not turn around, she
would not let anyone see she knew he was there—it

was surely imagination that she felt the flames of furious hot breath fanning the nape of her neck—she would simply keep talking.

'...associated with. But most decisive and helpful.' No, she was not imagining that the heat of His Lordship's regard was diminishing—the two faces opposite her were proof of that.

'Oh, Miss Marsh—Lord Burnham was right behind you, what if he overheard?' Miss Thomas whispered.

'He cannot have done,' her friend objected. 'His expression did not change. He is rather alarming, is he not? I was reminded of that painting of a great white bear on an ice flow that we saw at the Academy last year.'

'White and shaggy?' Lucy asked, bemused.

'No, not the bear, the ice—smooth and frozen and implacable.'

Yes, that was Lord Burnham. But he would have heard her unflattering comments—Lucy had no doubt his hearing would be inconveniently excellent. Now what would he do?

Chapter Four

'We should circulate,' Miss Moss said with a glance at the doorway. 'More people are arriving.'

Lucy half turned and saw a group of four young men, a middle-aged couple and, just behind them, Lady Sophia. The sight steadied her nerves a little. She had been employed to undertake a task and, unless her employer was so affronted by her tactless pronouncements that he sent her home with a flea in her ear and an empty purse, then she was going to do it.

Lady Hopewell moved to greet them as Lady Sophia, without a glance at the gentlemen, strolled across and began to talk to Miss Thomas.

'I will introduce you to my parents.' Miss Moss led the way to the couple and waited while they finished speaking to their hostess. 'Mama, Papa, this is Miss Marsh who arrived late this afternoon. Miss Marsh, my parents, Sir George and Lady Moss.'

Lucy bobbed a curtsy, forestalling anyone offering a hand to shake, and listened while Miss Moss recounted the tale of her arrival at the house party and Lord Burnham's rescue. 'Which was very kind of him, of course, but I have to say he seems a very cold sort of gentleman,' she said rather breathlessly.

'He is an earl, Clara,' her mother said with gentle reproof. 'Naturally he shows a proper distance in his manner.' She glanced around the room. 'And his sister is here, of course,' she added vaguely. 'So naturally he—' She broke off. 'So naturally he would think this a proper place to bring a young lady in difficulties.'

In other words she has worked out that Lord Burnham is highly unlikely to bring his chère amie *to stay in the same house as his sister, therefore I am probably as respectable as I appear.*

Lucy managed a smile. 'So thoughtful of him. Of course, it is a trifle awkward, but everyone has been most kind.'

'I am sure they have. Now, let me see, who else I can introduce you to.' Lady Moss cast a disapproving eye over the young men. They had been joined by some others and were gathered together at one end of the room, talking rather too loudly. 'Lady Hermione, I think.' She began to shepherd Lucy towards an angular lady of middling years wearing a startlingly vivid blue gown and an expression of equally vivid interest in what was going on around her.

'Daughter of the late Marquis of Fotheringhall, you know. Very much a bluestocking, but such an entertaining observer of the social scene,' Lady Moss murmured, then raised her voice to normal conversational levels. 'Hermione, dear, do allow me to present Miss Marsh who has only just reached safe haven here after quite an adventurous few days. Miss Marsh, Lady Hermione Felix.'

She went back to her family, leaving Lucy to be inspected by Lady Hermione through blue eyes for which her gown was a perfect match.

'Are you wearied to death of recounting your adventures or would you find another telling therapeutic?'

'I would much rather talk of other things, ma'am,' Lucy admitted gratefully.

'Excellent. Who here are you not acquainted with? I will not drag you about making introductions, but thorough character assassination does require a knowledge of whom one is discussing, does it not?'

'Most certainly,' Lucy agreed. Provided it was not her own character under scrutiny she was more than happy to hear Lady Hermione's opinion of the other guests. Particularly the young gentlemen, of course. 'As yet I only know the Moss family and Miss Thomas. Oh, and Lord Burnham, of course. I believe that is his stepsister over there in the primrose gown?'

Lady Sophia had posed herself prettily against the dark green wall and the young men began to drift in her direction, despite the fact she was ignoring them. Or perhaps because of it, Lucy speculated.

'It is. A pretty chit with more brains in her head than she allows to be seen, most of the time. One can understand why—most men flee in the face of feminine intelligence: a depressing fact of life.'

'Indeed. I have four close friends, all of them intelligent and skilled. Three have found husbands who appreciate them for what and who they are. They are men who are confident enough not to be intimidated by their wives' attainments, which seems like a small miracle when one considers how empty-headed young ladies are expected to be. The fourth maintains that she has no wish to wed, so they are all happy.'

'And you?' Lady Hermione raised one perfectly plucked eyebrow.

'I am very content to be single.' She had seen the happiness true love brought and she was practical enough to know that the chances of it happening to her were non-existent and wise enough to have learned to ignore the little spark of envy. Time to change the subject from herself—those blue eyes were far too intense. 'Who are the young gentlemen?'

'The very tall black-haired one with the large nose is Viscount St Giles. Next to him, on his right, with the red hair and the deplorably shiny waistcoat, is Benedict, Lord Easton. The good-looking blond youth with the Brutus cut is Philip Doncaster. The one attempting to simultaneously toss his hair and look languid is Lord Tobias Jerman—someone was once foolish enough to tell him that he resembled Byron. The somewhat rotund young man being strangled by his neckcloth is Algernon Tredgold and, finally, the intelligent one with the brown hair and the green and brown waistcoat is my nephew Terence, Viscount Overdene. The best of the bunch, but then, I am prejudiced.'

Which of those had caught Lady Sophia's fancy? Lucy wondered. Viscount Overdene certainly looked both intelligent and handsome. Mr Doncaster was even better looking. Viscount St Giles might have a personality that counteracted the nose and perhaps Lord Tobias had good qualities, despite the posturing. A poor taste in waistcoats and a degree of plumpness moved Lord Easton and Mr Tredgold down the list of probabilities, but one could never tell what might appeal to another woman. There were doubtless those for whom Lord Burnham's frosty demeanour was highly attractive.

'And are those the only single gentlemen?' she asked, creating a list in her head and ranking them within it.

'The only young ones whose antics might amuse us. There is Lord Burnham, of course. He is single, but twenty-eight and, therefore, one hopes, has reached an age of discretion. The Marquis of Petersbridge is just out of mourning. A very eligible catch, of course, if one does not mind a husband in his forties, so there may be some entertainment to be had in watching the girls batting their eyelashes at him.'

There was a small flurry at the doorway and Lady Hermione turned. 'Ah, more young ladies. The brunette in pink—oh, Lord Burnham, good evening.'

The man moved far too quietly for comfort, Lucy thought, arranging her expression into one of modest insipidity. She had good practice with that expression because it was the one she used most of the time at home. It usually deceived her parents into assuming only correct and ladylike thoughts were passing through her head.

'Lady Hermione, a pleasure to see you again. Miss Marsh, I hope you are comfortably settled?'

'Yes, indeed, thank you.'

'Do excuse me, I have just recalled something I must say to Terence. I hope to further our acquaintance later, Miss Marsh.' Lady Hermione drifted off across the room like a bright blue dragonfly—she was far too angular to be a butterfly, Lucy decided.

She turned back to Lord Burnham, expecting some cutting remark about her indiscreet comments earlier.

'You may wish to inspect the conservatory, Miss Marsh. It is a particularly fine one, and usually unoccupied at this hour.' He gestured towards an archway in the far corner of the room. 'Through there.' And then, just as she was on the point of telling him that she would look at it later, he strolled off in the opposite direction.

Lucy narrowed her eyes at his back. It was, she had to admit, a fine one—broad shoulders apparently in no need of buckram or padding on the part of his tailor, a trim waist, which certainly was not due to corsetry, and long legs. It did not make him any less infuriating, of course, but at least he was *decoratively* maddening.

And then she realised that his remark about the conservatory had not been a suggestion, it had been a direction. An order from her employer.

She meandered across to the archway, smiling at anyone who smiled or bowed to her, but not stopping. The opening led to a short passageway with a glass door at the end. It creaked as she pushed it wide and she found herself in warm heat, the air filled with the smell of greenery, moist earth and a drift of heavy, exotic scent. From the far side there was a tinkle of water. The sound of voices from the room behind her disappeared as she let the door swing closed. The hinges really did need oiling.

What am I supposed to do now? Wait for His Lordship to arrive and deliver a lecture, I suppose.

Lucy wandered through the glasshouse, ducked under drooping palm fronds, found the source of the exotic perfume in a white-flowered creeper and finally discovered the source of the water, a fountain trickling into a large raised pool against the far wall.

She perched on the rim of the basin, quite content to watch the little gold and silver fish that darted among the water weeds. It was peaceful here and she did not have to make any small talk.

The door creaked again and footsteps sounded on the tiled floor. She watched warily until Lord Burnham came into view, ducking around a large fern in a Chinese vase.

He would be angry with her, of course. But Lucy had found that being constantly considered to be in the wrong at home had given her an admirably thick skin when dealing with disapproval. She should apologise, though. It had been wrong to let her tongue run away with her like that.

She got to her feet as he approached, rather glad of the solid marble rim at the back of her thighs for support. 'Lord Burnham, I—'

'That was an excellent tactic, Miss Marsh, I congratulate you. Word will get back to my stepsister that you find me unsympathetic and that will make her far more willing to confide in you,' he said with the nearest thing to a smile she had yet seen on his face.

'Er...yes,' Lucy said, amazed. He thought that had been deliberate? She tried to look like a woman who was a mistress of cunning. 'I am glad you understand and did not take offence,' she said.

Oh. Goodness. That *was* a smile, a real smile. And it transformed a conventionally handsome face into something far more interesting, because the left side of his mouth quirked up slightly more than the right. The effect was somehow quizzical and...and charming.

'Is something wrong, Miss Marsh?'

Lucy realised she was staring. Probably her mouth

was open. 'No, nothing, it is just that you have some fallen flowers from that white climbing plant on your shoulder.' She reached out a hand to brush them off, he stepped closer and the far door creaked.

Lord Burnham shifted, half turning as though to shield her from the view of whoever had just come in. As he moved, Lucy tried to step behind him, found she could not because of the fountain basin and, off balance, toppled helplessly backwards.

The basin was about the size of a half-barrel and her head was above water as her bottom hit the base. With a splutter she scrabbled to sit up.

'Shh! Stay down.'

'What!'

A ruthless hand descended on the top of her head, pushing her down as Lord Burnham sat firmly on the basin rim, his back to her. A man's laugh, deep and warm, and the trill of feminine amusement came from quite close. They must be behind the fern in the Chinese pot, she thought, trying not to move abruptly when the little fish darted against her skin.

'Oh, Philip, how you do make me laugh!' The speaker was young—too young to be unchaperoned in a conservatory with a man.

As am I, Lucy thought. A fish nibbled delicately at her fingertip and she pushed it away.

'And how you make my heart beat faster, Elizabeth, you know you do. May I beg just one kiss?'

'Ooh, I shouldn't really...but, Philip—oh!'

'Miss Gainford. Doncaster.' Lord Burnham stood up, squarely in front of the fountain.

Lucy slid down until the water almost reached her nose, took a deep breath and prepared to submerge.

Were there snails? She really did hope there were no snails.

'Might I suggest that Miss Gainford's chaperon might not wish for her to be in here alone with a gentleman?' Lord Burnham said reprovingly. The footsteps halted.

'Er…yes. Quite right, sir. We got talking, didn't notice we were in here all alone, if you know what I mean. Then the heat of the moment… Come along, Eliz—Miss Gainford. Back we go…'

There was the sound of retreating footsteps, the creak of the door. Lucy sat up and plucked at the waterlily leaf that had attached itself to her cleavage.

'They have gone.' Lord Burnham turned and held out his hands, then reached down farther and took her arms just above the elbow.

He didn't want to hurt her hands, Lucy realised, allowing herself to be pulled upright. How thoughtful of him to remember and take care.

And then she was aware that she was soaking wet and dressed in light fabric that clung as though glued to every curve of her body. Water dripped down her forehead and off the end of her nose and, as she pushed back her hair, a fish dropped in a flash of silver into the water.

Lord Burnham was still holding her upper arms, his gaze fixed tactfully on her face. He was smiling, just a little.

If it had not been for his grip she would probably have ended up sitting in the water again, she realised. 'This is not amusing, my lord.'

It most certainly is not. I am alone with a man, in a

compromising position, soaking wet and I appear to have lost my wits, simply because he almost smiled.

'No, it is not, you are quite correct. Forgive me, Lucy.'

That smile had vanished, but the memory of it lingered and so did the warmth of his hands on her bare, wet arms. He had called her Lucy and she was within an inch of losing her head over a man, she realised, belatedly discovering why she felt dizzy.

It was ridiculous: she, Lucy Lambert, ordinary, unimportant, awkward and independent, did not even *like* men, let alone take leave of her senses over one. And she was standing up to mid-thigh in cool water.

'Of course, *Max*,' she said with enough of a sarcastic edge to bring both of them to their senses, she would have hoped. Although, of course, he was still in full possession of his and was simply teasing her. Or toying with her, or whatever sophisticated men of the world did with music teachers who had found themselves thoroughly out of their depth.

'Let us get you out of there,' was all he said as his hands left her arms, fastened around her waist and lifted her right out of the pool, over the rim and set her, with a regrettable squelch, on the tiled floor.

He is strong, she thought, all those unruly senses scattering again.

'Now what are we going to do with you?'

His hands were still on her waist, unmoving. Lucy thought he had forgotten he was holding her like that.

'You are going to let go of me, give me your coat and I am going to drip my way out of that door over there, which hopefully leads to the staff quarters, where I will climb the back stairs and ring for my maid,' she said firmly.

Then his gaze flickered down, fixed, and she saw him turn white.

Of course, she must be wet through. Max looked down. Down at the soaking cloth clinging to the slender body, the trails of water weed. The warmth and the scents and the sounds of the conservatory faded, leaving the slap of Thames water on stinking mud, the creak of oars, the bone-chill of winter. He felt once more the shock of seeing death for the first time, the sheer horror of recognising the sheet-white, mud-smeared face.

He felt the blood draining from his head, heard a high-pitched keening sound in his ears—and then the woman in front of him moved, spoke, and he realised that he was still clasping Lucy Lambert around the waist. Max released her abruptly.

Lucy, not Julia. Alive, not dead.

'I beg your pardon, Lucy.' Damnation, he had done it again, used her name. This was ridiculous. He did not knock young ladies into pools, he did not use their given names, he did not have nightmare hallucinations of drowned girls or of scrawled words blotched with tears.

I love him, but not enough. He says this is all my fault. I cannot live without him...

He was the Earl of Burnham and a man and he should behave like it.

'You will have to help me off with my coat,' he admitted. It had taken Hobson a good ten minutes to ease him into it and it was new, one of Weston's best.

Thinking about what contact with wet skin would do to the burgundy silk lining was another lifeline back to reality.

Max glanced around, but there were no convenient throws on the marble benches, not even a pile of sacking left by the gardeners. He would have to endure Hobson's silent displeasure.

He would also have to endure the expression of disdain for such foppish tailoring—he had no doubt that was how Lucy would categorise it. He turned his back on her and began to ease it off his shoulders. The shuddering nerves so close to the surface of his skin had almost calmed now. He took a steadying breath.

Cold, damp fingers hooked into the collar and pulled and then, as the coat began to slide off, seized the cuffs and tugged. By the time he turned back Lucy was enveloped in it, her hands hidden by the length of the sleeves.

'I hope it did not hurt you, pulling like that.' That was certainly no laughing matter, even if the sight of her swamped in his coat, the swallow tails almost touching the floor, was ludicrous.

'The doctor encourages me to exercise my hands daily, past the point of discomfort,' she said, chin up.

It occurred to Max that since he had reached adulthood, no one had ever answered back to him like this. Sophia wheedled and coaxed or threw tantrums, but in-his-face defiance like this was a novelty. And, curse the woman, it was an intriguing one.

'I will go and make certain that door goes to the back stairs and that the way is clear.' The squeak and squelch of wet shoes followed him across the tiles. 'In fact, I had best come with you and go to my own chamber—I can hardly appear in the dining room in my shirt sleeves.'

Lucy's instinct had been correct. The door, which was much plainer than the one by which she had entered, opened on to an uncarpeted corridor. Max strode along it, found the foot of the stairs and called back, 'Come on, there is no one in sight.'

They went up swiftly. When he glanced down there was a trail of moisture behind them, but it was a warm evening and hopefully it would evaporate before anyone came and wondered about it. A careless maid with the water cans, perhaps, would explain it.

Two floors up he opened a door and looked out. 'The coast is clear.' Then he realised that while he had at least half a dozen coats with him, a music teacher was unlikely to have a supply of evening gowns. 'Have you anything to change into?'

'Thank you, yes. I will contrive to appear downstairs shortly adequately dressed for the occasion.' Lucy stalked off down the corridor. He could not see her face, of course, but he strongly suspected that her nose was in the air.

With a sigh, Max opened the door to his own room and braced himself for Hobson's reaction. The man was a perfectionist and Max was all too aware that his appearance was seen by the valet as a direct reflection on his own skills and, by extension, his reputation.

'My lord?' Hobson stopped, clothes brush poised over the riding coat Max had travelled in. *'My lord.'*

'A damsel in distress and an encounter with a body of water, Hobson. I regret to say that the new Weston coat may return somewhat the worse for wear.'

Chapter Five

Max arrived downstairs just as the butler entered the drawing room to announce that dinner was served. As Lady Hopewell began to usher her guests into order he glanced around. No sign of Lu—of Miss Marsh.

Then, as Dorothea bore down on him, making little shooing gestures to urge him towards Lady Hermione, he saw her slip through the door. Her hair was still dark with moisture and had been pulled back into a severe knot to disguise the fact that it was wet, but her gown of pale fawn muslin was unexceptional for an unmarried lady and she looked remarkably composed.

'Burnham?' Lady Hermione tapped lightly on his arm with her fan. 'Are you quite well? I declare you are positively pale.' When he forced a smile and a rueful shake of his head she laughed. 'No, do not dissemble, it is the prospect of sitting next to me, I know it is. Why, I have even routed Wellington before now!'

'I am sure you are quite capable of it, but the explanation for my seeming a little out of sorts is quite prosaic. I had an accident and spilt something on a brand-new coat and my valet was, to put it mildly, displeased. I would wager he is someone else who could overcome the Duke. Not that he says anything, but he can sigh like a disapproving dowager.'

He steered her round to her place next to the Marquis of Petersbridge who was seated at the foot of the table.

Max settled himself and discovered to his horror that his hands were not quite steady as he shook out his napkin. He dropped it into his lap and spread them palm-down on his thighs, willing them to stillness. Shaking hands, pale skin—the effect of seeing Lucy soaking wet was worse than he had realised. The image of the dead girl's body on the Thames foreshore had been buried as deep as willpower could make it and yet it had taken only that moment to bring it all back.

Guilt, he supposed. He should not have taken the risk, should not have allowed himself to be convinced by Julia's talk of love. The sense of failure stuck like a burr in the soul even though he was an adult now, not a child to be frightened by phantoms.

Max took a deep breath, nodded to the footman who was offering wine and set himself to make conversation. At least with Hermione Felix one had to engage all your wits, which left no room for old nightmares he had thought himself long since hardened to. He reached for his glass, his hand steady now.

Lucy studied the other guests while she recovered her breath. A benefit of being the least important guest meant she was placed halfway along the table with an excellent view of everyone else. She was seated between a Mr West, who introduced himself as the Vicar of the parish and Mr Tredgold, who blushed every time she ventured a remark.

The Vicar seemed rather young for his position and she was not certain he had even attained thirty years. He was also gravely serious and darkly handsome which must, she supposed, make him the target for every hopeful spinster in the parish. That might account for his reserved manner.

She did a rapid count of the company and saw the number at table had been made up to twenty by two young ladies she had not encountered before. Her last-minute arrival had unbalanced the numbers and, she suspected, the Vicar had been invited at short notice to make up the number of men. Probably being summoned to dinner at short notice, and having to look appreciative of the honour, was an occupational hazard of holding a living in a country parish when one's patron resided close at hand.

But for now Mr Tredgold had escorted her in and it was to him that she must address her conversation.

'I have not yet been introduced to everyone,' she told him. 'Who is the lady on Lord Burnham's left?' She gestured discreetly towards a pale-faced blonde who was looking shyly down at her plate.

'Lady Georgiana FitzRichard.' He shifted slightly for the footman to serve the soup, then must have realised his reply had been somewhat abrupt. 'Her family lives somewhat to the north of here, I believe. Distant neighbours of Lady Hopewell.'

'And almost opposite us?' Lucy lowered her voice, although the auburn-haired girl in question was prattling so animatedly to her dinner partner that she was highly unlikely to hear.

'Anne Easton, Easton's sister.'

So this was everyone and, if Max was correct, Sophia's unsuitable swain must be among this company.

She should stop thinking of him as Max, although it seemed to make him less imposing, more of a human being. The name suited him, she thought, letting her gaze halt for a moment on his profile at the end of the opposite side of the table. Strong and to the point. He didn't look quite himself, but perhaps that was the candlelight. Or he might not be feeling well: he had certainly reacted strangely when she had emerged from the pool.

Then Lady Sophia laughed, a bright trill of amusement, and his head came round, just for a quick, frowning glance. That was it, of course. He was worried about his stepsister. It was time to begin earning her wages.

'Lady Sophia seems a delightful, light-hearted person,' she remarked to Algernon Tredgold.

He swallowed a mouthful of *potage de la reine* and nodded. 'Yes, very jolly girl. Sporting, game for everything. Archery, dancing, parlour games. No airs and graces.' He buttered a fragment of bread roll. 'Doesn't expect a chap to do the pretty all the time. You know, flirt and pretend to be dying of love.' He snorted.

That was interesting. Or perhaps Lady Sophia was tactful and knew that kind of behaviour would embarrass Mr Tredgold. She decided she could most definitely cross him off the list, unless he was a consummate actor.

Sir George Moss was married and did not look at all the kind of man who would indulge in an illicit flirtation with an unmarried girl—or anyone but his wife, come to that. The Marquis was possible, if Sophia found a brooding, older man attractive, and she supposed that after a year in mourning he might welcome the attentions of a pretty, lively young lady.

But if he *was* the man, then why the secrecy? A marquis, middle-aged or not, was a staggeringly good match, even for the daughter of an earl, and her mother and stepbrother might be expected to greet the courtship with heartfelt approval.

The remaining five young men were far more likely, although what was wrong with any of them that would cause Lady Sophia to keep her feelings a deep, dark secret, Lucy could not determine. Not yet.

The soup was cleared and Lucy turned to her other neighbour. The Vicar turned sloe-dark eyes on her. 'You have only just arrived, I understand, Miss Marsh.'

Yes, that confirmed it—a note must have been sent to the vicarage urgently requesting his attendance at dinner. She hoped he did not object, but young clergymen rarely earned much and the food was very good, so perhaps he regarded an evening of making conversation a fair exchange.

'Yes, I have. Very late this afternoon, in fact. I know no one present except Lord Burnham who was good enough to rescue me when my father was called away unexpectedly. But no doubt you are acquainted with all the regular guests here.'

'I am new to the parish so this is the first large gathering I have attended at the Manor,' he said gravely.

'Where were you before? In another parish?'

'I was a curate at Walcot for three years. This is my first appointment as Vicar.'

Walcot? The name was vaguely familiar, but Lucy

could not place it and she didn't like to ask, so she made an encouraging sound and listened to his description of this parish and its challenges.

'Do tell me about the village's unusual name,' she prompted as she watched Lady Sophia, trying to catch her exchanging a lingering look with someone, or watching one of the gentlemen too intently.

'Waterless, I believe, derives from the frequent failure of the wells in the Middle Ages. They are deeper now, but there is only a very small stream at the extreme southern edge of the parish, which makes things hard for the farmers,' Mr West explained.

Lucy listened with half her attention. Either Sophia was being extraordinarily discreet or Max—*Lord Burnham*—had been misled. Or possibly the object of her affections lived locally and was not at the house party.

She was pondering that thought, while simultaneously responding to the Vicar's polite enquiries about her own home, when she caught Max's eye. Without thinking, she smiled and then bit her lip at the suddenly arrested expression on his face. What on earth was she doing smiling at the man? What had provoked that?

Look at him, all starched up and disapproving. Now what have I done wrong?

Max looked away—without, of course, returning her smile—and Lucy focused on the Vicar. 'I live in London now, but I was brought up in the country,' she explained. She was saved from having to invent somewhere by the arrival of the footmen to clear plates for the next course and turned back to Algernon Tredgold.

'Do tell me all the gossip, Mr Tredgold. Are any of the other single guests betrothed or courting?'

'Courting?' He seemed startled by the concept. 'Oh, no. Not to my knowledge. I wouldn't know anything about that. I'm just here to get out of London, don't you know?' He went pink again and lowered his voice. 'Repairing lease.'

'Cards or horses?' Lucy asked sympathetically. Yes, she could definitely eliminate Algernon from the field.

'Cards,' he muttered.

Crossing Algernon Tredgold off the list was the sum total of her success so far that evening, Lucy thought as she followed her hostess out with the other ladies, leaving the gentlemen to their port. It was time to tackle Lady Sophia.

The old Lucy would have found a corner to hide in, but the new, independent Lucy, with a fee to earn, found herself rather bolder and, by careful manoeuvring, she was in position to take the seat next to Sophia on one of the sofas in the drawing room.

'Good evening. I am Miss Marsh and I believe you must be Lady Sophia Harker. You have probably heard how Lord Burnham very kindly rescued me.'

Lady Sophia turned with a look brimful of mischief. 'Whatever possessed him to do something so gallant? I would have thought dear Max had not a drop of romance in his soul. But to be quixotically scooping up young ladies and bearing them off to the depths of Dorset when he ought to be pursuing me with fire and brimstone—why, it is quite wonderful! I am very pleased to meet you, Miss Marsh.' She looked puzzled for a moment. 'Were you not wearing a different gown earlier this evening?'

'An accident—I trod on the hem and tore the flounce,'

Lucy said airily, making a mental note to mention that to some of the other ladies if she had the chance. 'But as for my arrival here, I can assure you, there was no scooping up involved. I cast myself on his mercy because I had heard Papa speak of him as the best man in a crisis and, very fortunately for me, he happened to be coming here and he knew Lady Hopewell would take pity on me. But why fire and brimstone, Lady Sophia?'

'I am quite in disgrace.' Lady Sophia wriggled herself into the corner of the sofa with the air of making herself comfortable for a good gossip. 'Max had forbidden me to come, you see, so I tricked him and here I am and now he has to pretend there is nothing wrong in case that causes talk.'

'Oh. But… Surely Lady Hopewell is a perfectly… I mean, why on earth should he take exception to you coming here?'

'The foolish man thinks I am conducting a secret love affair.' Lady Sophia dimpled a naughty smile and blushed a little.

'My goodness!' Lucy had no trouble sounding surprised. She was *admitting* it? 'You are?'

'Goodness, no.' The dimple vanished and with it Lucy's belief in the denial. Sophia was looking entirely too calculating, in her opinion. 'Max is such a stuffy old thing. I flirt a little, silly people gossip and the next thing I know he is planning to lock me up like some medieval maiden in a tower.'

Just for a moment Lucy had thought she was going to hear a name. But of course, it couldn't be that easy.

'How tiresome for you. But here you are, despite your stepbrother—I do admire your courage. Fancy travelling all the way from London by yourself. I would never contemplate such a thing myself.'

Lucy hoped some wide-eyed admiration might provoke more confidences. Although whether that *had* been a confidence or something Lady Sophia was happy to share with all the guests, she wasn't sure. The other woman merely smiled and wafted her fan.

'I must say, I do not blame you in the slightest for running away,' Lucy persisted. 'This seems to be a most delightful party. So many single young men,' she added, lowering her voice further.

'Tribbles, the lot of them,' Sophia said roundly. 'Algernon is a dullard, Tobias fancies himself to be a romantic hero—I can remember him when he had spots and his verse is execrable—Philip Doncaster is making sheep's eyes at Lizzie Gainford and the others are far too young to be interesting.

'But never mind the tiresome gentlemen, come and meet the other girls.' She jumped up and held out her hand to Lucy. 'Oh, what is wrong with your fingers?'

'An accident. Something heavy fell on them,' Lucy said shortly.

'Ghastly for you. What a good thing you didn't play the harp! Oh, goodness, so tactless of me—you didn't, did you?'

'No. I never played the harp.'

'Well, that's a mercy. And really, with gloves on, one can hardly tell. Now, here's Lizzie and Georgie. Darlings, this is Miss Marsh who has been cast adrift among us. Be lovely to her, I have just been so tactless!'

Lucy excused herself as the clocks struck half past ten. The group showed no signs of breaking up, but she was weary from the journey and the effort of keeping names and impressions straight in her head. There had been no sign of Max when she had extricated herself from the chattering group of young ladies and gone to wish her hostess goodnight. Perhaps he was playing billiards or cards. Or perhaps he, too, had retired. He had certainly not been looking particularly well at dinner time.

Which, on reflection, was odd, she mused as she reached the first landing. She would have thought he was as healthy as a horse and probably as strong as one. The memory of being lifted bodily out of the pool produced a both disturbing flutter of her pulse and a possible explanation—perhaps Max had wrenched a muscle in his back. It was easily done, even for the fittest person. Their local blacksmith had done it the previous year lifting a small bucket of coals when he was slightly off balance—and he was built like a barn door.

'Miss Marsh!'

Lucy jumped, then fanned herself with one hand. 'Ma—Lord Burnham. I thought you had gone to bed.'

'Clearly not,' he said. 'I was waiting to speak with you.' He stepped on to the landing, looked over the banisters. 'Still early, the others will not be coming upstairs for a while.' He led the way along the corridor. 'Come in here.'

In here proved to be the little sitting room attached to his bedchamber. Lucy hesitated on the threshold. To step inside a gentleman's bedchamber—even an annexe to it—was, effectively, to court ruin, even if they spent the entire time playing piquet while fully clothed.

On the other hand, ruined for what, exactly? She had no expectation of ever marrying, she had no gimlet-eyed mother or chaperon waiting to sweep in and demand that Max Did The Decent Thing. She wasn't even here under her real name.

Nor had she the slightest fear any longer that he might make advances. A man who could knock a girl into a fountain, then fish her out and regard her body, revealed by clinging wet clothing, with total indifference—he was not going to pounce on her now.

She sat down on one of the two armchairs as a small, treacherous voice in her head whispered, *Unfortunately.*

'Are you all right, Miss Marsh? I am afraid I startled you.'

'No. I am quite all right.'

I startled myself.

'And you?' she added. 'I am sorry if you hurt your back lifting me from that pool.'

'No, I did not.' He was pacing on the other side of the room. Not so very far away, with only the other armchair between them.

'I thought… You were very pale afterwards. I thought you looked unwell.'

'A passing headache.' He certainly looked perfectly fit now and was certainly back to his intense, tight-lipped state. 'What have you discovered?'

'Not a great deal. I am sure we can eliminate Sir George. Algernon Tredgold is surely not the man. He is shy and, frankly, not the brightest candle in the box. If Lady Sophia had fallen for the Marquis, I cannot imagine you would consider him so unsuitable that she would be driven to underhand tactics to see him and there would surely be no reason for him to encourage such behaviour. But that still leaves five young men.'

She hesitated, wondering if something that had occurred to her would provoke his anger.

'Out with it, Miss Marsh. What is making you bite
your lip like that?'

'I suppose he could not be a servant of one of the
guests? A groom or valet?'

Max narrowed his eyes at her, and she hurried on.
'Someone she might have met at another house party,
perhaps?'

'I find it unlikely. Improbable. But not impossible—
hush!'

But she had heard it, too—voices just outside the
door, both male.

'…game of cards? Aye, that I would. I'll just
straighten His Lordship's room so it is ready when
he rings—'

'Hobson.' Max strode around the armchair, seized
Lucy by the wrist and towed her into the next room,
closing the door softly behind him as the door from
the landing opened. 'My valet,' he breathed in her ear.

The soft light of an Argon lamp turned low burned
on the dresser, revealing that this was his bedchamber.

'He'll come in here, surely,' she whispered back. 'Is
there an exit from your dressing room?'

Max shook his head. 'He'll have the clothes press
open, so that's no good either. He'll check the window,
so not the curtains… Under the bed, *now.*'

Lucy scrabbled after him under the bedframe, pulling the valance down as she did so. With it in place
there was only a thin line of light showing. Max inched
towards the farther side and she wriggled farther in,
then froze as the door opened.

They lay flat on their backs, shoulder to shoulder,

like effigies on a medieval chest tomb, she thought. Carefully, she lifted her hand and found that, fortunately, it was a high bed. There was perhaps eight inches of space above her body.

The valet was clearly someone who liked to talk to himself, because he kept up a low-voiced running commentary as he moved around.

'Window, just ajar. Fresh water on the night stand. Aha, there's that collar stud…' Mentally, she followed him around the room, heard the door of the clothes press creak open— thank heavens they hadn't hidden in there—the dressing room door open and close. Then, 'Chamber pot…'

Light flooded in as the valance at the foot of the bed was lifted. She raised her head and squinted down the length of her body, across over the upturned toes of Max's shoes, and saw a hand reach in. There was chink of porcelain, the utensil was pushed back and the valance dropped.

At which point Lucy realised that Lady Hopewell's housekeeping was not as perfect as it had seemed. Dust tickled her nose.

'Going to…sneeze,' she whispered in Max's ear, then clamped her hand over her nose and mouth in an heroic, futile effort to stifle it.

He twisted in the narrow space, grabbed her shoulder and pulled her tight in against his chest so her face was buried in his neckcloth.

'Atchoo.' It was a very muffled sneeze, but she heard the valet stop moving, stand still. He was listening.

Chapter Six

Lucy knew she was going to have to start breathing in a moment, but the valet was still motionless, still silent. Listening. Right beside the bed.

'What the devil was that?' he muttered. Then outside, an owl hooted. 'Gawd, I'll be imagining ghosties next.' He chuckled. 'Best check the clothes for tomorrow, I suppose.'

Clasped against Max's chest, Lucy made herself relax, which was almost as impossible as holding back a sneeze. The Earl was lean and hard and should have been exceedingly uncomfortable to be half lying upon, but somehow she seemed to fit quite well. That meant she could feel his breathing, quiet and steady, hear the thump of his heart under her ear. That was steady, too, which was more than could be said for hers, which was pounding.

Fright, she told herself. That might have been the case, but intimate proximity to a man—this man—was contributing, too. And the smell of him. A hint of brandy from his coat, starch and white soap from his linen, a smoky, subtle tang that would be his cologne and under it a not displeasing muskiness that must be his skin.

A faint moan escaped her.

'Shh.' Max gathered her even closer. Now she was virtually lying on top of him, squashed between his body and the webbing and frame under the mattress. That had the effect, of course, of squashing her closer against his body.

He had noticed. He could hardly fail to, of course, but the noticing was more than intellectual. Lucy was a country girl and, however much society liked to think that young women knew nothing of such matters, she understood perfectly well what happened to the bodies of male animals during mating.

She noticed something else: Lord Burnham, the iceberg, was not at all icy. Not this close.

It was interesting and strange and stirred something inside her. She ought to be frightened, but she was quite certain that Max was not going to attack her. After all, he could have committed any number of indecencies with his hands if he had been inclined, but they had not strayed an inch. She found herself relaxing, safe.

This was torture of the most refined sort. Goodness knew what it would be like if Lucy was a curvaceous, attractive young lady. Unfortunately, the message that she was a rather ordinary, sharp-tongued female with as few curves as she had graces did not appear to have reached his body.

Why the blazes hadn't he called out, stopped Hobson coming in before the man had the door open? He had been caught off guard, Max admitted to himself. And that was inexplicable, because normally he was quick-thinking in an emergency. He told himself it was worry about Sophia, but he knew that, in truth, Lucy had distracted him.

Now he was aroused—and that was an understatement. He was hard and aching and furious with himself for getting into this predicament and for responding to it like this. The confounded woman was virtually lying on top of him—which was his fault—he'd hauled her so close when she was about to sneeze. Surely even a respectable virgin could not fail to notice the state his body was in?

On the other hand, he discovered as he fought for control, she was as relaxed and limp now as a sleeping cat. Perhaps she really was that innocent.

At last, at the point when he was distracting himself by cursing the fates for wishing such a conscientious and thorough valet on him, Hobson left the room. Max heard him walk away, then the loud click of the outer door closing behind him.

'Has he gone?' Lucy whispered, her breath tickling his ear and adding another few twigs to the blaze.

'Yes.' Max managed to slide her off his body, then reached out for the side of the bed frame and pulled himself out. 'Can you manage?' He did not want to haul her out by the hand.

'If I wriggle.'

Max stood up and held the valance clear, eyes fixed on the bed head. There was only so much wriggling he could cope with. The thought was bad enough, to say nothing of the breathy little sounds she was making.

Lucy emerged and began to brush down her skirts. 'Another evening gown ruined?'

'Not at all.' She twisted round to check the back. 'It

was only slightly dusty and I didn't feel anything catch or tear. Pringle will be able to brush it down. And the other one was not silk, thank goodness, so it will dry without watermarks, she says. The ribbons will probably need replacing, but that's all.'

Sophia would be furious at having one-tenth of the damage done to her own gowns, he knew. Lucy cheerfully brushed off the dust and carried on.

'You are not concerned that she will gossip with the other staff about this succession of mishaps to your clothing?'

'Of course not. Pringle is very loyal.' She began to stab hairpins back into her coiffure. 'This feels like a haystack.' She caught his slight huff of amusement. 'What is funny about that?'

'I was imagining Sophia under the same circumstances. She would be having a tantrum.'

'Your stepsister is a beauty, used to looking perfect at all times. It must be a great concern to her if she looks less than her best.' She shrugged. 'I am not a beauty, so I do not care.'

What was a gentleman supposed to say to that? *You are too modest?* But she was looking at him now with those clear brown eyes and he knew such flummery would be treated with the disdain it deserved.

'You are an original,' Max said, his tongue apparently several beats ahead of his brain.

That was received with a look that said, quite clearly, that he had disappointed her. Or possibly insulted her and she was trying to work out whether to be offended or dismissive.

At which point Max, who *always* thought before he spoke, plunged in, feet first. 'Hedge sparrows. Those little ones the country folk call dunnocks. They hide away under hedges and look small and brown and non-descript. But when you study them they are subtle and charming. And they have a beautiful song.'

What the devil was wrong with him? Dunnocks? Hedge birds? He was lucky that the chamber pot was empty because, when Lucy had taken in what he had called her, she was going to look for a blunt instrument.

'Oh,' she said softly. 'I know the birds you mean. They *are* charming. What a very kind thing to say. Thank you.' And she smiled up at him, transforming her irritated expression into something else entirely.

They stared at each other for a moment, then she said, 'What is it?'

Max, already in the hole, began to dig himself in deeper. He knew it, but he seemed dunnocks power-less to control his own words. 'I was thinking that I would like to kiss you.'

'You would?' She didn't scream or faint or slap him.

He was dreaming, of course. He, Max Fenton, Earl of Burnham, connoisseur of lovely women, renowned for his self-control, had apparently lost his head. 'I would,' he said simply.

Lucy tipped her head to one side, considering him. Blinked. 'Yes, please.'

So he kissed her. As his lips touched hers and her hands came up to rest against his chest, an inner, cyn-ical Max thought fleetingly that perhaps she was not the innocent she appeared, or that this was a cunning ploy to entrap him.

The little gasp she gave as he drew her closer, sealed his mouth over hers, silenced the cynic. No one could feign this innocence, this curiosity with its endearing earnestness. She tasted of the tea served after dinner and, faintly, of tooth powder. Her skin smelt of Castile soap and her hair of rosemary.

She stood quite still, her hands flat against his lapels, and moved her mouth experimentally against his, making a little humming sound as she explored. When he ran the tip of his tongue along the seam of her lips she opened to him and the hum became a little gasp, but she did not recoil.

But he must, he knew that in the part of his brain that was not lost to all sense. Lucy had no idea what this would lead to, but he knew, only too well. Regretfully Max lifted his head, stepped back and sought for the right words.

Instead, Lucy found them. 'That was…interesting,' she said prosaically. Women had been known to feign a swoon at the intensity of his kisses. Not Miss Marsh. 'Rather nice, but very unexpected. I had wondered what all the fuss was about.'

All the fuss? Rather nice? 'I must apologise,' Max said stiffly. 'I do not know what came over me.'

A wicked dimple appeared at the corner of her mouth. 'You don't?'

'Are you unshockable, Miss Lambert? Miss Marsh, I mean.'

'No, of course not. All sorts of things shock me. Cruelty and unkindness—and tripe and onions. But I do understand the facts of life. From a purely practical standpoint, naturally,' she added seriously.

Max had a suspicion that she was teasing him. No one ever teased him. *Not since Julia.*

'Anyway,' the provoking woman said, walking back

to the sitting room, 'where were we before your valet arrived?'

'You were suggesting that my stepsister might be engaging in a liaison with a servant.' That was as effective as a bucket of cold water over the head for subduing any lingering traces of arousal.

'It does happen.' Lucy perched on the arm of a chair and began to rub and stretch her fingers. He doubted she even realised she was doing it. 'Servants are people, too. And just like those who employ them, many are individuals with interesting minds, decent moral standards—and physical attractions.'

'Thank you, Miss Marsh. If I wanted a lecture on the rights of man I would read the works of Thomas Paine. However, we have no need to invoke the possibility of a misalliance between an earl's daughter and a groom. I am quite certain she would not have had the opportunity to encounter any of the staff of the guests here. No, she is secretive because none of that collection of young bloods is a suitable pretender for her hand and she knows it. Sophia is a considerable heiress.'

He stood by the fireplace, one foot on the fender, feeling a ridiculous urge to maintain a dignified pose, to keep control of the situation. In front of a woman who had been rolling around under a bed with him while his valet checked the chamber pot, for goodness sake? The woman who had driven his body into a state of aching arousal just by lying on him?

'Very well.' Lucy gave her fingers one last stretch and stood up, brushing her skirts down. 'I will take them one by one tomorrow and see what I can discover.'

'Miss Marsh... Lucy—'

'Yes, Max?' She turned, one hand on the door handle.

'What happened just now—I would not have you fearing that I would take advantage of the situation.'

The look she sent him was level and cool. 'You would certainly not get the opportunity to, Max, believe me.'

She eased the door open, peered cautiously around the edge and then was gone, leaving him staring at the blank panels.

Of all the confounded— Then he felt something very like laughter welling up inside him. *Pompous ass. She certainly told you what was what. And took what she desired from that situation, too.* If she had not wanted to kiss him he would have known about it in no uncertain terms, he was quite certain. And she was a good judge of character—she knew he would not presume on that kiss.

Much as he might want to. The certainty of that came as the final unsettling moment in a very long day.

'Would you be so good as to pass me the cherry preserve, Lord St Giles?'

It had taken Lucy an uncomfortably long time to get to sleep the night before, but at least that had given her the opportunity to decide on her strategy. She would work systematically through the young gentlemen and make notes of conversations with them, what others said of them and how they and Lady Sophia behaved together. Finding the Viscount next to her at breakfast, she concluded that she might as well begin with him.

'The cherry? Certainly, Miss Marsh.' He passed the silver dish, looking rather like a very amiable heron with his height and beak of a nose. 'Do you have sufficient toast?'

'Ample, thank you.' So, polite to the least significant female guest. Neatly turned out for what would probably be a morning of walks or other recreation in the grounds, no objectionable habits apparent. So far, so amiable. His clothes were very good quality, of tasteful cut and appropriate colour. The sapphire in his cravat last night, the intricate links of his watch chain and the fine, but sombre, antique intaglio ring on his signet finger seemed to show he was not so short of funds that he needed to seduce an heiress.

That might signify a good tailor and large outstanding bills. And he might hold on to his last few pieces of jewellery to appear solvent, of course. She should not leap to conclusions.

Lucy wondered what Max had against him or whether it was simply that he was apparently friendly with the rather louche Lord Tobias and Lord Easton, he of the dubious waistcoat.

'The post, my lady.' Formby came in with a substantial pile on a silver salver.

'Excellent. Deliver it to those of our guests who are here, Formby. Everyone—do not stand on formality, feel free to read your letters.' She began to flip over her own pile.

There was nothing for Lucy, of course, but an envelope was placed beside Lord St Giles's plate.

'Do, please, open it,' she urged, seeing him glance at it, pick up his knife, then restrain himself. The handwriting was very feminine. 'Unless it is a beastly bill, of course!'

'If you do not mind, Miss Marsh. Thank you. I will just take a quick look in case it is something urgent.'

He slid his knife under the seal and opened out the folded page.

Reading someone else's letters was something no lady would ever contemplate, but, Lucy reminded herself, she was here as a spy, not a lady. She buttered her toast and slid her gaze sideways.

Yes, definitely a feminine hand and, at the bottom, a signature she could just make out.

Your Jane XXX

Lord St Giles stroked his fingertips over the words, sighed, then folded the letter again and slid it into the breast of his coat. There was the trace of a gentle smile on his lips and Lucy fixed her attention firmly on her toast.

It was the smile that convinced her that she could cross him off her list. It had not been the smirk of a man who had made a conquest, nor that of someone amused by an infatuated female. No, that had been as tender as the brush of his fingers over the signature.

The Marquis came in, said good morning to his hostess and went to the sideboard. When he came back he approached the seat next to Lucy. 'May I?'

'Certainly.' She moved the conserve dish aside for him and tried not to let her disappointment show. She had hoped for another member of The List, as she was beginning to think of the young men.

Sandwiched between a marquis and a viscount, she was glad that her friends' remarkably good marriages had at least left her comfortable with gentlemen of rank. Hopefully they would not realise they were making small talk with a humble pianoforte teacher.

A humble pianoforte teacher who had been kissing an earl in his bedchamber the night before.

Even as she thought it, the man in question strolled in, greeted the assembly and went to peruse the chafing dishes.

Was she blushing? Lucy touched her cheek, but it was difficult to detect heat through the fine cotton of the crocheted gloves she wore. No one was staring at her, anyway. She had woken that morning half convinced that the kiss had been a figment of her imagination. Now, she told herself that her imagination had never been that vivid. She could still feel the pressure of Max's lips down to her toes.

There had been the evidence of the gown, as well. Pringle was proving to be an absolute godsend. She had not turned a hair when she came to undress Lucy and was confronted with another distressed garment and, that morning, had announced that it was as good as new after a brushing and a light sponging.

'I don't think much of their housekeeping here, miss,' she'd said with a sniff. 'If you got that dusty tripping over in the corridor, I hate to think what it's like under the beds.'

Lucy hadn't known whether to laugh or hide her face. Now, catching Max's gaze across the fruit bowl as he sat down opposite her, she wished she could share that observation with him. But perhaps he didn't have a sense of humour.

I could never fall for a man with no sense of humour.

The thought shocked her so much that she dropped her teaspoon into the saucer with a clatter.

I am not—I couldn't be. I don't want to fall for any man and certainly not this one.

There was only one outcome of developing an attraction for an earl—heartbreak, or ruin followed closely by heartbreak. This was physical attraction, of course, nothing more.

She made herself look at Max again. He looked back from beneath heavy-lidded eyes. Either he hadn't slept well or he was plotting goodness knew what. It did not seem to bode well for whoever he was thinking about with that calculating expression.

You could freeze ice cream with it, she thought fancifully in an effort to distract herself from her own unruly imaginings. It would be a novel flavour at Gunter's in Berkeley Square. *Iced Earl: a tart and stimulating experience.*

The whimsy made her smile and Max's expression changed, lightened. Goodness, did he think she was smiling at him, attempting to flirt?

The arrival of the rest of the party in a flurry of chatter and greetings, dropped napkins and attentive footmen, distracted her. When she glanced back, Max was deep in conversation with Lady Hermione.

The lifting of his regard felt almost physical. Lucy buttered another piece of toast that she did not really want and cut it into small pieces while the other guests settled themselves around the table. Then she located Lady Sophia and set herself to watch the remaining men on The List while she nibbled at the toast.

Sophia smiled sweetly at her stepbrother and then applied herself to gossipy chatter with the young ladies nearest her. They were all clearly aware of the gentlemen and the effect they were having on them, but both sides kept up the pretence that no flirtation was happening. Lady Sophia seemed to be attracting no more, and no less, covert attention than her friends.

Were the lovers so very skilled at hiding their feelings—or was Max wrong in suspecting a serious liaison? Perhaps Sophia's eagerness to attend the party was simply a wilful girl's rebellion at having a treat refused and the hints her friend had given the chaperon merely troublemaking.

What would flush a lover out of hiding if one really did exist? Lucy recalled the intruders in the conservatory the evening before: perhaps she could eliminate at least one of the gentlemen, after all.

What she needed was half an hour of quiet thought to work out who to approach first. She abandoned the toast and got up with a murmured, 'Excuse me', to the gentlemen on either side before slipping from the room, unremarked, she hoped.

She should have known better. No sooner had Lucy found a window seat in the small Blue Salon to curl up on than the door opened. It was shielded from the window by an ornate Chinese screen so she hoped whoever it was would think the room empty and leave. But, no. The door closed and Max came around the screen.

'You wanted me?'

Chapter Seven

Did she want him? Well, yes, was the honest answer, although the rational, sensible part of her brain was jumping up and down and shouting, *Run!*

'Um?' It was hardly an intelligent response, but at least it was non-committal.

'You smiled at me rather secretively over breakfast. I thought you wanted a private word.' Max strolled across the floor and leaned one shoulder against the opposite end of the window embrasure.

'Oh. No, not at all. I was thinking about ice cream.'

She had discovered how to disconcert the Earl, it seemed. After a long moment during which he was almost visibly examining her words in his head, Max said, 'Ice cream? At breakfast?'

'Yes, I adore it, don't you? I like the unusual favours—parmesan cheese, burnt sugar and ginger.' It was a fib, she had never tasted any of those, although her friend Jane had once regaled her with mouth-watering descriptions of the delights to be sampled at Gunter's.

'But possibly not all at once,' Max murmured. 'How do you intend on spending your day?'

'I should report that we can rule out Lord St Giles: I saw his reaction to his morning correspondence and the man is in love. I hope to eliminate Mr Doncaster as well, this morning.'

'On the basis of his appearance in the conservatory with Miss Gainford?'

'Exactly. I was just considering how to find a way of raising the subject without appearing to pry, because, of course, he may be flirting with her as a cover for his interest in Lady Sophia.'

'Or he may simply be a rake and be leading both of them on,' Max observed. 'And have you decided how to approach the problem?'

'I shall begin by luring Miss Gainford into discussing Mr Doncaster's manifold charms and hope she will betray her feelings. I shall then try to find some opportunity to talk of her with him, although that may be more difficult to arrange. Perhaps I can manage it during dinner.'

Max nodded. 'That sounds the best way to go about it. You must be careful not to reveal that you saw them together.'

'I might have seen them entering or leaving. I can hint.'

'You appear to have a talent for this.' Max straightened up and wandered over to a side table where a mass of roses had been arranged. He extracted a half-open red one from the middle, snapped the stem short and slid the flower into his buttonhole.

'A talent for spying? I hope not, it sounds rather unsavoury as a general principle. But I am enjoying the puzzle, I find. I never… When I could play, when the music filled me, occupied my mind, I confess I did not pay a great deal of attention to the world around me. My friends, of course, but mysteries and puzzles—I do not think I noticed those before.'

'Your music was totally absorbing?'

She had bent her legs so she could clasp her hands around her knees and Max sat down at the end of the window seat in the space that created.

'Yes.' She hesitated, wondering whether he was merely being polite or was actually interested. 'It made me selfish, I can see that now. I paid very little heed to anyone else. My friends were very understanding.'

'And your parents?'

'Hymns, sacred music, pure and sentimental ballads were all acceptable. Fortunately one of my friends, Verity, is the daughter of a bishop and was possessed of a good pianoforte. My parents were delighted that I spent so much time in such a worthy household.'

'Your friend Verity who is now the Duchess of Aylsham. I see.' No doubt he had been wondering how an ordinary person like herself was friendly with a duchess. Max rested his head against the folded-back shutter and looked out at the lawns. 'Miss Gainford has just wandered past clutching a slim volume and looking mournful. Or that may be lovelorn. Or perhaps she is attempting to show a romantically sensitive disposition.'

'Unkind,' Lucy chided as she twisted to see. 'No, you are quite correct, I do believe that is extreme sensibility—there, she has stopped to pick a rose and clasp it to her bosom. I do hope it is free from earwigs.'

Max snorted. When she looked at him he was grinning. It took quite five years off his apparent age.

Lucy smiled back, caught by another of the rare moments of charm.

'I have not seen you smile as much as I have today,' Max said. 'You are not feeling prickly?'

'Prickly? Oh. No. No, I am not. Perhaps the puzzle of Lady Sophia's lover is distracting me.'

'From the pain of your hands?'

'No,' she said shortly. The physical pain was manageable and improving. But Lucy doubted whether the anguish of losing her music was ever going to fade.

'I think I understand,' Max said, as though she had explained. Then he was expressionless again. 'This might be an ideal time to talk to Miss Gainford and see if she is in a mood to confide.'

'Yes. Could you open this window for me?'

Max pushed up the bottom part and Lucy was able to swing her legs over the low sill and hop down on to the terrace.

'Thank you!'

She ran across the flagstones until she reached the balustrade and saw Miss Gainford was already crossing the lawn towards the low-spreading branches of a great cedar of Lebanon. Lucy waited until she had disappeared under the shelter of the boughs and strolled after her, taking care to tread softly until she reached the tree.

'Oh! I am so sorry—have I disturbed you?' She did not wait for an answer, but crossed to the iron seat against the trunk and sat down at the other end to her quarry. 'It is so beautiful out here and away from all the shallow chatter about gossip and beaux, don't you think?'

Either Miss Gainford was too well mannered to tell her to go away or she actually welcomed some company, because she smiled wanly and laid down her book. She placed the rose carefully on top.

'Miss Marsh, is it not? Yes, when one's heart is full of genuine sentiment, one does not welcome idle chatter about flirtation.'

'I do so agree with you.' Lucy managed a sigh that she hoped conveyed yearning and fine feeling. None of her friends as they fell in love had drifted about speaking like this, but she should not be unfair—there might be genuine, deep emotion here. 'Forgive me asking, but are you separated from someone? It must be very hard if there is someone you would wish to be with, but you must hide that feeling.'

'Oh, no.' Miss Gainford had forgotten to be languid and her smile was eager now. 'No— Oh, can I trust you not to betray me, Miss Marsh? There is no one I can confide in here.'

'You may trust me, Miss Gainford,' Lucy assured her. After all, even if she was able to tell Max that Miss Gainford was indeed involved with Mr Doncaster, he would keep it to himself.

'My parents wish me to marry the eldest son of our neighbours in Hampshire, but he is the most stolid creature—good-natured enough, but a positive *block*. And I love another,' she added with a dramatic tremble in her voice.

'Someone unsuitable?'

'Oh, no. Well connected, financially secure and of such good character…'

Can we be talking about the same man who leads unmarried girls into the conservatory for a tête-à-tête, I wonder? But I am not going to spend the morning coaxing a name out of her.

'Might I guess? Mr Philip Doncaster?'

'Ah!' Miss Gainford's hands flew to her mouth. 'How did you know?'

'I guessed. I saw a glance between you, saw how he looks at you, and my judgement of his character, on very short acquaintance, made me wonder if it is he.'

Oh, Lord, now I am talking like a sensation novel myself!

Miss Gainford nodded shyly. 'Is he not wonderful?'

'I am sure he is. Are you promised to each other?'

'We are.' Miss Gainford tugged on the thin gold chain around her neck and a ring threaded on it emerged from her bodice. 'This was Philip's grandmother's. He has great prospects in the legal profession,' she added in an awed voice. 'His prospects will soon be secure and then he will speak to Papa.'

'I wish you every happiness. But I disturbed your quiet contemplation and will go. Be assured, I will do nothing to harm your romance.'

'No, please stay and talk, Miss Marsh.' Sharing her own confidences seemed to give the other girl more assurance. 'Will you not call me Lizzie?'

'Thank you. I am Lucy.'

'And I think you, too, have a secret of the heart. Am I right?'

'Me?' It emerged as a squeak.

'Lord Burnham.'

'Oh, goodness, no. He merely took pity on me when I was stranded in London. He is an acquaintance of my father,' Lucy said with a casual air and sinking heart. 'That is all.'

'Really?' Lizzie sounded disappointed. 'But the two of you exchange such looks. And he watches you, when you are not looking. It is very romantic.'

What?

'I assure you, there is no such feeling between us,' Lucy said, trying to sound puzzled and not in the least defensive. 'I am concerned he will report to my father that my behaviour and deportment is unsatisfactory. I am unused to such elevated company so I suppose he feels some responsibility to keep a watchful eye on me. But my goodness—*romantic*? He is far above any aspirations a squire's daughter might have, believe me.'

Was she protesting too much? *That kiss. That look of understanding in the little salon just now...*

'Oh, how disappointing. I suppose, being in love myself, I want everyone else to be, too,' Lizzie said, laughing at herself, it seemed.

'A generous thought.' Lucy managed a smile as she stood up. 'I will leave you to your romantic musings.'

She was halfway across the lawn before she realised where she was going—to find Max. How foolish... But then, perhaps she ought to report the progress she had made. Unless Mr Doncaster was an expert deceiver he was highly unlikely to be the man in Sophia's heart, so that was one more to cross off The List.

The window into the Blue Salon was still open, so she ducked through and down on to the window seat, her feet in light sandals soundless on the cushioned surface. Before she could straighten her skirts and jump down the door opened. Lucy knelt quietly on the seat, hoping not to appear the kind of hoyden who scrambled in and out of windows.

But the newcomer did not come around the screen. 'Oh, there you are, Max. I have been looking everywhere for you, you really are the most provoking man.'

It was Sophia—and Max must be sitting on the other side of the screen. She could either try to climb back out without making a sound or she could stay where she was and hope Sophia did not come around the screen and find her, compromisingly alone with Lord Burnham.

'If I had any idea I was so urgently needed, my dear, I would have flown to your side,' Max drawled.

'Beast,' Sophia said amiably. 'I need you to frank some letters for me.'

'I do not know why I should do anything for you, except pack you straight off to your mama in Bath under the escort of two strapping footmen and the dourest chaperon I can find.'

'Oh, don't sulk, Max. What do you expect me to do when you virtually lock me up and forbid me such an innocent pleasure as a house party?'

Wisely, perhaps, her stepbrother did not answer. 'Bring me the letters, I will frank them for you when I have finished reading *The Times*.'

Sophia was clearly hoping for a stimulating argument. Lucy could hear her moving restlessly about the room, the swish of her skirts punctuated by the rustle of Max's newspaper. Could she tiptoe out unseen? Sophia sounded to be close to the door. Lucy settled back on to the window seat, then almost leapt to her feet when Sophia spoke again.

'And you should not be so high and mighty, Max,

bringing your latest mistress with you. She seems very nice, I must say, but hardly up to your usual standard. Besides, I thought your *belle amies* were always married ladies or widows, not spinsters.'

'Miss Marsh is *not* my mistress.' There was the sound of a newspaper being folded with some emphasis. 'She is a young lady who found herself in a difficult situation and I did what I could to assist, given that I was distracted at the time by you running off like a petulant schoolgirl.'

Sophia muttered something. Then, 'I should have realised. She really isn't pretty, is she? And you always have beautiful mistresses, someone told me. And there's her hands, poor creature. But she is very pleasant, for all that.'

'There are times, Sophia, when I think the best thing would be for me to marry a lady of iron will and the utmost propriety who will teach you to behave as a young lady should.'

'Your Miss Marsh, for instance?'

'No. *Not* Miss Marsh. Pleasant ladies of genteel origins do not make suitable wives for earls. A lady of impeccable breeding will be required. In addition perhaps I should look for someone with a large dowry. It would be useful to save me from being bankrupted by your spending.'

'I knew it! You are going to propose to Lady Cynthia Probert, aren't you?'

'She is very suitable. I wish you could see the necessity for suitable marriages, Sophia. You have commonality of station, of wealth, of acquaintances and culture. There is clear understanding on both sides from the beginning and the assurance that your spouse is who they seem. Our parents had marriages that worked very well, did they not?'

'Well, yes, if all you want is monotony and blandness.'

'I would say tranquillity and stability—and for children, too. I was happy growing up and I have seen the awful consequences for everyone when there is no stability.'

'It sounds dull,' Sophia said petulantly. 'Max, Lady Cynthia is the crossest creature in creation. She'll turn you into even more of a stuffy old man than you are now! Oh, I despair of you—what you need is to fall in love and then you might be human!'

The echoes of the door slamming rattled the porcelain plates hanging on the wall. Lucy bolted out of the window again while the sound still rang.

Well, that would teach her to thinking yearningly of Max's—no, the *Earl's*—kisses, Lucy thought bitterly as she rounded the corner of the house and saw the young ladies of the party. Two were playing shuttlecock and battledore on the lower lawn, with a net slung between two posts, and the others were seated on rugs, watching.

She hesitated, reluctant to join them. She felt too sore and too cross with herself for being such a ninny as to imagine that one kiss meant anything to a man like the Earl of Burnham. Then Miss Moss saw her and waved and she changed her mind. It would be rude to turn and walk away and an hour or two spent in the company of the sort of young ladies who were ideal partners for a titled gentleman would be salutary.

Miss Thomas and Lady Georgiana were playing very seriously, their faces fixed with concentration.

'Oh, well done, Mary!' Clara Moss called as Lucy sat down beside her and her friend's shot had the shuttlecock sailing over Lady Georgiana's head and into a bush. 'Do you play, Miss Marsh?'

'Lucy. And, no.' She lifted her hands. 'Not that I am sorry on such a warm day.'

'Oh, I forgot. Do forgive me.' Clara looked chagrined at her own tactlessness, then brightened, seeing a way to make amends. 'Have you not brought your parasol out? Here, use Mary's for the moment, it would be dreadful if you caught the sun.'

Clara settled down to the game again, calling encouragement or uttering groans of sympathy when her friend lost a point.

Lucy tilted the parasol so that it shielded her face and tried to make sense of her feelings. Only there was no sense to be made. Had she lost her mind? To be thrown into a tizzy after being kissed by an earl—her first kiss—why, that was entirely to be expected. To be excited more than embarrassed when someone made utterly incorrect assumptions about the feelings the Earl in question might have for her—that was surely a danger signal? And to be utterly cast down when he made it clear to his sister that she, Lucy, was a *pleasant lady of genteel origins* and in no way fit to be the wife of an aristocrat? Now that reaction was more than dangerous.

She was, she hoped, pleasant. Her upbringing had certainly been genteel and a day ago she would have agreed wholeheartedly with anyone stating that she was quite unfit to be the wife of the Earl of Burnham. Her head was still firmly of that opinion, but her heart, or possibly some demon of irrationality that had taken possession of her, was thoroughly miserable.

Perhaps it was some sort of delayed reaction to her injury? She pondered that for a moment, willing this feeling to be easily explained. She had heard that people who had a dreadful shock sometimes did not fully react to it until much later. Certainly before, when she could still play, when her music possessed her, it had never occurred to her that she might marry.

Mama and Papa, of course, expected their daughter to make a good match—by which they meant to a dull, respectable, God-fearing man. An attorney, perhaps, or a clergyman. Quite how they expected this to happen was not clear. Possibly, Lucy thought with a flash a bitter humour, they expected eyes to meet across a pile of hymn books. But, no, that would imply undesirable emotion, not rational choice.

Verity, Prue and Jane had not made rational choices—they had been pitchforked by emotion into happiness and it seemed to be the most wonderful of accidents. But without that, the prospect of becoming a spinster had seemed no hardship, not if she had her music. One day she would inherit everything and then she would live alone, quite happily, she had thought. *If I had my music...*

Some of the young men strolled down from the upper lawn to watch the game and the girls brightened, began to laugh and flirt. Perhaps, now the music had gone, she was making up for all those years of not flirting, of not looking yearningly at men and, by the most unfortunate timing, she happened to be kissed by Max.

It is like those goslings that hatched out in a basket by Mrs Philpot's range at the farm, she thought. *The first thing they saw was Toggle the cat and they decided he was their mother and followed him everywhere. I was kissed by Max and now all I can see is him.*

It was very unfortunate, but simply dealt with, she decided, closing the parasol with a snap and sitting up straight. She would ignore this…yearning, or whatever it was. It would go away and Max would go away and everything would be just as it was before.

Or, if it were not, she could pretend until it was so.

Chapter Eight

Lucy told herself with fierce determination that there was no choice. She had accepted her changed life, now she must adapt to this, too. She was a single woman with damaged hands and without looks or dowry or family support. She would never marry and she was not going to attract any man as his mistress. Not that she would contemplate such a thing for a moment. All the business of dowries and settlements in marriage was bad enough with its overtones of the marketplace, but the thought of selling herself… No.

Someone sat down close by with a murmur of apology for disturbing her. Lucy smiled brightly, murmured, 'Not at all', and, 'Do you have sufficient space on the rug?' before she saw it was Philip Doncaster occupying the edge of the blanket.

'Oh, Mr Doncaster. I'm afraid Miss Gainford is not with this group.'

He turned so sharply to look at her that he had to put out a hand to stop himself sprawling on the grass. 'Miss Gainford?'

'I am sorry if I was tactless.' Lucy glanced around.

'Nobody can overhear us. It is just that I thought that you and Miss Gainford had an understanding. But perhaps I am wrong?'

No, she was not, judging by the way the tips of his ears turned pink. 'Ah... Er... Well, I am dashed fond of Lizzie, you see. But...'

'But?'

'My father wants me to marry Miss—er...someone else. But I love Lizzie.' He glanced around, the picture of guilt. 'You won't tell anyone?'

She would have to, but it would go no further than Max. 'I do not gossip, Mr Doncaster. Your secret will not reach your father through me, I assure you. But how do you intend to carry on your courtship? You do not plan to elope, I hope.'

'Certainly not.' Suddenly the young man about town looked as sober as a judge. 'I have been working in my uncle's chambers at Lincoln's Inn as a clerk. My godfather is a barrister also and he has promised to take me into the practice with a partnership in a year—he is not far off wanting to retire from the Bar, you see. I plan to convince Mr Gainford that I can support his daughter as he would wish, with every good prospect for my future career. If I show Papa that I am truly dedicated to advancing myself and that I love Lizzie, I have hopes he will relent about my betrothal and continue my allowance.'

'But until then you must avoid every appearance of scandal, I can see that. No meetings in the conservatory, then,' Lucy said before she recalled that he could not know she'd been there. 'I saw you go in there the other evening.'

The blush spread down over his cheekbones.

'Miss Gainford is seated under that cedar of Lebanon on the top lawn. It is in full view from the house, should anyone choose to look hard enough—there can be no harm in you sitting with her, I'm sure.'

He scrambled to his feet, grinned at her. 'You are a sport, Miss Marsh.'

She smiled as she watched him walk away. Yes, definitely another one crossed off The List without any awkward encounters over dinner. Now she had to compose herself sufficiently to report to Max. To *Lord Burnham*, she reminded herself.

Max let himself out of the garden door and looked down the slope to the party playing at battledore and shuttlecock. There was no sign of Sophia, which was a concern, but all the young men were visible, so doubtless she was just sulking. Lucy was deep in conversation with young Doncaster, establishing his feelings for Miss Gainford, no doubt.

He turned away, followed the wall of the house to the corner and then struck off, crossing the carriage drive and making for the stable block. Dorothea had told him to take his pick of the saddle horses, should he wish to ride, and now, unsettled by that confrontation with Sophia, he was in the mood for exercise, the more physical the better.

It was typical of his stepsister to turn and attack when she was criticised, but he did not like the way she had fixed on Lucy, although he had not picked up a suggestion that any of the other house guests suspected a liaison. And what did the minx know about his mistresses? But she was correct, Lucy was as unsuitable for his *chère amie* as she was for a wife.

And why was he even thinking about her in either of those roles, damn it? He should be thinking about Lady Cynthia Probert, the ideal candidate to be the future Countess of Burnham. The problem was, Sophia was quite correct. Lady Cynthia was a pattern card of propriety and as dull as…as dull as that implied. She would not do.

Somehow he had to balance the need to find someone fitted for the role with the need for that person to be pleasant to live with. And that, he knew, was quite different from being in love with that person. His Uncle Robert had married for love, a merchant's daughter from a nearby town, and he recalled asking his father why they always seemed so cold with one another.

'She did not learn fast enough to fit into his position in society and her gaucheries began to embarrass him and she saw that and became angry and defiant. The love that had made him deny our father's prohibition was rubbed away and all that was left was resentment,' his father had explained.

It had puzzled him then: surely love was supposed to last and to be a true touchstone of the worth of the beloved? And then he saw Julia, bedazzled, betrayed and quite unfitted for the life she found herself in and, finally, despairing.

But it was time he stopped looking for another Julia, a wilful beauty with blue eyes and far more courage than sense. She would have made a most unsettling wife, unless, of course, she had loved him. Which she had not. He heard her voice in his memory as he walked through the great archway into the stable yard.

Oh, Max! You are far too young for me even if we

are the same age. I want a grown man—the man I love.
I am going to live happily ever after, you wait and see.

And he had waited and not betrayed her secret and
Julia had died because of his misplaced sense of loy-
alty. Ruined, abandoned and desperate, she had found
oblivion in the cold waters of the Thames and his pun-
ishment for sentimentality and muddled thinking had
been to identify her and to open her final letter when
it eventually reached him.

Surgeons could cut away diseased flesh, but no one
had discovered how to cut away a memory, to keep it
from returning in nightmares.

'My lord?' The groom's voice jerked him back to
the present. 'May I show you around the stables? Or
would you like to take a horse out now?'

'Thank you. I thought to ride at some point during
my stay here. I prefer something with some character
and a turn of speed.'

'I have just the thing for you, my lord. The grey in
the centre box. Jerry!' A lad looked out of a nearby
stall. 'Run out Windrift.'

The grey was a stallion with obvious Arab blood betrayed by the dished nose and the flowing tail carried
so high. He took exception to the stable cat, the mount-
ing block, the dung barrow and a passing blackbird,
but when he was trotted up to Max he dipped a soft
muzzle into his extended hand and did not try to bite.

'Very nice. Does Lady Hopewell intend to breed
from him?'

'Not sure, my lord. He's a bit of a handful, to be honest. More than her ladyship bargained for, I reckon.'

Interesting. Max wondered if she might be willing

to sell. If Windrift rode as well as he looked, he was a tempting proposition.

He thanked the man and strolled back to the house. Luncheon would be called soon and then he would have to spend the afternoon being a considerate guest, taking part in whatever Dorothea had planned. And tomorrow he would have accumulated sufficient credit to escape for a ride, he hoped. Get away from worrying about Sophia, fighting ghosts and guilt, fretting that he might have placed Lucy in a difficult situation and exposed her to insult. And escape, somehow, this nagging sense that something was missing in his well-ordered life.

Lucy spoke once to Max when she found him by her side entering the dining room for the midday meal. 'As we hoped, that name can be crossed off The List,' she murmured, then moved away to take a seat next to Lady Sophia.

She might want to tip the glass of lemonade that the footman poured for her all down Sophia's pretty sprig muslin but, if she wanted to gain her confidence, she had to forget what she had overheard her say to Max.

'Would you care for some salad?' she offered, taking care to wield the serving spoons without a fumble. It was humiliating to be pitied for her hands.

'Thank you.' Sophia looked slightly taken aback by the friendly tone. 'Yes, please. May I pass you the cold salmon?'

'Please.'

'There is to be an archery contest tomorrow,' Sophia said as she helped herself to the fish. 'I am so looking forward to it and I think the weather will stay fair, don't you?'

'It looks as though it will—there is hardly a cloud in the sky. You will be taking part? I imagine you have a very accurate eye.'

Sophia dimpled a smile. 'I have! I should not boast, but I do pride myself on being a good shot.'

'Then perhaps I should lay a wager on you.'

'That would be such fun! We could wager for pennies, or forfeits.' She raised her voice. 'Oh, do listen, everyone! Miss Marsh has had such a good idea. We are to wager on the archery tomorrow—just pin money or trifles or some such thing. Will that not be amusing?'

There was a buzz of agreement and the men immediately began to argue about the stakes and who should act as bookmaker.

'Tredgold for bookie,' Lord Overdene suggested. 'He's the only one of us who can add up straight.'

This was obviously an in joke among the younger men and there were roars of laughter in which Algernon Tredgold joined.

'So clever of you, Miss Marsh,' Sophia said. 'I am certain to win.'

'And what will you wager on yourself?' Lucy asked. 'Perhaps you will offer odds in kisses? Who do you favour to bet on you and win?'

Sophia laughed, a delicious trill of amusement that had the men turning to look at her. They all smiled.

She kept her voice low, but her smile was wicked. 'These gentlemen? Oh, come, Miss Marsh, you cannot believe that I would welcome a kiss from any of them? Dimwits, poseurs or just too ordinary for words, I assure you.'

Was she protesting too much? Somehow her opinions had the ring of truth, but as Lucy was all too well aware, Lady Sophia was skilled at deception. The archery match would be useful, she decided. Sophia would surely wish to impress a man she admired and her willpower would have to be extraordinary if she did not watch him to see his reaction to her prowess.

The afternoon was spent strolling in the gardens, reading and taking in the shade. The young men discovered the lake and its boathouse, wheedled the ancient gardener into finding them the key and then spent a noisy, wet, but apparently entertaining hour or so discovering which of the rowing boats and punts had holes in the bottom.

'Quite a few of them,' Lucy observed to Miss Easton as two very wet young men walked past on their way to the house to change.

'That is my brother under the pond weed,' Miss Easton remarked. 'Benedict! Make certain you have no newts in your unmentionables!'

The other young ladies either blushed or collapsed in giggles as Lord Easton turned as red as his hair and strode off without replying.

'Oh, dear,' Lady Hopewell lamented as she joined them under the shade of the rose arbour. 'I had meant to have the boats overhauled before you all arrived and it quite slipped my mind. I do hope some, at least, are sound.'

'Is it quite safe, Lady Hopewell?' Lady Georgiana

enquired, averting her gaze from another pair of wet and laughing men.

'Perfectly—if one takes out a boat that isn't leaking, that is! I shall have the gardeners remove all the dubious ones and clean those that are sound. The lake is very shallow almost everywhere, which is why we have the punts. When the young gentlemen have had their fill of falling in, I expect they will be eager to show off their prowess with the punt pole. There are some little islands to explore as well, and a folly.'

That sounded amusing, if one could rely on the wilder spirits not to attempt water jousting or to try ramming each other, Lucy thought as she stood up, gathered up the blanket, strolled across into rather deeper shade where the sun would not be in her eyes and settled down again.

She had pleasant memories of islands in lakes after being a bridesmaid at Verity's unconventional wedding to Will, which had taken place on the tiny islet where they had been stranded and comprehensively compromised.

'Pleasant thoughts, Miss Marsh?' Max folded himself down elegantly on to the rug beside her.

She must have been smiling to herself, she supposed. Now she struggled to keep the curve on her lips and not freeze into rigidity. Lucy took several deep breaths and willed her shoulders to relax, reminding herself that she was *pleasant and genteel* and that she must not read anything into Lord Burnham choosing to sit beside her, other than good manners and amiability.

Amiability? Yes, he did appear rather less chilly than normal. It must be the sunshine.

She pulled herself together. 'Yes, very pleasant,

thank you. I was recalling the Duke and Duchess of Aylsham's wedding.' She glanced around, but no one was very close to overhear.

'The one that set society on its ears, with the guests arriving by rowing boat?'

'Yes. I was a bridesmaid.'

'And the aquatic adventures of our fellow guests have not dissuaded you from setting sail here?'

'No. There is the archery tomorrow afternoon and that will give the staff the opportunity to remove any boats that are unsafe.'

'You will be taking part?'

'In the archery? No.' She managed a smile. 'I have never learned to shoot.'

'Your hands?' Max asked. She liked that he did not avoid the subject.

'No, the fact that I never learned. Although now I do not think I could manage it anyway. My parents do not approve of frivolous sports for girls. Any sports, in fact, because they draw attention. And besides, as my mama always observes in horror, archery so often gives the gentlemen the opportunity to come very close to demonstrate. It was declared quite indecent.'

All he said was, 'I see.' Lucy decided that it was quite clear that he did not. What would an aristocratic male know about the life of a girl growing up with parents obsessed with the idea that pleasure was ungodly and that appearing virtuous and unblemished was the best their daughter could aspire to in life?

'Excuse me, I must speak to our hostess about a horse.' He stood up abruptly and walked away to Lady Hopewell's side.

Lucy watched him go. There was something about

the ease with which he had risen, the muscles in those long rider's legs that made her feel warm all over. Far warmer than sitting in this shady spot could account for. She pulled her gaze away and met that of Miss Easton, who grinned and then fanned herself in an exaggerated manner.

Goodness, Miss Easton thought she had been... Well, she had been. Ogling, that is. It was disgraceful and she should be ashamed of herself. Melissa would say it was natural, human, merely a question of appreciating a fine physical specimen. But Max was not a *specimen*. He was a very attractive man, although when she had begun to think that, she could not quite recall. Before he kissed her? Afterwards? Certainly not *during*, because then she had been incapable of any thought at all.

'Tea is here, everyone!' Lady Hopewell called, and Lucy went to join the others, thankful for something else to think about. The footmen had carried down some hampers, jugs of lemonade and trestle tables with white cloths to set the food out on.

Lucy filled a plate and went to sit by shy Lady Georgiana who could be counted upon not to admire passing gentlemen, or their legs. Or, if she did, she kept it to herself.

Dinner was very pleasant. Lady Hopewell had changed the seating plan and Lucy found herself between Mr Doncaster, who appeared to regard her as already a friend, and Sir George, who made intelligent conversation about the local wildlife.

Lucy was feeling positively relaxed until the dessert was served. Lady Hopewell raised her voice and an-

nounced, 'I have a treat for after dinner. As you may know, I have recently purchased a really wonderful new pianoforte and I propose that we have a little concert. It is one of Broadwood's grands. I thought I would mention it now so that everyone could think what they might like to play.'

'Is that a good make of pianoforte, do you know?' Philip Doncaster asked.

'Yes. They make instruments of the highest quality,' Lucy said, her stomach tightening. Suddenly the confection of cream, strawberries and little almond biscuits in front of her seemed impossible to eat.

A Broadwood grand. Even the pianoforte at the Bishop's Palace, which Verity used to let her play, had not been as good as that. Piano students learning to play were tolerable for her to listen to now, but if one of the guests was a good player—and Max had said that Lady Sophia was—then listening was going to be a nightmare.

Lucy kept up the conversation with Mr Doncaster until Lady Hopewell rose to lead the ladies out. She would make herself invisible while they all discussed what they were going to play. That would lead to the usual polite squabble over who would perform first and nobody would notice her.

'Lady Sophia should play first, she is so accomplished,' Miss Moss said.

'Oh, no, she should play last so as not to show the rest of us up,' Miss Easton protested. 'I shall go first because everyone will sound better once I have played.'

Lucy found herself a corner and hoped that her dark cream gown against a beige silk sofa would render her

Chapter Nine

Max looked around for Lucy, then saw just the hem of her gown showing beneath one of the draperies that framed a niche in the panelled walls. Of course, she would not want to make herself conspicuous by being the only one of the young ladies not able to perform.

He found a seat in an unoccupied row at the back of the audience and settled himself, wondering vaguely why, whatever their appearance or style, the gilt chairs provided at balls and receptions were, without exception, uncomfortable after ten minutes.

Miss Easton began with a lively country air. She was more than competent, he thought, and the pianoforte itself produced a beautiful sound. He normally endured, rather than enjoyed, musical interludes at house parties, but this evening might prove the exception.

Miss Easton was succeeded by Lady Georgiana, pink-cheeked and with the air of rushing to the dentist to get it over with. But, despite appearances, her playing was competent, if without the personality or vigour of Miss Easton's. She also kept to one short piece and retreated, blushing even harder, to friendly applause.

Next came Doncaster and young Overdene. Doncaster played and Overdene sang a comic song that stayed carefully on the right side of saucy. There was much laughter and calls for an encore, so they finished with a sea shanty and then bowed themselves off to be followed by Miss Thomas.

Now, she *was* good, Max decided, re-crossing his legs in an attempt to get comfortable. Not as good as Sophia, but quite delightful to listen to as she played her chosen piece of Mozart.

He glanced over to see what Lucy made of it. Surely she would appreciate such fine playing?

For a second he thought she had gone, then he saw the trailing hem of her skirts and realised that she must be sitting hunched up on the upholstered bench. He looked back at the stage, then back at the alcove. Young ladies did not sit in public with their feet up like that. Was she ill?

Max slid from his chair and padded quietly across. No one appeared to notice him.

Lucy was huddled on the bench, her arms around her knees, her face buried in her skirts. He realised that her arms were crossed so that she could put her fingers in her ears. Her shoulders were shaking.

'Lucy,' he whispered, going down on one knee beside her. 'Are you unwell?'

She started so violently that she almost pitched off the narrow seat into his arms. There were no tears on her face as he had feared, but it was white and strained and utterly miserable.

'Sorry.' She scrubbed a hand over her face and sat up.

'Come outside, you need some air.'

Max put one hand under her arm and guided her out, along the corridor and on to the terrace. The sound of music pursued them and he closed the door.

'Thank you.' She drew a deep, shuddering sigh. 'I am so sorry to have troubled you.'

'Nonsense. What is wrong? Should I fetch your maid? Or the housekeeper?'

'No. No, it was the music, that is all.'

'I thought it very good, although, obviously, I am no expert as you are.'

'It was beautiful,' Lucy said, her back half turned to him. 'Intolerable.'

'I do not understand.' There were still tremors running through her. Even in the moonlight he could see, even though she tensed slender shoulders against them. He wanted to hold her, but he had no idea whether his touch would make things worse. 'Can you explain?' Perhaps talking of it might help her.

'I will try. You will probably not understand. Even my close friends find it hard. When I play… When I *played*, the music possessed me, my mind and my body. It was…all enveloping, part of me. Now I can still listen to it, hear it, but it is not the same. It is like being suddenly blind or dumb, but I do not know how to explain it. How would you describe purple to someone who has never had sight?'

'I don't know.' He felt uncharacteristically helpless. This was not something he could make right, nor could he walk away and ignore her misery. Perhaps talking about it would help. 'Could you explain more?'

Lucy shrugged. 'Can you imagine a feeling that sweeps through you, body, mind, soul? Something that takes you over, something transcendental? Something

that you have done, created with your body, your skill. And then it has gone and you are left with the memory of it and you need it again. Perhaps it is like a drug. Like opium.'

Max knew exactly what it sounded like to him—a truly wonderful orgasm. But you could hardly offer that as a suggestion to an innocent. Because that was what Lucy was, even if she kissed with a sensuality that was surely instinctive.

He could not have closed the door properly because it swung open with a faint creak, allowing the music to float out, faint on the soft evening air. Lucy shivered, turned with a graceful swirl of skirts, and Max had an idea. She could no longer play, but—

'Lucy, can you dance?'

She looked back at him, puzzlement clear, even in the moonlight. 'Not very well. Mama and Papa rarely went to the assemblies and when my friends danced together I was the one who played for them.'

'Will you humour me and try?' Max held out his hands.

'Dance? Here? But why?'

'Because I would very much like to.'

She had that expression again, the one that told him she thought he was either all about in his head or planning something dubious, but to his surprise she stepped forward and let him take her hands.

'I warn you now, I will tread on your toes.' She said it lightly, but he could feel the tremor still running through her and the glance she gave towards the door was haunted.

At least it was a waltz tune, which meant he could hold her and the rhythm was strongly marked, which

helped. Max put one hand on her waist and lifted her hand in his, feeling the stiffness in her fingers. Her other hand rested lightly on his shoulder.

'One two three,' he murmured, starting to move.

Lucy caught the beat immediately, as he guessed she would. They circled cautiously as he counted out loud, then he felt her catch hold of the steps and he stopped speaking, let the music talk. She had stopped trembling and when he looked down he saw her eyes were closed, her lips slightly parted.

Then the music ceased, they drifted to a halt and she stepped forward, as though instinctively, and rested her head on his shoulder. Max slid his arms around her and just stood, feeling the softness of the relaxed body, trusting against his, listening to the faint sound of her breathing.

He wanted to kiss her, he realised, just as he knew he must not. Kisses raised expectations and he could not do that again to his prickly music teacher. Lucy showed no obvious signs of developing a *tendre* for him, but then, she was a very private person. He knew what it was to love hopelessly, to hide it, to have his heart broken, and he was not going to risk hers by being thoughtless. This was bad enough, this intimacy here in the shadows, the owl hooting in the trees, moths floating white against the night-flowering plants.

Lucy murmured something and he bent his head to hear. 'I felt it,' she repeated, her face still pressed to his lapel, her breath warm over his shirt front. 'I felt it, right through me. It was different from playing, not so intense, but still wonderful. Oh, *thank you*, Max.'

She came up on tiptoe, so suddenly he was caught

off guard, and kissed him on the mouth, her arms twined about his neck.

Yes. Then...*no.* He put up his hands and unlocked her grasp, stepped back. 'No. It is bad enough that we are out here. I am sorry if I gave you the impression that I wanted—'

Instantly, the soft, melting woman changed into something of fire. 'I was saying *thank you*, that is all. *Thank you* for a few moments of joy. I do not think for a moment that you *want* anything from me except what you hired me for. Or do you think I want to entrap myself an earl? Let me assure you, my lord, that if I *was* such a conniving female you are the last man I would set my sights on.'

Max let her rage at him. There was not much else a gentleman could do and explaining himself was only going to make everything very much worse. Joy? Was that what he had felt, too, as they had circled in the moonlight? Was it even an emotion that was safe to feel, to desire? Contentment was safer, not a fleeting emotion that left pain behind it when it was taken.

He watched Lucy stalk off towards the door, then she stopped and turned.

'But thank you for giving me my music back, even if it is in a different form. Thank you for listening and understanding.'

'Lucy—'

'But I still think you are a stiff-rumped authoritarian who looks down on the rest of us sadly genteel creatures from the lower ranks.'

He gave her full marks for not slamming the door.

Lucy ran upstairs, not certain whether to float or stamp. That dance. The way the music had flowed

through her… It had been different from playing, far less intense, but still marvellous. She had been immersed in the music, a part of it, responding to it, and Max had given her that, had cared enough to take her out of the ballroom, seek to comfort her.

And then he had reacted to a spontaneous kiss, a gesture of thanks, as though she was seeking to compromise him.

And it *had* been spontaneous, Lucy decided, searching her conscience. She certainly had not intended to do it. She hadn't even thought about it, she had just done it.

At least there was no danger of him getting close enough to her for either of them to do anything unwise ever again. She just wished that her nostrils were not full of the scent of Max, that her lips did not taste of him and her body did not ache to dance again. Dance in his arms.

Melissa was right, men were the devil.

The next morning Lucy kept well out of everyone's way in the library. She would observe Lady Sophia and the gentlemen during the archery contest that afternoon, but for now, with no clues to follow as to who might be Sophia's secret love, there was not a great deal she could do.

The only constructive idea she had was that a man willing to carry on a clandestine liaison with a respectable young lady might be the sort of person who was a menace to the female servants. While she was dressing she had asked Amy to find out if any of the maids had been accosted or harassed, but it was too soon to hear what she had discovered.

Lucy told herself now that she was thinking of more

tactics to discover the man but, after half an hour of gazing blankly at the ranks of book spines, she had to admit that all she was doing was brooding on Max. Max and the miracle that had happened when she danced. Was it only with him or would the same magic be there with any partner? For the first time in her life Lucy was hoping her hostess would decide to arrange an informal dance.

Which just left Max for her to daydream about, she acknowledged ruefully. But that was what daydreams were all about. They were impossible fantasies and she was a working woman with no room in her life for those.

After luncheon there was an interval for everyone to change into whatever outfits they considered most suited to archery and then they assembled in the hall.

Lord Easton, who announced that he was a member of the Toxophilite Society of London, appeared in a green coat with a white waistcoat and breeches. His hat was black with a green feather and he had a leather belt around his waist supporting a quiver full of arrows. He had his own bow and began boring Lord Tobias with a lecture on how green was the only colour to be worn and how he had gone to great pains to find a glove-maker who could make archery gloves to the right specification. Lucy suspected he was also rather fond of the way the colour set off his red hair.

Lord Tobias tossed his long black locks and announced that it was all too exhausting and he would sit in the shade and compose verse on the subject.

'That's because he couldn't hit a barn door with a pitchfork,' Philip Doncaster murmured to Lucy. He was

wearing riding clothes with gloves and a wide leather belt with a quiver. 'Borrowed this from Easton,' he confided. 'I *think* I could hit the barn door if I stood six feet from it. Beyond that… I wouldn't put your wager on me.' He grinned and strolled off down the slope.

Lord St Giles was also looking competent in green and Lord Overdene, although only in riding clothes, seemed equally at home handling a bow.

Lady Hopewell emerged from the house, deep in conversation with the Marquis and carrying a much larger bow, almost as tall as she was. Algernon Tredgold hurried along behind with a large schoolroom slate and chalk, clearly intending to take his bookmaking duties seriously.

Then the female guests appeared, all in a cluster. Lady Sophia was dressed in what was clearly the feminine equivalent of Lord Easton's club uniform. Her green gown was narrow skirted and tight-sleeved, with little Tudoresque puffs at the shoulder. Her hat, green with a black feather, was tilted provocatively to the left and she had a belt with a quiver, a leather wrist brace and gloves.

Lady Hermione was in a similar outfit, but the other women were all in walking dress. Whether that meant they were inexperienced archers or had simply not packed specialist clothing, Lucy was not sure. If she were to place a bet, she thought it would be on Lady Hermione who looked calm and very competent.

Three targets had been set up on the lawn, the pale straw clear against the dark green of the shrubbery, perhaps twenty yards behind them. White flags fluttered from stakes set between the targets and the shrub-

bery, presumably, Lucy deduced, to mark the edge of the danger area.

'Now, everyone, cluster around!' Lady Hopewell called. 'We are using light bows today, so if anyone wanders off, be sure to stay beyond the line of the flags and then you will be quite safe.'

'That is a very fine bow you have there, Lady Hopewell,' Lord Easton said. 'May I try the pull?'

'Of course. But we will not be using it in our little competition. I only brought it out to show Lord Petersbridge. It was my late husband's,' she explained as Easton took hold, drew back the string and gasped at the effort. 'He had it made as a replica of a medieval longbow and the range, in the hands of an expert, is almost four hundred yards.'

Easton, looking as though he had almost put his back out, handed it back hastily to the Marquis, then flushed when one of the other men sniggered.

Lucy looked around for Max as the group clustered round the bench where Algernon had set up his slate. But there was no sign of him. That was probably all for the best; she would not have to avoid him and could relax, but it did mean there was one fewer pair of eyes watching Sophia and the men.

Finally, it seemed, all the wagers had been placed. Lady Sophia was the clear favourite with Miss Easton second and Miss Thomas third. 'What are the stakes?' she asked Algernon Tredgold.

'One shilling. That was all Lady Hopewell would permit,' he told her.

'In that case, please put me down for one shilling on Lady Hermione.'

He raised his eyebrows, but made a note on a piece of paper and adjusted the odds on the slate.

The ladies took it in turns to shoot, dropping out if they missed the target twice in succession. That soon whittled the number down to Lady Sophia, Miss Easton and Lady Hermione, who was proving a more consistent shot than Miss Easton, Lucy thought.

'Neck and neck, Lady Sophia and Lady Hermione,' Lord Overdene, who was keeping score, announced. 'Three arrows in succession to decide the match. Lady Hermione first.'

Her first two arrows hit the gold, side by side in the centre. The third just missed gold and thudded into the red.

Sophia stepped forward with a modest smile that Lucy thought verged on smug. She scanned the audience, but it seemed the gentlemen were more concerned with their wagers and she could see no sign of a proud or possessive look.

Sophia took her stance, nocked her arrow and sent it straight into the centre of the target.

'Bullseye!' Miss Moss exclaimed, clapping. She was shushed as Sophia took aim with the second arrow. It landed squarely in the red.

Lips compressed, Sophia took out her third arrow, drew and hesitated for just a fraction too long. It hit the target side by side with her second shot.

To her credit, Lucy thought, Sophia was a good sport, smiling and congratulating her rival, with no excuses made.

Now that the ladies' match was over the gentlemen were clustered together, tossing a coin to establish the order in which they would shoot.

Having no opinion on who was likely to be the best shot Lucy decided to preserve her winnings on Lady Hermione and moved to a secluded spot in the shade of a chestnut tree to think what to do next about Lady Sophia's mystery lover. The man who had seduced and abandoned her friend Prudence had been a very plausible character, apparently. Prue was no fool and if she could be misled, then even the bright and apparently sophisticated Lady Sophia might be also.

A burst of cheers pulled her attention back to the match. Mr Doncaster had scored a bullseye and his backers were celebrating. Which marksman was Sophia watching? She scanned the excited faces under wide sun hats and scalloped parasols.

Sophia was missing.

Chapter Ten

Sophia might have gone up to the house for some reason, of course, but a glance showed nobody walking away on the long expanse of grass. A quick head count showed that all the gentlemen were present.

Where could she have gone? As Lucy looked around she realised that the curve of the shrubbery almost reached the lawn at this point. Sophia could have vanished into the greenery within seconds if she had chosen her moment carefully.

And at the other end of the arc of the planting were the stables and the yards leading to the servants' part of the house. Was she meeting a groom or a valet? Lucy edged back from her sheltering tree and sidled into the shrubbery. Nobody took any notice.

Once there she found herself on a gravelled path wide enough for two people to walk abreast. It wound off between the plantings, deliberately beckoning the visitor to explore, she supposed, as she hurried along it, her light shoes making little sound.

On the path in front of her was a flash of green and, when she stooped to pick it up, she saw it was

an arrow with green feather flights. Sophia's arrows had been fletched in green and the little quiver she had carried them in had swung loose at her hip. If she had been hurrying it was possible that an arrow might have bounced out unnoticed.

Lucy picked it up and hurried on. The path wound around a number of wrought-iron seats, taking far longer than a direct line. She could hear the laughter and applause from the archery match and an occasional collective groan. From glimpses through the undergrowth she could see that she was now almost in a direct line behind the targets—and there was still no sign of Sophia.

'Bother the girl.' She could go and look around the stables, she supposed, walking towards the high wall that was visible at the end of a short side path.

The thud of hooves came just as she reached the track that lay between the edge of the shrubbery and the wall. 'Miss Marsh! Are you lost?' It was Lord Burnham astride a very handsome grey horse and looking dangerously fit, capable and masculine in a snuff-brown coat and low-crowned hat. 'Or are you playing the part of Cupid?'

'What?' Was he scrambling her thoughts again? 'Oh, you mean the arrow. I found it on the path.' Lucy kept her voice down. 'Max... My lord, I have lost track of Lady Sophia. She left the archery and, I think, came into the shrubbery.'

He swung down from the horse, tossed the reins over a branch and joined her. 'They are still shooting? Ah, yes, I can hear them.'

'And see them. But all the men are there and Sophia dropped this arrow from her quiver on to the path, so

she must have been hurrying to meet someone else entirely.'

'The stables? I wonder.' Max took a step back towards the horse, then turned again and went to the edge of the planting, pushing back the low branches. 'Best to check she has not returned before I start taking the place apart, stall by stall.'

Why she was suddenly uneasy, Lucy did not stop to examine. 'Max, don't—'

She was too late.

Max shielded his eyes and studied the group, counting heads. Yes, Lucy was correct, everyone appeared to be there—except Sophia.

Behind him he heard Lucy stir. 'Max. Don't—'

A tall figure stepped up to the mark, drew and someone shouted, 'Stop!' just as the man loosed his arrow.

It was somewhat unnerving, being in the line of fire, but the distance from the targets— The thought, all thought, was lost in a sudden whistling sound and a blow to his left upper arm that sent him staggering back.

He hit the ground before the pain struck, shocking a gasp from his lips, then his head slammed back into something hard and the world went black.

Max came swimming back up into consciousness. Distantly there were the sounds of raised voices and he realised that Lucy was kneeling beside him.

'Lie still, I'll get help.' He heard her push through the bushes and then shout, 'Here! Help! Someone's shot!'

Someone's shot, he repeated to himself. *Hell, that is me.*

Through a mist of pain he lifted his right hand, groped towards his shoulder and found blood, but no arrow shaft.

'No, lie still or you'll make the bleeding worse. It was a hunting arrow, I think, and barbed, but it cut through the flesh of your upper arm, it has not stuck in. I'll pad it with your neckcloth—I took that off while you were unconscious. But you hit your head on a tree root when you went down and knocked yourself out. No! Lie still, you may be concussed.'

She did something that felt competent   and painful—with a wad of fabric and then what must be his neckcloth. 'There. Now, I will feel underneath, make certain you aren't bleeding at the back.'

At least the thing wasn't in him and hadn't hit his chest. He had seen the arrows designed to take down a stag and a man would be lucky to survive that. He felt Lucy slide her hand under his shoulder, blinked and her face came into focus, intent and frowning. She winced and he realised this must be hurting her damaged fingers.

'Shh. Don't try to speak,' she said soothingly, slipping her hand free. 'There's virtually no bleeding, I cannot believe how lucky you were.'

'Lucky? Six inches to the other side and it would have missed me entirely,' he said with some bitterness.

He could hear running feet now, thudding across the lawn and, from the side, shrubs being pushed aside.

'Max!' That was Sophia's voice. He forced his eyes open and saw her white face and, behind her, the Vicar... West, that was the man's name.

'Don't need last rites yet, Vicar,' he said. It came out as a croak as his head spun.

Then they seemed to be surrounded. Bodies, voices, chaos. One voice cut through, clear and confident.

'Get hurdles or a door to use as a stretcher. Send a groom for the doctor. Someone run to the house, tell the staff to prepare a bed on the ground floor: he mustn't be tilted up the stairs. Bring clean soft padding. Hurry! And the rest of you get back, give him air.'

It was Lucy, he realised. She sounded urgent, angry and yet fully in control. *Lucky someone is*, he thought as darkness swept over him again.

'Max.' Sophia rushed forward, fell to her knees beside her stepbrother's sprawled body and seemed about to throw herself on his chest.

'For goodness sake, be careful!' Lucy pulled her back. 'I have bandaged the wound, but if you hurl yourself at him you will only dislodge the dressing and it needs to be tight.'

Sophia burst into tears and cast herself into the arms of Mr West, who appeared to be the only person prepared to pay her any attention.

Lucy became aware of a furious, low-voiced argument.

'If you hadn't shouted at me, I would have hit the target.' That was Lord Easton.

'You shouldn't have been using that bow at all—the range is far beyond the warning flags. Totally irresponsible behaviour.' When she spared them a glance she saw the other man was the Marquis, clearly angry, berating Easton who was white-faced and still clutching the powerful hunting bow.

'Oh, do be quiet,' she barked out.

Easton glowered at her, but Lord Petersbridge nodded. 'Quite right. Now is not the time for recriminations. Ah, here they come with the stretcher. Ladies, might I suggest that you all go back to the house?'

That reduced the crowd somewhat. Four footmen came running with a door, followed by a maid, her arms full of pillows.

Lucy arranged the pillows on the door then the men eased Max on to it, lifted it and began to walk back.

'The doctor has been sent for, Miss Marsh.' Lucy realised the maid who had brought the pillows was Amy. 'And they are making up a bed in the little parlour off the library.'

'Thank you,' Lucy said absently, her attention on watching the men to see the door was kept level, that Max wasn't stirring. It was a flesh wound, she told herself. There wasn't much bleeding, and the doctor would be here soon. Those positive thoughts, somehow, were not very soothing and he had hit his head with such force...

The doctor arrived soon after they had managed to get Max on to the bed. Formby, the butler, pulled a screen around and Max's valet undressed, him, cutting away the clothes on his upper body with scant care for the expensive tailoring.

Lucy stayed on the far side of the screen, as much to stop Sophia from rushing to the bedside and weeping all over Max as out of maidenly modesty on her own part.

He must have come round, because they heard the doctor asking questions and Max's voice replying.

'Come along, we should leave.' Lucy put her hand on Sophia's arm.

'Leave him? How could you be so callous? My place is by his side.'

The doctor said something, and Max's reply was short, basic and very much to the point.

'Out.' Lucy dragged Sophia from the room. 'He does not want us listening to this. I am sure the ability to say just what he feels will be a great help.' She shut the door firmly on a sentence that she suspected was essentially Anglo-Saxon in origin. 'It is a flesh wound and it will need rather a lot of stitches, I expect.'

'You are hateful.'

'Possibly. But I know that when I hurt my hands it made it worse having everyone fussing round me and having to pretend to be brave and not cry out and upset them.'

Sophia shook off Lucy's light grip. 'What were you doing alone with Max in the shrubbery, anyway?'

'I became bored with sitting watching the archery so I took a walk. Your brother was riding back to the stables when I came out on to the path. He went to look and see if you were still with the archery contest.'

'A likely story.' There were tears spiking the ends of Sophia's lashes and her voice was shaking. 'You are trying to entrap him, don't think I cannot see what you are about. And to think I quite liked you.' She turned with a flounce. 'I shall tell everyone. I would leave at once, if I were you.'

Lucy stared at her retreating back, the skirts of Sophia's archery outfit twitching with every jerky stride. The attack, so sudden, so personal, took her breath and

she sat down on one of the hallway chairs and stared blankly at the door of the room where Max lay.

'What a spiteful little madam.' Amy marched over and stood beside her. 'What has she got to hide, I wonder?'

'What do you mean?' Lucy blinked back tears and focused on her maid.

'If she was worried about His Lordship she'd be outside this door, like you are. She's carrying on like that because she's trying to distract you from something. My sister used to be just the same, cunning little minx.'

Startled, Lucy thought that over. Yes, in retrospect Sophia's tantrum did seem almost artificial, as though she was winding herself up to make a scene, not expressing her genuine emotions. But what could she be trying to hide? She could not have known that Lucy was following her, nor did she know that Max had asked Lucy to discover her secret lover. If one existed.

But Lady Sophia *had* sneaked away from the archery party...

The door opened and Mr West the Vicar came out. He looked up and down the hallway and seemed surprised to see them. 'Oh. Miss Marsh. I came out to reassure Lady Sophia that Lord Burnham's injury is far less severe than might have been feared. The bleeding has stopped, thanks to your prompt action. But is she not here?'

'She was very upset.' Lucy gestured towards the front of the house. 'She went that way.' He turned to leave, but she stood up. 'Can you tell me what the doctor says?'

'Oh, yes, of course. It appears to be a flesh wound through the muscle of the upper arm. No major blood

vessel has been cut and no joints damaged. It was
most—' He broke off, clearly searching for a word suitable for a lady's ears. '*Unpleasant*, stitching it. However, if infection can be prevented, then Lord Burnham
should make a complete recovery. The doctor was able
to remove all the fragments of cloth in the wound and,
of course, they were very clean. The blow to the head,
however, was forceful and there is always the danger
of a concussion.'

'Thank you.'

Lucy watched as he strode off in the direction she
had indicated. 'You know, I wonder—'

'He is very concerned about Lady Sophia, isn't he?'
Amy said at the same moment. 'Oh, excuse me, Miss
Marsh.'

They stared at each other.

'You know, if we put two and two together, it is not
impossible that it makes four,' Lucy said slowly.

'Or even a pair,' Amy agreed with a grin.

'Come on.' There was no need to specify where
or what for and any scruples about spying were more
than smothered by Sophia's clumsy attempt at blackmail. 'Tread softly.'

They did not have far to go. Just around the corner,
the Ladies' Small Drawing Room was a little chamber
that no one seemed eager to use. It had a dull view of
the lawn and was tucked away from the main recep-
tion rooms. Ideal for a tryst, in fact.

Amy crouched so she could peep through the key-
hole. 'There's a screen just inside the door,' she whispered.

They eased the handle down and the door opened
without a creak. From the far side of the room they

could hear Sophia and Mr West in what sounded like urgent conversation. They squeezed through the narrowest possible gap, then pushed the door to again.

'…sure she suspects something. I can only hope I have frightened her into leaving.'

'Dearest, that was not well done.' The Reverend West sounded fond but stern. 'Threats are wrong and besides, you have probably only aroused Miss Marsh's suspicions.' There was a sound suspiciously like a sob. 'You know you should not have come here, Sophia. We must not meet alone again and we must put these feelings behind us.'

'How can we?' Sophia demanded. 'These feelings? It is not *feelings*, Anthony—I *love* you. You told me you loved me. That is not a feeling, that is…*everything*.'

'Oh, my darling—'

Lucy couldn't stand it any longer. She stepped out from behind the screen, gesturing to Amy to stay where she was.

Sophia gave a small scream as Mr West stepped protectively in front of her.

'Lady Sophia, I have no desire to cause you difficulties, but really, attempts at blackmail ill become you. Surely the Vicar here is a most respectable suitor to present to your stepbrother?'

Sophia burst into tears.

Mr West drew himself up like a man facing a firing squad and announced, 'I fear that my birth is irregular.'

Wild visions of gynaecological disorders flitted through Lucy's head, then she grasped what he meant. 'Your parents were not married? But clearly you are respectable and educated. You are in Holy Orders, your bishop considers you a fit and proper person to min-

ister to a congregation.' She tried to remember what little she knew about the appointment of clergymen to parishes. 'You have, I imagine, a patron?'

'I have. Lady Hopewell holds the advowson of this parish and was kind enough to take an interest in my career. Even so,' Mr West continued, 'I am not a suitable match for the daughter of an earl.'

'Then it is a pity you allowed the attachment to develop this far, is it not?' Lucy enquired tartly.

'You are quite correct to reprove me. As you may have overheard, I was attempting to explain to Lady Sophia how impossible—'

'Oh, I hate you both!' Sophia burst out. 'Anthony, you should stand up and claim me, not hide behind this beastly propriety. What does it matter if you are dismissed from your post? I have *thousands* of pounds. And you...' she turned on Lucy as the Vicar spluttered and tried to interject '...you are a spy and a hypocrite.'

'Miss Marsh.' Amy put her head around the screen. 'Lady Hopewell and some of the ladies are coming and I think they heard Lady Sophia just now.'

'Come in, quickly, Pringle.' Lucy contemplated fleeing through the nearest window and scrabbled frantically for some explanation that she could offer for what was going on. 'Lady Sophia is upset because of Lord Burnham's injury. We are trying to soothe her—'

'Liar!' Sophia declaimed as Lady Hopewell, followed by Lady Moss and Lady Hermione, swept into the room.

'What on earth is going on? I thought someone screamed. There is not bad news of Burnham, is there? I thought it was only a flesh wound. And who is a liar?'

'She is.' Sophia, doing credit to leading actress

Sarah Siddons at her most dramatic, flung out an accusing hand. 'Miss Marsh is Max's mistress and she is trying to blackmail me into keeping quiet about it.'

'I am no such thing,' Lucy protested hotly. 'Lady Sophia is distressed, she does not know what she is saying.'

'She is threatening to say that Mr West here and I are…are *involved*. In order to silence me.'

'I have no intention of saying any such thing.' *Not to anyone but Max, at least.* The Vicar was looking desperate. If he confirmed Sophia's story he would be corroborating a lie, to admit it was a fabrication would be to compromise his love and disgrace himself in front of his patron. To do him credit, she thought, it was probably the danger to Sophia that was most concerning him.

'I believe that Lady Sophia, anxious about Lord Burnham, misunderstood Miss Marsh who came across us as I attempted to calm Lady Sophia.'

'What the devil is going on? Sophia?' It was Max, barefooted, clad only in breeches with a bed robe thrown over his bare shoulders, revealing a considerable amount of muscled torso and a glimpse of white bandaging.

Lady Moss gave a faint shriek, Lady Hermione raised what Lucy, staring distractedly at the scene, could only describe as an appreciative eyebrow and Lady Hopewell rushed to his side.

'Burnham, you should not be out of your bed. Sit down, this moment. The doctor will be furious.'

'I will go to my bed when I discover what my stepsister is shrieking about, why Miss Marsh is as white

as a sheet and why the Vicar is looking like an early Christian martyr.'

'The last is easy to answer,' Lucy said. Her nails dug into her palms and the damaged tendons sent a stab of pain through her hands that, somehow, steadied her. 'Mr West is attempting to calm your stepsister down and make her behave more rationally. It would appear to require the patience of a saint.'

She saw Max put out his right hand to steady himself against the door frame and resisted the urge to go to his side. He had his pride. After a moment he walked to the nearest upright chair and sat down, just as a chattering group—all the remaining guests, it seemed—flocked into the room, staring round with barely disguised curiosity.

Sophia drew herself up, clearly emboldened by an audience. 'I was trying to make your…your *paramour* realise that her presence is a disgrace and that she is most definitely not wanted here now.'

There was total silence, then Lady Hermione said brightly, 'What nonsense. The shock of Burnham's injury has disordered your mind, Sophia dear. What do you know about irregular relationships? Nothing, I should hope. You should go and lie down and take a composing draught and perhaps you will be more yourself in time for dinner.'

Lucy watched Max. He, very definitely, did not look at her.

'Sophia will apologise to Miss Marsh before she goes anywhere,' he said.

'I will not! I will *not*. She is hateful.' Sophia burst into tears and cast herself on the Vicar's chest. To his

credit he held on to her and made soothing noises: Lucy would have been tempted to drop her on the floor.

She saw understanding dawn on Max's face and, finally, he looked at her. She tipped her head slightly towards the pair and nodded. His eyes widened.

There was, she realised with relief, another door out of this room. 'I think we are beyond apologies. Excuse me.' She was out and the door closed behind her before anyone reacted.

The next room was merely an antechamber off the hall, and she was halfway up the stairs before Amy caught up with her.

'That lying little madam! I could have boxed her ears for her,' the maid said indignantly. She was bristling like a mother hen confronted by a cat. 'I told them, I did. I said, "My lady's as virtuous as she could be and anyone who says different is a nasty liar." And that Lady Hermione, the bony one, she said, "Well said, young woman."'

'But you tipped His Lordship the wink, so he'll know why the silly chit is telling those lies.'

'Yes,' Lucy agreed wearily. Her initial rush up the stairs had slowed to a trudge. No one had come hurrying after her with protestations of belief in her virtue, of course. 'Lord Burnham is not going to tell everyone why his stepsister is attacking me—he will not want people to know that she is entangled with a country vicar of irregular parentage.'

'I had better pack, don't you think, Miss Marsh?'

'Yes. I expect Lady Hopewell will be glad enough to get rid of me and will send us to the nearest town in the gig. But not until I am given what I am owed by Lord Burnham,' she said with sudden decision. 'This

household may believe he is paying me for my body, but it is true he did employ me to find him an answer and I have done that.'

'Quite right, miss,' Amy said stoutly. 'Look, there's a footman. Hey, James, fetch my lady's valises down right away. We're leaving.'

Chapter Eleven

Max leaned back in the chair and concentrated on not slumping. He was damned if he was going to fall flat on his face in front of an audience on top of everything else. Lucy, at least, was out of this for the moment and he had to deal with this mess first before he could go to her, much as he wanted to. Through a sickening headache he could see clearly enough that to do so would only add credence to Sophia's tale.

I have to get rid of Sophia and her confounded clergyman before she says anything else and digs the hole we are all in any deeper.

'West, kindly take Lady Sophia to the room I am currently occupying. I will join you in a moment.' He waited until the door closed behind the white-faced Vicar. The man would be several shades paler before he'd finished with him.

'My sister is hysterical. Miss Marsh is not my mistress, but she is my agent: she reports to me on confidential matters that I am not going to discuss here.' Was that enough? He could hardly explain that Lucy was spying on Sophia or he risked her ruin, too.

Lucy's white, set face danced before his eyes like the after-image caused by staring at something too long in bright sunshine. She had discovered Sophia's secret for him and she had kept it to herself in the face of a vicious attack on her own reputation. He was not certain how he was going to be able to repay that. But his shoulder was throbbing as though someone was prodding the wound in rhythm with his pulse, he was dizzy and knew he was not going to be able to stay focused on more than one thing at a time: his stepsister had to come first.

His statement had produced a buzz of speculation. He could see mystification on several faces—mainly the young ladies—speculation on those of the older guests and intense interest among the younger men.

'I would appreciate your arm to get back to my bed,' he said to Petersbridge. The Marquis was possibly the most sensible, and certainly the most influential, of the guests.

'Of course.' Lord Petersbridge got him to his feet with minimal discomfort. Once they were outside and halfway along the hallway he added, 'Anything I can do?'

'Calm down the speculation. Sophia is…upset and saying things she does not mean. Miss Marsh is a thoroughly respectable young lady.'

'Of course.'

Petersbridge didn't exactly pat him on the hand, but the soothing tone set Max's teeth on edge. He believed Max was lying to protect Lucy—the lesser of two evils—and the Marquis approved of that. If he assured everyone else that it was all a hum, he would

be about as convincing as the Prince Regent would be swearing off rich food and wine.

The Vicar was standing outside Max's temporary bedchamber door, which was closed. 'Lady Sophia is within, my lord.'

'Then you can relieve Lord Petersbridge of his burden and help me inside.'

He ignored Sophia until he was sitting propped up on the bed. 'Well?'

The response was a stifled sob. 'I wish I was *dead*.'

'Mr West? Might I hope for some sense from you?'

'My lord. Lady Sophia and I formed an attachment— of the utmost propriety, I assure you—when we met in Bath. I was the curate at St Swithin's where her mother attended, the Walcot parish being more convenient than walking to the Abbey. However as soon as I realised who she was, I knew that such feelings must not be acted upon, that I am an impossible husband for Lady Sophia and that we must forget that we ever met.'

'And yet here we are.'

'Indeed,' the Vicar said miserably. 'I have attempted to explain to Lady Sophia the impossibility of our situation, but in her innocence, she fails to grasp it.'

Max closed his eyes. The throbbing in his head was getting worse and the prospect of being left alone in a darkened room was enticing. He forced the lids open again. 'You appear to be a gentleman. Lady Hopewell is a fair judge of character. What seems to you to be the bar to you making an honourable proposal? The match would be very far from brilliant, of course.'

'My parents were not married,' West confessed. 'Not to each other, that is.'

'Ah. You know who your father was?'

'Yes. My mother was his daughter's governess.'
West sounded bitter. 'He died some years ago.'

And there was a definitely unclerical satisfaction in
that statement, Max thought.

'And your prospects?' Not that they were relevant—
not now he knew West's background. It was no fault of
the man. He seemed decent enough, but this was Sophia's future they were considering here.

'They are those of any country clergyman with no
family connections. I work hard, I would seek advance-
ment and I have a generous patron in Lady Hopewell.
But even if I were to accept the allowance left to me
by my father, I cannot support a wife.'

'But I am an heiress,' Sophia said. 'Max, I keep telling him that and he will not listen.'

'That only makes it worse,' West said.

An honourable man, it seemed. 'You appear to be
intelligent. Tell me, what possesses you to think yourself in love with Sophia?'

'Max.'

He ignored her.

'Lady Sophia has been over-indulged, I know—'

'Anthony!'

'But she has a kind heart and a good mind and a
warm, if impulsive nature. I cannot tell what makes
anyone fall in love. Can you, my lord? All I can say is
that I love her with all my heart and I will not see her
ruined on my behalf.'

'In that at least you have my blessing,' Max said.
'Sophia, you know this is impossible. Do you want
your children to be merely the offspring of some obscure country vicar?'

'I want them to be Anthony's children,' she retorted.

'You will lose your station in society, your friends, the way of life you are used to. And don't start reminding me about the size of your inheritance, I am perfectly well aware of it. Do you think this man is going to let you drag him off to London to be your lapdog?'

'Oh, Max!'

'Every feeling revolts, my lord.'

'There, Sophia. If you have any true affection for West, then you will not try to force him to do what his conscience very clearly tells him is wrong. And you will tell everyone that your accusations about Miss Marsh were a joke that misfired. Do you hear me?'

Sophia fled.

West looked at Max. 'I will do what I can, my lord.'

It was the right decision, even West admitted that. Sophia would not be happy as the wife of a humble country clergyman and he had to stop her throwing her life away. This was not like Julia, infatuated by a wicked rake, but even so, the results for Sophia of a marriage she would surely come to bitterly regret would be a long life of discontent. He had to protect her from that.

But even so, he could not shake off the memory of the look of blank unhappiness in West's eyes. The man genuinely loved her, Max realised. He was going to do the right thing, but it was stabbing him in the heart and Sophia was beside herself. *Lord, what fools these mortals be!* That was what Puck had said, watching the lovers in *A Midsummer Night's Dream.* Love was risk and pain and disorder.

An hour later, when Hobson had repaired the damage to his bandages caused by Sophia hurling herself

on to his chest in an excess of emotion, there was a tap on the door.

'Unless that is someone ignoring the doctor's orders and bringing me brandy, send them away, Hobson.'

His valet came back. 'Miss Marsh's maidservant, my lord. She has a note.' He hesitated. 'She appears somewhat agitated.'

'Let her in.' He knew he should speak to Lucy, but if Sophia had done what she promised, the fuss should have died down by now.

'My lord.' Pringle thrust a folded note at him and Max unfolded it one-handed.

My Lord,
I would be obliged for the fee which we agreed
for my duties here. I will be leaving for London
immediately.
L.M.

'Why is Miss Marsh returning to London, Pringle?'

'Because of what they are saying, of course.'

'I told my stepsister to explain her ridiculous accusation.'

'My lord! You really should not get up again!' Hobson was positively flapping, as though to shoo a flock of geese.

'I am trying to sit up, Hobson. Dealing with insanity while flat on my back is impossible. Another pillow— Thank you. Well, Pringle?'

'They don't believe her. Not the young gentlemen, nor most of the young ladies, anyhow. They think you've ordered Lady Sophia to change her story.' She bit her lip. 'And there's ever such a big pile of letters

waiting to go to the post. I think some of them have been writing to tell friends the gossip.'

When it came to it and you were drowning, there was no point in struggling. He would do his best to make this work and he was certain that she would, too. They could be civilised about this, learn to live together somehow. It felt very…cool and, oddly, that no longer felt desirable.

'Please ask Miss Marsh to join me here, Pringle.'

'In your bedchamber, my lord?' Hobson protested.

'Hobson, either Miss Marsh is my mistress, in which case there is no further damage to be done, or she is not, in which case I am hardly in a fit state to leap from my bed and ravish her, now am I?'

Hobson stood guard just inside the door, as though to defend his master's virtue with a clothes brush.

Ten minutes later, Lucy sailed in, bonnet firmly on her head, lips tightly compressed.

'Thank you, Hobson. You and Pringle can wait outside.'

'At least you are conscious and sitting up in bed, not flat out and delirious, which is what I had expected after your appearance in the Small Drawing Room,' she observed tartly.

'This has got out of hand,' he countered. 'Oh, sit down, for heaven's sake.'

Why was he angry with her? Because she was stubborn, of course. Because she would not agree to what he… He almost thought, *wanted*. The word startled him and he tried to work out why. *Ought to do* was the correct phrase, not *wanted*.

'Yes, my lord,' Lucy said with a mock meekness

that jerked him away from the disconcerting train of thought.

'And stop perching on the edge of the chair like a scullery maid in disgrace. We had best announce our betrothal.'

'Our... No.' She stood up.

'You are effectively ruined, Lucy.'

'Lucy Marsh may be, if she took any notice of such nonsense. Lucy Lambert, teacher of the pianoforte, is not.'

'You want to risk it? Before, when I came up with this insane scheme, I thought you could fade away again afterwards. Now you are the focus of all eyes. They have seen your hands, they have seen *you*. All it will take is for someone to say in the course of conversation that their daughter is doing so well with her new pianoforte teacher, despite the poor lady having injured her fingers, and it will be all over town.'

Yes, she had thought of that, he could see it in her face and, from the haunted look in her eyes, it would keep her awake at night now. 'I will take that chance.'

'You do not *want* to marry me? You would gain a title, wealth—' Even as he said it he knew that those things would not weigh with her. Or perhaps they would weigh her down. You could not measure the things that seemed to matter to Lucy—friendship, music, independence...

'And the reputation of someone who entrapped an earl into marriage,' she stated, as though slamming down another brick into the scales against what was important.

'Lucy, come here.' Max held out his hand and, reluctantly, she stood and moved to the side of the bed.

He caught her hand and felt her tense, but she did not pull away.

'I will tell them all that we were already secretly betrothed and you agreed to help me because we were concerned that Sophia had made an unwise connection. Now we know the man in question is the eminently virtuous Reverend West, who naturally refuses to presume on her unwise attachment, you were about to return to London to await the formal announcement of our betrothal.'

'No.' Under his fingertips her pulse was rapid, like a tiny creature caught in his hand.

'My honour demands—'

'The sacrifice of my self-respect? I doubt it. There is one reason I would marry and this is not it. This is the very opposite of it. I will not marry to observe the decencies, to make you feel better—not that you *would* feel much better once this had begun to sink in. I am going to leave now. If you do not give me the money you owe me, then we will have to walk to London, finding rides on farm carts where we can.'

Was that true or did she simply not wish to risk him having an excuse to see her again in London? Did he want an excuse? He would have expected to feel relieved and somehow he could not. She was trembling now, he could feel it, but could not tell whether it was anger or distress. What did she mean about a reason to marry? Not love, surely, not sensible, prickly Lucy? Love was a burden, love deceived and bound you.

He wanted to pull her into his arms and kiss away her objection, whatever it was. He let his thumb trail lightly over the inside of her wrist, exposed by the short gloves, and a little gasp escaped her.

'Hobson!'

'My lord.' The valet appeared from his discreet retreat in the dressing room.

'I am getting up. Find me something that will go over these bandages and a sling.'

'You cannot!' Lucy jerked her hand free, sending painful shocks up his injured arm. 'What are you going to do? Have men no common sense at all?'

'Miss Marsh. I have a headache which you are making worse. I have a flesh wound that is aggravating, but which will be a mere nuisance in the morning and only mildly troublesome if I wear a sling. It appears that, if you are set upon ruin, then the only way I can prevent it is by exposing my stepsister to public humiliation. So be it. I gave her every opportunity to behave as a lady should. Now, I suggest that unless you wish to assist me in getting into my breeches, you leave.'

Lucy left with as much dignity as she could muster.

'Miss? What's happening, Miss Marsh?' Amy was hanging over the banisters.

'I have to think. Stop packing while I do.'

She had to be logical about this because the emotions involved were simply too painful and destructive.

If Max told everyone about Sophia and the Vicar, then they would both be embarrassed and upset.

But... Nobody seeing Mr West would imagine for a moment that he would have done anything to actually ruin Sophia and she had been given every opportunity to say she had been mistaken about Lucy, so she deserved a little discomfiture. Lady Hopewell was not going to hold this against her choice of vicar, she imag-

ined, and if he did lose his post she could trust Max to make certain he did not suffer for it.

And… *If I do leave now it would put Max in a difficult position. It would seem like an admission that I have been his mistress and that he could not manage his private life effectively and discreetly.*

What was more… *I could never be absolutely certain that I would not be recognised and exposed. I would have to move to some unfashionable place—Manchester or Norwich—where society ladies were unlikely to hire me.*

Finally… *None of this is my fault. Why do I have to suffer for it? I might have developed a ridiculous* tendre *for that man, but that did not cause any of this.*

No, not finally… *What is best for me is to stay and have Max set the record straight. But what is best for Max? That, too, I think. No more deception, no awkward pretences and lies that might be exposed.*

It was going to be unpleasant and she felt sorry for Sophia, not least because, if she really did love Mr West, then her heart would be breaking. But being unhappy was no excuse for making anyone else suffer, Lucy decided.

But there was that proposal of marriage… She made herself think about it when she reached the end of her very logical and dispassionate assessment. It had never, for a moment, occurred to her not to refuse and yet it had been as if she were two persons. One was the sensible, honourable woman who would not dream of presuming on a man's sense of obligation and forcing a marriage that was so unequal. A second knew that he made the offer out of duty and not love and that was why she'd refused. *If he loved me…* But she

did not love Max, much as she might desire him and, increasingly, like him. She had seen the dream made real and she could never accept second best, or inflict it on someone else.

'Put out my evening gown, please, Amy. And ring for hot water. We are staying, at least for tonight.'

The atmosphere in the drawing room lifted the fine hairs on Lucy's arms as though a thunderstorm was about to break. The younger ladies were wide-eyed, the older guests were gathered together as if awaiting an artist to paint a group portrait and, in the centre of the room, Sophia was laughing, surrounded by the young men.

'It was very naughty of me,' she said with a gurgle of amusement that positively invited the chorus of denial. 'I only meant it as a joke because darling Max was so stuffy about me flirting with Mr West and now I have embarrassed the poor man and he has fled back to his vicarage and Max's headache is worse and as for poor little Miss Marsh—'

Lucy cleared her throat.

'Oh, there you are!' Sophia dashed over, ribbons fluttering, and seized Lucy by the hands. 'I was just telling everyone how dreadful that my silly little revenge on Max got so out of hand. I never dreamed for a moment that anyone would believe you were his mistress and it's so awful, I am having to apologise to *everyone*.' She beamed at Lucy, but her eyes were bleak. 'Say you forgive me, do.'

'Of course I forgive you,' Lucy said, smiling through gritted teeth. 'Just as long as you stop squeezing my hands,' she added quietly.

'How dreadful of me—I forgot. But we are friends again? Say we are.' She linked arms with Lucy and turned back to face the room. 'See, everyone, Miss Marsh forgives me. Isn't she wonderful?'

So, Sophia had seen the danger she was putting herself in and Max had not needed to publicly shame his stepsister to save Lucy's reputation. That was an enormous relief. 'Your brother was very anxious about you,' she said, slowing down before they reached the young men.

'There was no need and I do not forgive him. He had broken my heart and I will make him regret it. But I am sorry I picked on you, truly I am.'

She meant it, Lucy realised. Of course, Sophia had no idea that Max had engaged Lucy to spy on her and she still did not realise that she was Miss Lambert, the music teacher she had tricked in London. It was Lucy's guilty conscience about her own role in all this that had made it so easy to think that Sophia had acted out of personal spite.

'Come and talk to me,' she said, angling away towards a deserted part of the room.

'Really?' She was nervous, Lucy could tell. All the bright, brittle confidence was gone.

'Yes, really.' She sat on a little sofa with just room for the two of them. 'Now, tell me, are you truly in love with Mr West? Or is it a flirtation?'

'I love him and now he is being all noble about things I don't care about, and Max just doesn't understand.'

'Smile, or everyone will think we are arguing,' Lucy said with a laugh. 'But he could never rise much beyond this parish, unfair though it is. His birth is no fault of

his, but he would be miserable thinking that he had torn you from the life you are used to, wouldn't he?'

Sophia nodded. 'It isn't even that Anthony *wants* to be a clergyman. Oh, I know he is a good one and he cares for people, but it was the only path open to him. His education was excellent because his mother insisted that he take his father's money for that and he agreed because he wanted to support her all her life. But if Lady Hopewell had not known her and offered this living once he had some experience in the church, I do not know what he would have done.'

Lucy suspected that more than half the Anglican clergymen were only clerics because it was one of the few respectable openings for younger sons of good family to earn a modest living. Was there any other occupation that might make Anthony West a more suitable husband for Sophia?

'Let us join the others and, with any luck, they will all have the tact to forget about this.'

'I hope so. I hate having to pretend that I don't love Anthony. You are kind after I have been so horrid.' Sophia stood up and shook out her skirts, then froze. 'Oh. Max has come down.'

Lucy was on her feet, too, staring. 'He shouldn't,' she said, but she was hardly aware of what she was saying, she was so focused on the man in the doorway.

Max was in full evening dress, his coat draped across the shoulder of his injured arm and Hobson had somehow fastened it to the black sling she could see against the deep crimson waistcoat. He was pale, which made him seemed icier and more aloof than ever, like a wounded hero facing his enemies, she thought fancifully.

'How romantic he looks,' Sophia said.
Lucy nodded.
'The beast,' Max's loving stepsister added.

Chapter Twelve

There was a surge of people towards Max, led by Lord Easton. 'I'm sorry, Burnham. I was reckless and I'm just damn—apologies, ladies—I'm just relieved it wasn't any worse.' He shuffled his feet, looking very young all of a sudden. 'When you are better you are very welcome to punch six bells out of me at Jackson's Salon.'

'I heal well,' Max said. 'I might get those punches in before we leave here.'

There was laughter at what Lucy recognised as one of those incompressible male remarks that, instead of actually promising bloody retribution, signalled forgiveness.

'Now, do not crowd the poor man, you will set his head to aching again,' Lady Hopewell chided. 'Come and sit by me, Burnham.'

'Delightful as the prospect is, Dorothea, I have been flat on my back all afternoon and the prospect of a little mild exercise is tempting.'

She laughed and let him go to saunter around the room, exchanging a word here and there before stop-

ping to talk to Lord Overdene and his aunt, Lady Hermione.

Lucy and Sophia strolled in the other direction and ended up with a group of the younger guests who were debating what to do the next day.

'What will the weather be like, I wonder?' Miss Gainford said.

'It will remain fine, I asked one of the gardeners.' Mr Doncaster seemed pleased to have the answer for her. 'The other men assure me he is a local weather prophet and can be relied upon. The breeze will cease, the sun will shine and parasols will be on parade.'

'Then we will take to the boats and explore the lake,' Sophia announced. She sounded her usual lively self, but Lucy thought she could detect the strain under the rallying tone. Sophia was a good actress and she had enough pride not to show her feelings, now that the shock of having her dreams so abruptly crushed had lessened.

'Have you not been out on it before?' she asked. 'I thought you were very familiar with this house.'

'Not since I was quite a child. The weather has never been quite right, or we were doing something else or there was no one I trusted not to hand me a frog or tip me out into the water.'

There was general laughter and Miss Easton embarked on a lively account of how her beastly brother once put two newts down the front of her dress in church and she had screamed in the middle of the sermon.

'Lucy?'

'Hmm? Oh, sorry, I was thinking—I am not sure about what. It has been rather a long day.'

'You were gazing at…at Terence Overdene, I do declare,' Sophia said. 'He is dreadfully intellectual, you know,' she added. 'Perhaps, like me, you prefer a man with some thoughts in his head beyond race horses and the knot in his neckcloth.' That was said in a murmur with a nod towards Lord Easton.

'I haven't really noticed Lord Overdene,' Lucy said with perfect honesty. She had been looking at Max, she realised. Thank goodness there was another personable male in the same direction. 'I was just letting my attention wander. Oh, good, dinner has been announced.' She had every intention of slipping away immediately afterwards. It had been a long, hot, fraught day.

The weather-forecasting gardener deserved his reputation, Lucy thought, as the guests gathered around the breakfast table. The sun was shining, not a whisper of a breeze stirred the flowers in the urns on the terrace and the staff had already set the windows open and were lowering blinds on those facing south.

'The boats and the punts are all clean and watertight,' Lady Hopewell announced. 'The estate carpenter has removed those that leaked and has had his lads rowing around to check the rest. I had thought we might have a picnic luncheon on the bigger island if everyone would like that.'

There was a chorus of approval and someone suggested boat races, which seemed a popular idea.

'I am punting,' Mr Tredgold announced. 'Someone else can keep the odds this time.'

The men, including the Marquis, Sir George and the languid Lord Tobias, announced that they would compete, which left Max to act as bookkeeper and referee.

There were four punts and six rowing boats among eight competitors, so it was decided to have two heats of rowing and a final for the first and second in each, followed by two punt races on the same principle.

'Formby, please proceed to send over the rugs, chairs and trestle tables and so forth and advise Mrs Pettigrew that all the guests will be present at the picnic,' Lady Hopewell ordered. 'I shall have to think of trophies to present and one for the ladies' archery yesterday.'

An hour later Lucy was handed carefully into a punt by Sir George and the little flotilla of ten small craft set off for the island, laden with guests.

As they rounded a headland in the lake she saw that, unlike the island that had been the catalyst in Verity and Will's romance, this one was low and long with a little wood in the middle. There were spreading grassy banks that formed something very like a lawn and on it some of the groundsmen were erecting little striped tents. Maids were shaking out rugs while footmen set out trestle tables and chairs.

'Our hostess has clearly planned this well in advance,' Sir George said, handling the long pole with commendable grace as the rowing boats pulled ahead of the punts. 'There is quite a little garden party set up already.'

In fact, it was more like a fête on a village green. There was a flat area set aside for quoits and skittles, two shady awnings, a discreet tent for a ladies' retiring room, another tent for Mrs Pettigrew, the cook, and her little force of kitchen maids and the lads to fetch and carry. A wide plank swing was swaying gently be-

neath a sturdy horizontal bough and, as the first boat grounded gently on the shingle beach, Miss Easton and Miss Moss were helped out by one of the footmen and ran laughing towards it, already pulling off their wide sun hats so they could sit side by side.

As the punt scraped to a standstill two more footmen, bare-legged below their knee breeches, stood on the soggy margins of the grass to help the passengers alight.

Lucy wandered up the gentle slope. Max had set up a board and was pinning up what she assumed were the competitors and the running, or rather, rowing order for the races, and the older ladies were settling themselves in the shade.

'Do come and play quoits,' Mary Thomas said, skipping down to the water's edge. 'Lizzie Gainford and I and Mr Tredgold, Mr Doncaster and Lord Overdene are playing and, if we had another lady, we would have three pairs.'

Lucy was uncertain how well she could toss the rope rings, but she was willing to try it and within a few minutes they were in the thick of a tightly contested match, shouting encouragement to their partners, booing the opposition and once or twice sending the rings rolling down the hill to be retrieved from the lake by the good-natured footmen.

'Thank you so much.' Lucy took a dripping quoit from James, who was grinning, and walked back to the game. 'I think they are enjoying themselves, too.'

The game was finally settled with Lizzie and Mr Doncaster first, Lucy and Lord Overdene second and Mr Tredgold and Mary third by a long way, owing mainly to his total inability to aim true.

Lord Overdene looked round at a call from the main tent. 'The boat race order has been settled by the look of it. Come on, let's see what the opposition is like.'

It was agreed to hold the rowing races first. Max was chalking up odds on a blackboard that was considerably larger than that used for the archery and must have been brought from the old schoolroom, as well.

As wagers were placed the Marquis emerged as the favourite for the punting and Lord St Giles for the rowing. Lucy hazarded sixpence on Sir George for the punting and sixpence on Algernon Tredgold in the hope of raising his morale after his quoits defeat.

He was with the first four rowers against Lord Overdene, Lord St Giles and Sir George and they all removed their coats, jammed their hats more firmly on their heads and marched off down to the boats.

'Miss Marsh?' Max was standing right beside her. It was the first words he had spoken to her since she had refused his offer. He looked outwardly composed, but his eyes were questioning.

Lucy swallowed and found her voice. 'Lord Burnham?'

'Would you start the race for me? You need to raise this handkerchief, then let it fall. I will stand at the finish line with a footman as a runner to bring back the results.'

'Yes, of course,' she agreed, deflated. What on earth had she expected him to say? 'But why me?'

'Because I can rely on you to get them in a straight line first,' he said and walked off towards the far end of the island where a flag had been erected as the finish post.

So that was the answer! Foolish, romantic creature that you are, she scolded herself.

Was it even a compliment? Perhaps. Lucy shrugged and went down to the water's edge. 'Get straight, gentlemen!' She waited while there was some backing and splashing, then raised the handkerchief and they were off.

To everyone's surprise, but, she suspected, not his, Algernon Tredgold won by half a length with Lord St Giles second. The next four were won by Lord Easton with Mr Doncaster second. By now the betting on Mr Tredgold was increasing and Lucy risked another sixpence before the rowers lined up for the final. Their blood was up and she had some trouble getting them in order, but they were finally off, the younger men and several of the ladies running along the shore to cheer on their favourites.

'Mr Tredgold,' the panting footman announced when he arrived back, closely followed by the rowers on the water and the runners on land.

After a rest and considerable back-slapping and teasing of Mr Tredgold the first four punters lined up: the Marquis, Mr Doncaster, Lord Tobias, languid as ever, and Lord Overdene.

Mr Doncaster fell in after six yards, Lord Overdene spun round in a circle and ran ashore before pushing off and giving chase to the Marquis, who was clearly an experienced punter, and Lord Tobias who, to Lucy's amazement, was staying level with him. It was, the panting footman announced, a dead heat.

The second race was won by Sir George with Lord St Giles second.

'Would you like to start the final, Lady Hermione?'

Lucy passed her the handkerchief without waiting for a reply and walked along until she was halfway to the finish line. The start was all very well, but she wanted the excitement of the finish of at least one race.

It was clear from the start that punting needed skill and experience and more than a young man's fitness. Lord St Giles fell behind from the start, but Lord Tobias, his hat discarded, his hair rippling in the breeze, full shirt sleeves billowing, was holding his own with his two seniors. As they came level she began to run to follow them and, at the last moment, the Marquis bent his knees, pushed hard, and his punt slid ahead of Sir George to pass the flag first.

Laughing, Lucy cannoned straight into a solid obstacle that grunted and then held her upright.

'Oh! Max—I am sorry!'

Max kept his balance, but he staggered sideways. 'Lucy. I should have known.'

She was still laughing, despite the collision. Her cheeks were pink, her eyes were bright and her bosom was rising and falling with the exertion.

Max was conscious of a sudden stab of anger, largely at himself and his own doubts and worries. All that drama and emotion the day before and now Lucy was laughing, happy. It seemed that her refusal had been genuine and she was deeply relieved not to be betrothed to him. He had agonised over that in long sleepless hours last night. It appeared he had wasted the time and emotional energy.

'Miss Marsh.' He was suddenly acutely aware of James, the footman, just a yard away. 'James, run back

with the result, will you? Lord Petersbridge, Sir George
and Lord Tobias.'

The man took off at a brisk trot. He should have
followed but, somehow, his feet were staying firmly
rooted to the slightly muddy turf.

'Did I hurt you?' Lucy asked. 'I'm so sorry. No? Oh,
I'm glad. That was exciting, wasn't it? I would never
have imagined that Lord Tobias would be so good.'

'I suspect that he has spent a good deal of time in
a punt with his notebook, drifting around looking romantic with a capital R,' Max said. 'That young man
is not such an aesthete as he would like us to believe.'
No, she hadn't jarred his shoulder, but there was something decidedly odd with his breathing and he realised
that he was still holding Lucy by the upper arm.

'Let us walk back.' It came out more abruptly than
he meant.

'Yes, of course. You should go and rest in the shade.
Shall I take your arm?'

'*No.* No, thank you.' What the devil was the matter with him? The arrow wound had settled down and
was showing no sign of infection, and he always healed
well, anyway. It wasn't fever. Perhaps he was suffering concussion from that blow to the head after all.
That and a sleepless night. 'We do not want to miss the
prize-giving,' he said more moderately and offered his
arm, making it quite clear he had absolutely no need
to lean on her.

They began to stroll back. He really did feel decidedly strange. Reckless, almost rebellious, not that he
had anything to rebel against. There was a faint breeze
whispering in from the water now, bringing with it the
scent of cut grass, a hint of jasmine and warm woman.

'Is everything all right? Have the others accepted that there really is nothing to Sophia's ridiculous tale?'

'I believe so, now that they see she and I appear to be firm friends and they have had time to digest the fact that she really is enamoured of someone of whom you do not approve. And quite how ridiculous it would be for me to be your mistress, as you said.'

Perhaps that had not been the most tactful way of putting it. Max found himself hoping that there would be dancing that evening. That would cheer her up. He wanted to see Lucy dance, see her face light up as it had just now. And then he could take her in his arms and feel that thrill of happiness shiver through her again. Just to calm his anxieties about her, of course.

Before he could explore that desire any further she said, 'Lady Sophia is throwing herself into the spirit of the day.'

'You say that as though it is a bad thing. Personally I am delighted that she isn't sulking. And, if she is happy, then it just goes to show that it was a whim, a foolish infatuation.'

'Of course it doesn't,' Lucy retorted, the old, prickly female back again. 'If it had been that, then she would sulk at being caught out and told off. If she loves Mr West, then she will try to hide it. She will not give up. Why should she, if he is the man to make her happy?'

'Love in poverty to a man with a disreputable ancestry? How long would that last? I have had more experience of the world than you, Lucy. I have seen the effect of reckless marriages for love, or what passes for it.'

'His parentage may be disreputable—and I would wager that any fault was his father's—but Mr West is not. He is too proud and honourable to live off Sophia's

money—why don't you find him a better position? He has no religious calling to be a clergyman. You could discover his strengths and help him to find something that would earn more and which would suit him. Thousands of people live very happily outside the orbit of those who would turn their noses up at a man for something that happened before he was born.'

'How do you know what he feels about the clergy?' Max demanded, feeling attacked. Dammit, he *was* being attacked. And lectured.

'I took the trouble to find out, which is more than you did,' Lucy retorted. 'This is Sophia's happiness at stake, her whole life. Don't you care?'

They had almost reached the rest of the party. Max slowed down. 'And I know what happens when a girl is blinded by what she thinks is love, when she puts her trust in a man who is not a suitable husband for her. A broken heart—if such a thing exists outside fairy tales—is a small price to pay for her life.'

He had said too much and either shocked or intrigued Lucy, he could tell by the jerk on his arm as she took a beat before she matched his pace again. The group surrounding the victors of both the races swallowed them up and he made himself smile and clap the two men on the back, join in the laughter as Philip Doncaster emerged from a tent attempting to dry himself with a small towel while fully clothed and tease Lucy when the extent of her winnings on Algernon Tredgold were revealed.

Under cover of the banter and the arrival of Doncaster's valet with dry clothes and an armful of towels, Max watched Sophia and Lucy. They were both good actresses, he realised. If you did not know his stepsis-

ter well, you would believe the smile, the laughter, the flirtatious little games she played. You would not see how brittle that smile was, how bleak her eyes became when she was quiet for a moment.

As for Lucy, she had been exasperated with him, he knew, but now she was smiling and defending Tredgold against accusations of employing whatever methods racehorse trainers used to give their beasts an advantage. Only days before she had been reserved, almost shy with everyone—and cross as crabs with him. That, at least, had not changed.

He saw Sophia was watching him intently. He raised an eyebrow and she pursed her lips as though he had done something wrong. His conscience was clear, he told himself. Making hard decisions was what being head of a family was so often about. It was his duty. So why did he feel guilty? No, this was not guilt—it was as though he had lost something.

Chapter Thirteen

M ax took a seat in Lady Hopewell's boat for the return to shore and allowed her to fuss over him. Dorothea was an old friend and her gentle nagging was
almost soothing. She was quite correct—he had spent
a long day, mainly on his feet, and it was only yesterday that he had been injured.

'I cannot imagine why you are not flat on your face
on the turf, Burnham,' she scolded as he stepped ashore
and handed her out of the rowing boat. 'You must have
the constitution of a horse and it is a miracle that you
are not throwing a fever.'

'It is only a flesh wound,' he said as they walked up
the long slope towards the house.

'Well, I think you should change into something very
comfortable and spend a peaceful evening in your room.
I will have them send up the decanters—although doubtless the doctor would say that alcohol will only raise
your temperature—and a good dinner. And a pile of
all the latest books that have arrived from Hatchard's.'

'That sounds very tempting.' It made him feel eighty
to admit it, but everything ached now, including his
brain.

'I am sure you will feel much better for it. Certainly more rested than if you spend the evening with this collection of sad romps, dancing.'

'Dancing?' Just what he had hoped. Max's vision of a cosy evening by the fireside being pampered began to sound less tempting.

'Yes. I engaged the excellent little string band that plays at the local Assembly Rooms. But do not worry, you will not hear a thing from your bedchamber.'

And no doubt, if I ask, they will find me a gout stool, a nice rug for my knees and an ear trumpet.

'Dancing? Oh, I think I can manage to sit and enjoy watching that,' Max said. A good dose of the willow bark powder that the doctor had left would see him through the evening.

'Well…if you are certain. I don't know what Dr Williams would say.'

'He would have said I could not manage today's picnic, I imagine. Doctors make their money with doom-laden prognoses from which only their skill can rescue the sufferer. Don't worry about me, Dorothea, I will go and rest now.'

And he would. A bath, an hour flat on his back on the bed, a mouth-puckering tumbler of medicine and he'd last the evening. There were two young ladies to keep an eye on. He told himself that he couldn't trust Sophia not to lure West to the house if there was dancing and, as he had given Lucy the notion that dancing would cure her distress at listening to music, then he had a duty to make sure that really worked when she was in a ballroom with other men. Yes, definitely it was his duty.

* * *

'This is a lovely gown, Miss Marsh.' Amy spread out the skirts of the remaining evening dress that Verity had passed on to Lucy.

Amy was still not very skilled with hairdressing, but she was an excellent needlewoman. She had altered the gown to fit and changed the colour of the ribbons from dark brown to an amber that was almost gold, to bring out the tiny dots of gold that were sprinkled across the cream silk fabric. There were two flounces at the hem, puffed sleeves slashed to show a glimpse of gold lining, and a daring, very plain neckline that, when she was laced into the corset that was made to go with the gown, actually gave Lucy a hint of cleavage.

'Do you think this is too…exposed?' She tugged at it. 'You could whip a length of lace around it in a moment.'

'Absolutely not, miss. You'd ruin the elegance of the cut,' Amy said, very much Pringle the lady's maid. 'It's a pity you haven't got a necklace to do it justice, though.'

'I'll put Grandmama's gold locket on some of the narrow amber ribbon.' Lucy rummaged in her small jewellery case. That might prove some distraction from what felt like an expanse of bare flesh. It hadn't felt so bad when she had tried it on in Verity's bedchamber…

She would brave the music, she had decided. Perhaps one of the gentlemen would ask her to dance and, if they left her a wallflower, then she would creep off to one of the antechambers and dance all by herself. It was different from being able to play, but the music would still run through her, lift her. She rather thought that Max had restored happiness to her.

It was a good thing he would not be there this evening, not after such a strenuous day of being active without any rest. She was coming to look for his presence, feel the need to be near him, and that was dangerous, even though he was still infuriatingly authoritarian, cold and conventional.

Amy found her shawl and draped it perfectly from elbow to elbow and Lucy went down to dinner. She was halfway down the final flight of the broad staircase when she stopped, struck by an unpleasant thought: any day now she would find herself back in London, rather better off financially, considerably healed in her mind, but restored to her new life of a music teacher, living in modest respectable lodgings. Her friends would ask her to dinner, to their parties, but she was going to miss this life of ease and elegance.

'You look as though you have lost a guinea and found a groat, Miss Marsh.' Mr Tredgold looked up at her from the foot of the stairs, chubby and beaming in his evening black and white. His victory in the rowing race appeared to have transformed him. 'I hope nothing is amiss. I have to thank you for your support of me—I hear that you placed an early wager, which must have been an act of pure kindness over hope.'

Lucy laughed and came down the rest of the steps to his side. 'I merely remembered something just now that had slipped my mind. And as for the rowing, why, I declare that you are a dark horse, Mr Tredgold, keeping the secret of your prowess like that.'

'I used to be a very good rower when I was a boy,' he confessed, offering her his arm. 'Then I grew sadly stout—the fleshpots of Oxford, you know!—and recently I resolved on a course of exercise on the river

invisible. It appeared to work, or at least the others were too tactful to suggest she play something.

By the time the gentlemen joined them it was agreed that Miss Easton would be first, Lady Sophia, last, and Lady Hopewell would decide the rest of the order, including any gentlemen who wished to play.

The men were polite enough not to linger over their brandy and the entire party trooped through to the ballroom where the pianoforte was installed on a low dais and chairs had been arranged for the audience.

Lucy managed to go in last and found an alcove to sit in. Probably it was a favourite trysting place when balls were in progress, just secluded enough for a flirtation, but not so cut off as to be shocking.

No one took any notice of her, they were all too occupied admiring the instrument, choosing seats and bickering gently over who was playing what.

She would be all right, she told herself. She could put her fingers in her ears and nobody would notice.

Anne Easton stepped up on the dais, settled herself at the keyboard and began to play.

at home. I have not my old form yet, and it was a good thing the course was no longer, but I think my style gave me an advantage. Or possibly,' he added with a chuckle, 'the sight of me in the lead so startled the others that they caught crabs and lost their rhythm.'

'It was most impressive,' Lucy assured him as they reached the doors into the drawing room.

'Will you be dancing this evening, Miss Marsh? Might I hope you will partner me for a set?'

'Why, yes, certainly, with pleasure. And I hope I will not reward you for my winnings of a whole crown by treading on your toes.'

They were both laughing as they walked in. The first person Lucy saw was Max looking at her with a coolness that had her chin coming up and which fixed the smile on her lips as though it had been glued.

'Do excuse me a moment, Mr Tredgold.' She swept across the floor. 'Why are you here?'

'As opposed to where? York?'

If he so much as twitches that eyebrow at me, I'll...

'Your bed. You should be resting, you stubborn man.'

'I do not require a nursemaid, Lucy.' There was something in his eyes as his gaze met hers that stirred all the unsettling feelings she had been striving to suppress.

'I do not know *what* you require,' she said tartly.

Max spoke so quietly that she hardly made out the words. 'No, I do not suppose you do. I'm damned if I do either.' Then, 'But Algernon Tredgold is what you fancy?'

'He is a very pleasant young man and he was the cause of my winning a whole crown this afternoon.'

'Hardly a very prepossessing figure of a man.'

'So what if he is not?' she demanded inelegantly. 'Men do not have to cut fine figures any more than ladies have to be beautiful to be worthwhile human beings. It is a pity you have not suffered some losses or setbacks in your gilded life, then you might be less superior and more sympathetic, my lord.'

The lovely gown made a highly satisfying swish as she swept round and stalked back to Mr Tredgold. 'I am so sorry, I just recalled something I had to say to Lord Burnham.'

If Algernon noticed that colour was burning in her cheeks he was too tactful to say anything and at that moment the remainder of the guests came crowding into the room and they were swept up in the conversation.

Lucy received three more requests for a dance before dinner was announced and was feeling quite dizzy with anticipation, especially when Lady Hopewell let slip that she had instructed the musicians to play at least one waltz.

Lady Moss looked dubious. 'Are you certain that the mothers of all these young ladies would approve? I know it is danced at Almack's these days, but even so...'

'I know just what you mean, my dear. But all the gentlemen are known to us and the party is too small to allow any romping to go unnoticed. If danced with discretion I find it a most elegant dance. I am sure your Clara would shine in it—she is so graceful.'

Lucy noticed that Miss Moss, out of sight of her mother, had just collapsed on the sofa in a fit of giggles at something Lord Overdene had said. Graceful?

Well, perhaps. She did not believe she would be either, although she had felt so in Max's arms the other evening. But this was only a private party, not Almack's, and matchmaking mamas would not be observing the young ladies with hawk-like stares, ready to pounce on the slightest misstep in behaviour or deportment. Everyone could relax.

Dinner brought her Sir George and Lord Tobias as neighbours and, disconcertingly, Max seated opposite. Sir George, who seemed to have only just noticed her damaged hands, was so tactful in assisting her with everything from her linen napkin to placing the butter just so that she was hard-pressed to thank him civilly. Unless she overstretched her fingers or tried to do anything too fiddly, she was managing now to forget her injuries for hours at a time.

'Thank you. No, I can manage perfectly, Sir George.'

'What happened?' Lord Tobias asked abruptly, ignoring the convention that he should be conversing with his right-hand neighbour during the first course.

'Something heavy fell on them.' Lucy remembered just in time not to say it was a keyboard lid.

'Painful. Can you still write?'

'Yes, although it is uncomfortable.'

'Dreadful not to be able to write. I do not know what I would do if I could not.'

Sir George was cheerfully conversing across the table—it appeared that the casual picnic atmosphere was carrying through to the evening—so Lucy decided she could ignore convention, too.

'You write poetry, I believe?'

Lord Tobias nodded, then had to toss back his hair.

It was very thick, black and glossy, Lucy thought, but it must be a dreadful nuisance. Lord Byron's locks were wavy, she had heard, so they must have been easier to manage. 'I must congratulate you on your punting. I believe it is a lot more difficult than it looks.'

'I learnt on the river when I was at Cambridge. It is a knack more than anything,' he said with surprising modesty.

'Tell me about your poetry,' she asked recklessly. Normally asking young men about their verse was risking mind-numbing boredom, but Lord Tobias shook his head.

'I would if it was better, but I am not satisfied. I wish to write like Byron, but I know I am setting the bar too high. Yet I must attempt it.'

'You have a theme in mind? Or a hero to write about?' She had expected him to talk incessantly—this was like winkling cockles out of their shells.

'You are truly interested?' he asked and she saw he was younger than all his romantic posing had led her to believe. Perhaps it was a mask to shield his uncertainty about his talent.

'If I gave you some to read, would you tell me honestly what you think?' Yes, he was most certainly younger than the twenty-five or six she had first thought.

'I am no poet, but, yes, I would tell you my honest opinion if you think it would be worth anything.'

'You would understand, I think,' he said seriously, looking at her. 'You would feel it, know if the rhythms are not right. Like music.' His smile took her by surprise and she smiled back. How interesting that two of the people she had almost dismissed on first sight—

Mr Tredgold as awkward and uninteresting and Lord Tobias as affected and foolish—had proved her wrong.

'Will you dance this evening?' Lord Tobias asked as the footmen cleared the first course and she told herself she must make conversation with Sir George.

'I will, although I am sadly out of practice.'

'Then you will save at least one for me?'

'I would like that very much,' Lucy said, smiling as she turned to her other partner and found Max regarding her with what looked like frigid disapproval.

For what? Talking to the wrong partner? For smiling?

She turned the smile on him, very sweetly. So sweetly that he seemed at risk of choking on the wine he had just drunk.

Sir George also claimed a dance and, with so many partners already, Lucy felt an unexpected confidence when they all went through to the ballroom.

The small string band was good and Sir George, who claimed her for the first country dance, was a steady, if rather ponderous, partner. It was not as easy as dancing in hold had been and the effect of the music flowing through her was not as magically all-consuming. Or perhaps that was the effect of dancing with Max, a theory she preferred not to explore too deeply.

Anyway, Lucy told herself as they all clapped and then took their positions for the next dance of the set, she was enjoying this, it felt soothing and invigorating both at the same time and it proved that the magic she had felt when Max had waltzed with her on the terrace had not been a product of the moonlight.

He was not dancing, of course. It was foolish of him

to be here at all, when he should be resting. If he threw a fever tomorrow, it would be entirely his own fault. In fact, his arm was probably hurting him, which was why he was looking so severe at dinner.

Algernon Tredgold claimed her for the next set, but he was not as accomplished a dancer as Sir George and trod on her toes three times. Magic was decidedly lacking, but he was cheerfully apologetic and the set passed without too many small mishaps.

There was a short interval while the musicians sorted their music, consulted together and the viola player retuned his instrument. The ladies sat and fanned themselves and the windows were opened on to the garden, bringing in fresh air and the perfume of night-scented stocks.

Lucy saw Max rise and walk over to the little stage, murmur in the ear of the lead violinist who nodded. The musicians settled themselves and the gentlemen began to fan out around the room, seeking their next partner.

'Miss Marsh?' Lord Tobias was at her side.

'My dance, I believe.' She turned to see Max looking, not at her, but at the younger man.

'I had promised Lord Tobias—'

'But not the waltz, I think,' Max said, his eyes still holding Lord Tobias's gaze.

'No, not the waltz. I hope for one of the later dances, Miss Marsh.' Lord Tobias made a small bow and strolled away to Miss Thomas.

'I had not promised you a dance and, anyway, you should be in your bed, not exerting yourself at this hour,' she said crossly. Lord Tobias had not even protested.

She should not have mentioned beds. There was not the slightest flicker of either amusement, let alone anything like desire, on Max's face, but somehow she was convinced that he was thinking of those crowded moments under that bed, of the kiss.

'I assure you, Lucy, I have rested upon my bed, taken a headache powder and generally behaved in the most sensible of manners,' he said, leading her out on to the dance floor.

And now I cannot turn tail and walk off or it will look to everyone as though we are quarrelling.

'Sensible? Of course, my lord, you are always *sensible.*'

The musicians struck a chord, partners took their places and Max gathered her neatly into hold without even a wince.

'I try to be,' he said very seriously as they began to dance. 'I really do—it makes life so much simpler. But recently I find myself wanting to behave in the most irrational manner.'

Oh, there it is, that wonderful feeling, the music flooding through me. So much better than the others, like a cloudy day when the sun comes out.

What had Max just said? She must learn to dance and to think at the same time. 'Irrational? I suppose Lady Sophia's behaviour, however understandable in a woman in love, is enough to make a strict brother, one who has no concept of the emotion, wish to respond irrationally.'

What did he just murmur under his breath? It was hard to tell because they were close to the orchestra now. *Sophia is hardly the problem?* No, it must have been, *Sophia is quite the problem.*

Lucy closed her eyes and found it was not simply the music that was taking over her senses. She was very conscious of Max's hands—light where he held her own, firm where he touched her waist—of the faint scent of starch and soap and the whisper of something citrus and sharp. And the music seemed to fade and the scent became greener and there was the tinkle of water and she opened her eyes.

'We are in the conservatory.'

'It is cooler in here. I was becoming quite dizzy.' He danced on, sweeping her around palms and pots and a statue of a mournful-looking Greek female clutching at her slipping robe in an attempt at modesty.

He was dizzy? She certainly was and Max appeared to have no trouble keeping in step and maintaining his balance.

'Max.'

'Yes?' They came to a halt in front of a bench next to the little fountain.

'You are *not* dizzy.'

'Are you calling me a liar?' He seemed amused rather than outraged.

'Yes.'

'I want to kiss you, Lucy—heaven knows why, given that you would probably impale me on your prickles—but I do. Which tells me I am dizzy and probably suffering from the blow to my head.' Max lifted his hand away from her waist as though freeing her to run from him.

Chapter Fourteen

Lucy stared at Max, up at him, because they were still in the dance position. This close she could see that he had shaved with meticulous closeness, that the slight indentation in his chin *was* a dimple when he smiled— even if it was ruefully—and that those cool grey eyes had intriguing little flecks that were almost black.

'I did not hit my head, I am not dizzy.' *Well, not very.* 'And I would like to kiss you,' she responded. Clearly, she had lost all common sense, but that did not seem very important.

'You understand that I am not attempting to seduce you? That I do not take innocents as lovers? It is just that I feel this quite irrational urge to hold you.' He sounded bemused, which was rather endearing.

Not a word I ever expected to apply to this man...

'Yes, I am quite clear on that. You have made it un- flatteringly plain that you cannot imagine why you should wish to kiss me. Let me say in return, I have no idea why I should wish to embrace an arrogant, au- thoritarian, chilly man like you.'

'I do not feel chilly, Lucy. Not in the slightest.'

She swallowed. Neither did she. 'I doubt that kissing will have a cooling effect, but we could try.'

Max did not reply, only lowered his head slowly, watching her, until their lips touched. She remembered the last time, how his mouth had moved on hers, how his tongue had slid along the seam of her lips, and now she was ready for that, anticipated him, opened to him on a sigh and leaned into his body as his tongue touched hers.

No, he was not at all cold, this man. He was hard as she pressed herself to him, his mouth was hot and she was burning up with the need to be closer to him. She wanted to climb him, wrap herself around him, drown in the delicious sensations his lips were creating.

Everything seemed to be connected, from her mouth to her breasts, to low in her belly, to the wicked little pulse between her legs and from her fingertips in his hair to her toes pressed hard against the unyielding tiled floor.

When he lifted his head a moment or possibly an hour later, she sat down with a bump on the cushioned bench, her knees trembling.

Max stood there, his hands on her shoulders, eyes closed, then he gave himself a little shake and sat down beside her.

'Max...'

'Yes?' He sounded braced for almost anything.

'When I had to hide in the pool that first evening and you lifted me out you seemed so strange, as though you were unwell.' *Or somewhere else entirely.* She had thought about his reaction since, as she had come to know him better. That pallor had not been the result of pulling a muscle in his back lifting her.

She thought he was not going to answer her, then he said, 'You were soaking wet, your clothes were plastered to your body and you were pale. There was weed in your hair. I once saw someone who had drowned in the Thames. A woman. They laid her out on the stinking mud, her gown clinging to her, her hair dark with the water, a strand of weed across her face.'

'Someone you knew?' Of course it was. There was hard-reined emotion under the flat description.

'Her name was Julia. I loved her.'

'Oh. Oh, Max.' Lucy curled her fingers into his hand. 'Were you betrothed?'

'No. It was ridiculous—*I* was ridiculous. She was twenty, I was seventeen and at that age the difference is immense. She was already a woman, I was a romantic boy. She fell for a man, a fortune hunter, and ran away with him, although I pleaded with her not to trust him. She made me promise not to tell anyone and, like a fool, I agreed.'

'Did…did he kill her?'

'He might as well have done. Her father refused to give him money, refused his consent to a marriage, so he discarded her like a worn-out shoe after five months. She was pregnant, the doctor at the morgue said. I had come up to London searching for her when her letters stopped coming. I felt responsible, because I had not told anyone where she had gone, and with whom, until it was too late. I asked the river patrols and they took me to see that night's haul of bodies. They had not even taken her up from the water's edge when I got there.'

His voice was still flat. 'There were bruises on her face.'

'What did you do?'

'I sent for her father, but he wrote back, said she was already dead to them. I had enough money for a simple funeral, so I arranged that in the nearest church, a strange little place by the river. And I saw what damage an ill-considered love affair can do, why it is so important that there is equality of rank and fortune, acceptance by society and family. Otherwise the risk for a woman is too great.

'A week later a letter reached me. Julia had written it before she...before she went down to the river. She said it was all her fault, that she did not love him enough, that she had thought it was all that was needed to be happy and she was wrong and now she did not know how to go on.

'It had been my fault that she was not stopped and I will not make the same mistake again. I should have known, after all, because one of my uncles made an equally reckless match and they are both unhappy in it.'

'Max, the Reverend West would never abuse Sophia, you must see that in him.'

'It is almost the opposite case. He would come to resent her, her money. His pride is already engaged and he will not take her fortune. And she has no idea what it would be like to live outside her own social circle, to scrimp and save. I want her to be happy, contented, secure.'

Was he right? How could she tell when she hardly knew either of the lovers involved? But for that one tragic incident in his past to have created such certainty, such emotion, proved something to her—Max had felt deep guilt and she had no idea how to help him.

It is not your problem to solve, the voice of common sense said firmly. But yet, for some inexplicable reason, it was...

'Max, I am so sorry.' There were no words, but perhaps touch could soothe, just a little. She lifted her hand to stroke it down his cheek, saw her gloves and, without thinking, stripped them off. She needed to touch him, feel him.

He turned his face into her palm, pressed his lips into it, and with a little sob, she curled her other arm around his neck as he stood, bringing her with him. Something caught, tore, but she hardly heeded it.

The need to comfort had become something else, something entirely new, a sensation close to the ecstasy of making music when everything was right and it flowed from her fingers and possessed her utterly.

She could hear music now, swelling, building—

Someone screamed, a sharp, indignant screech. Max swung round, putting her behind him as he had that other evening in the conservatory, but there was no pool of water to conceal her now.

'Lord Burnham—and *Miss Marsh*. It is true after all! Girls, go out this minute.'

It was Lady Moss, Lucy saw through the fronds of the palm that Max had almost pushed her into. It was not, she realised, very effective cover, judging by the expression on the faces of Lady Moss, her daughter, Miss Thomas—all the young ladies, in fact, plying fans, their cheeks flushed. They had come through from the ballroom to cool themselves, which was why the music had suddenly become louder.

The young ladies ignored the instruction and stood in a little gaggle like nervous, nosy chickens.

'Max, what *are* you doing?' That was Sophia. 'Oh...'

And then Lucy realised that, despite being hot with embarrassment and kisses, there was cool air on her shoulders. What she had felt catch and tear was the little train that fell from the back edge of her neckline. It had ripped away, taking one puffed sleeve and a section of bodice with it, exposing much of her right breast and her stays. She scrabbled to pull it together, her fingers clumsy on the fine fabric, and her gloves fell to the floor.

'Girls, out this moment.' Lady Moss shooed them towards the door with little success. 'Burnham, I had thought better of you and as for you, Miss Marsh, ripping off your clothing in the conservatory! To think I gave you the benefit of the doubt earlier, that I allowed you to associate with my daughter, with the daughter of my friends who had entrusted her to my care. Hussy!'

'Miss Marsh is my betrothed and cannot be blamed for my own lack of self-control.' Max finally managed to get a word in edgeways.

'No, I am *not*.' There was silence except for the jolly strains of a lively country dance being played, presumably to a near-empty ballroom, given that everybody seemed to be in here, staring at her. 'Lord Burnham is being gallant. We are not betrothed.'

There was another door, the one she and Max had escaped though that first evening. Lucy turned and walked towards it. She felt Max take her arm and brushed him away.

Someone said, far too loudly, 'Look at her hands.'

The door banged behind her and she saw it had a latch which she flicked over. That should stop anyone following her. She ran upstairs, found her bedchamber and tumbled in, turning the key in the lock.

Amy was perched on the end of the bed, peering carefully at the heels of a handful of silk stockings.

'Pack, at once. We are leaving.'

'Now, Miss Marsh?'

'Hurry. There's an inn in the village, I can hire a gig to take us into the nearest town with an inn that the coach stops at. Then—'

She broke off at a knock on the door. 'Lucy, open this door.' It was Max.

'Go away.'

Silence. Knowing Max, she doubted that he had done what she asked. She turned to Amy and whispered, 'Keep packing, I will help. He can hardly stand out there all night.'

'What has happened?' Amy asked, but her hands were already busy rolling the stockings, as her eyes scanned the room, assessing what had to be done.

'A misunderstanding—and a scandal. Are the valises still down here?'

'Yes, miss.'

'What about your things, Amy?'

'I'll just have to go and get them when the coast is clear. Or… Come into the dressing room and look at this.'

Lucy followed her, feeling queasy. Max was still out there, she was certain. And of course he had said they were betrothed. He was a gentleman and so he had done the honourable thing, in public this time, even if it was also something that went directly against what he believed about suitable marriage partners.

But women could have honour, too, and marrying a man simply because of a few kisses in the conservatory and a ripped gown was as logical as trying to train a cat to ride a pedestrian curricle. It did not help that when Max had said *betrothed*, something inside her had fluttered with joy.

'Fool,' she muttered as Amy opened the shutters over the narrow window.

'See, miss?' There's a balcony outside, just like there is outside the bedchamber window. But that one has nothing close to it—this one is paired up with the room next door. I reckon we could climb across.'

Lucy opened the window and leaned out. They were two floors up with only darkness below. Her stomach swooped, but she knew Amy was right—the gap was about two feet and the balustrades were wide and looked in good repair. 'Who is next door?'

'Nobody, miss. And the door for the bedchamber that dressing room belongs to opens out on to the cross-passage at the back. I found it the other day when I needed some blue thread and I thought I'd see if someone's maid was there to borrow from. But it's empty.'

'Right. That's what we will do.'

Half an hour later Amy hitched up her skirts and climbed out of the window and on to the balustrade. Lucy held up a candle as she took one stride across, then dropped down on to the narrow balcony.

'The window's open, I suppose they don't think anyone can get in at this height,' she whispered. 'Pass the bags across, miss.'

That took only a moment, then it was Lucy's turn. She had put on her most sensible shoes and a plain walking dress, but even so, as she stepped across in the near-dark, she half expected to hear a rip as her heel caught in her skirts and she overbalanced to fall on to the stone terrace below. Then she was down beside Amy, helping get the valises through the window.

The key was in the lock. Amy eased open the door. 'All clear, miss.'

They tiptoed along the passage to the back stairs and Lucy held her breath while Amy ran upstairs and came back ten minutes later with her own valise.

The way down was clear. 'Everyone's in the kitchen clearing up, or up in the ballroom,' Amy murmured as she lifted the latch and they were out into the yard.

They made their way to the stables, then down the track where Max had been riding the afternoon of the archery contest. As Lucy had hoped, it gave out on to a lane and the gate had no lodge with a keeper to stop them.

'That way,' Lucy decided and gave a sigh of relief as they came to a larger lane with a rickety signpost pointing to the village of Staning Waterless. 'It can't be too far, I heard the church bells quite clearly the other day—the ringers were practising.'

Their luck held. The Hopewell Arms provided them with a gig and a lad to drive them into Blandford Forum and the assurance that they would be in ample time for the early-morning Mail coach to London from The Greyhound in the market square.

Yawning, they caught it at five o'clock and managed to secure inside seats. It saved Lucy the cost of a night's accommodation and the high price of a post chaise for a journey of at least a hundred miles and, she hoped, gave them sufficient of a start in case Max was still set and determined on putting honour above either sense or his own principles.

It did, however, give her more than ten hours with no privacy to think about what had happened.

Betrothed. Her heart had leapt at the word and she was not so good at self-deception not to understand exactly what that meant. She did not only desire Max's kisses, she wanted him. If their respective stations in life, if their circumstances had been more equal, she would want to marry him.

Which means I am in love with him, I suppose. How had that happened? She hadn't liked the man—she was still not certain that she did. He was too controlled, too authoritative, too… Just *too much*, she supposed.

And yet, he has his good points, she mused as Amy curled up in the opposite corner and fell asleep, buttressed at the side by a serious-looking gentleman who looked like a lawyer.

Max had a strong sense of responsibility and it was clear would do anything to protect his stepsister— whether she wanted it or not. He was honourable. He was intelligent and, she suspected, there was far more of a sense of humour lurking under that glacial expression than he allowed to show. He had kissed her, but only when she had made it clear she wished him to, and he had not taken advantage of her inexperience and simply carried on, swept her away on the tide of her own innocence.

And there was something about him, not simply his good looks, that stirred feelings she had not been aware she possessed. Feelings that must have been buried by the music. Or perhaps Max was part of the music…

'Unlock the door? But—'
'Dorothea, they have been in there since almost

midnight last night. It is now midday. Do you propose leaving them to starve? Would that be more proper?' He felt desperate. It had all gone wrong and that was his fault. His fault for wanting to kiss Lucy, his fault for making her unhappy.

His fault for not understanding himself when he saw her all too clearly. She was attracted to him, but was strong enough in her own beliefs to reject even his most pressing attempts to make reparation for his errors, while he felt as though the past and the present, his desires and his fears, were all tugging at him, clamouring for his attention. As Dorothea was now, he realised.

'I am not accepting a lecture from you on propriety, Max Fenton! You bring your paramour to my house when you knew full well it was not that kind of party—'

'I did no such thing. If you believe that I would when my own stepsister is present, then you have formed a very strange idea of my character in the years we have known each other. Now, do you unlock that door or do I kick it down?'

Chapter Fifteen

Max was angry enough to kick a door down—or shoot a lock off, come to that. He had spent the night on a chair outside Lucy's bedchamber door because he knew she would bolt if she had half the chance and what sleep he had was racked by the old, familiar nightmare of Julia's letter.

He had endured breakfast being glared at by Lady Moss, regarded with disapproval by the older men and with something like awe by the younger ones. The young ladies, herded down to the far end of the table—presumably in case he leapt on them with lustful intent—blushed and giggled.

He had stood up, leaving his food half-eaten, and addressed them. 'I will say this once more. Miss Marsh is not my mistress. I have every hope she will be my wife. If I hear remarks, inside this house or out of it, to the contrary, I will act as appropriate.'

Then he had stalked upstairs to relieve Hobson at the door.

'Not a squeak, my lord. Not so much as the creak of a floorboard.'

Now he had run out of patience. The sooner he extracted Lucy and made her see sense, the sooner he could begin to repair what damage he could. Bitter reality told him that as marriages went it could hardly fail to be a disaster on a personal level, but that was beside the point.

With a tut of disapproval, Lady Hopewell produced a ring of keys and unlocked the door. Max stepped inside and closed it firmly in her face. She promptly opened it and followed him in.

'Lucy?'

The bed was made up. The room empty. He went across to the dressing room. That, too, was empty. Hiding? What would that achieve? The clothes presses were bare, there was no one and nothing under the bed except a prosaic china utensil that brought back inconvenient memories.

'There is nothing of hers here,' Dorothea said. 'But how? There is no other door to the corridor and we are two storeys up.'

Max opened the bedchamber windows on to a tiny balcony, more an architectural feature than a practical place to sit. The corresponding one in the room to the right was a good ten feet away. To the left was the little balcony from the dressing room window and next to that—

He looked down and breathed again. No crumpled body on the flagstones of the terrace.

'Whose room is next door?'

'It is empty. There was a leak in the ceiling from a blocked gutter.'

Dorothea was still talking about falling plaster as Max went out, turned right and right again and found the door, unlocked. The window to the dressing room stood open and there were marks in the lichen on the balustrade of the balcony.

'They left this way,' he said as Dorothea came to stand beside him.

'But why take such a risk?' she demanded. 'If she is your betrothed...'

'She is not my mistress and, as she continues to make clear, she has no wish to be my wife.'

'Yes, but—'

'She is an innocent and I should not have kissed her. The disarray to her gown was due to it catching and tearing, not to unbridled lust,' he added acidly when Lady Hopewell opened her mouth as though to protest.

'If she likes you enough to be kissing you in the conservatory, then why will the foolish girl not marry you?' she retorted. 'You are an earl, for goodness sake. She is clearly gently born, but hardly the sort of young lady I would have imagined you marrying.'

No, and I made that more than clear to her only moments before we were interrupted, Max thought. Lucy must have thought that his pouring out of Julia's story was to emphasise just why he had no intention of marrying her, however much he might enjoy her kisses.

Now she was gone, back to London, he supposed. She would revert to her true name, continue with her pianoforte tuition. He could forget her and put up with a newly acquired reputation for debauched behaviour in respectable ladies' conservatories. Another little scandal would come along soon to eclipse this, he thought with a mental shrug, making his way back to the other bedchamber.

Dorothea tugged the bell pull and when a footman

appeared sent him off to see whether Pringle's things had gone from her room. A sensible thing to check, of course. The two of them could have taken refuge in the servant's room until daylight.

The man was back within minutes. 'Everything gone, my lady. Not so much as a hairpin that I could see.'

'Well, you have had a fortunate escape, it seems,' Dorothea remarked when the footman had gone.

'Indeed? From a young lady too principled to take advantage of an offer made out of a sense of obligation? And you would have me just wash my hands of her now? They left in the small hours—where are they now? I shall take out the horse you were considering selling to me. Miss Marsh may not wish to marry me, but I am damned if I'll leave her wandering the lanes of Dorset.'

He strode out, taking consent for granted and ignoring Dorothea's *tut* of disapproval for his language. His old acquaintance was growing puritanical with middle age, he thought darkly.

How did the infuriating female think she was going to get herself and her maid back to London without his money? Walk? The thought of the things that could happen to young women on their own in a journey of over a hundred miles made his blood run cold.

Max rode out of the same gate he had used the afternoon he was shot, taking it steadily. His arm hurt like the devil after the previous day's activity, followed by a thoroughly uncomfortable night in an upright chair outside Lucy's door, and he did not know how long he would have to be in the saddle now.

The earth at the gate on to the lane was shaded by a big elm and had remained moist, holding the imprints of two sets of small-sized shoes. They pointed towards the direction of the road to the village and he used his heels to send the horse into a trot that took him into Standing Waterless in ten minutes.

A groom was brushing down a neat bay cob in the stable yard and touched a finger to his hat when Max rode in. 'Morning, sir.'

'That's a good animal.' Max noticed a gig to one side, fresh mud splashes on the sides. 'Is he for hire?'

'Aye, sir. But not until this afternoon. He's been out as far as Blandford Forum and back this morning.'

'Ah. So the governess my sister dismissed did find a conveyance.' He leaned down and lowered his voice, man to man on the subject of foolish women. 'I come home and find the household in uproar, the governess dismissed for a mere nothing, the children in tears… I am concerned, as you might imagine.'

'Not to worry, sir. I got them to The Greyhound in plenty of time to catch the Mail.'

Max tipped him and, feeling somewhat relieved, turned his mount. Then something occurred to him. 'Is anything owed for the hire?'

'No, sir, I thank you. The young lady paid just what was asked without a murmur and something for me, too.'

So where the devil did she get the money from? And had she enough for the Mail? He did some calculations as the horse cantered along the wide grass verge. Over a hundred miles, two of them—hopefully inside—a couple of bags, food and tips. She would need at least four pounds, perhaps five.

She must have had more than he realised and, when she threatened to leave before, had demanded what he owed her because otherwise she feared she might not receive it. A wise precaution, but not a very flattering reflection on her opinion of him.

At The Greyhound the man in charge of the booking office was helpful. Yes, the two young ladies had secured inside seats and he was able to tell Max that the other two inside passengers on their way to London were Mr Promfret, a highly respected local attorney, and Miss Hatch, a most respectable spinster.

Max turned his horse's head back towards Waterless Manor. There was nothing to be gained by chasing the Mail on horseback, not when it seemed that Lucy had organised her escape most effectively—and with considerable good luck in her timing.

But I know where you live, Miss Marsh–Lambert, he thought as he rode. *If you think this is the end of the matter, you are very much mistaken.*

It was four o'clock in the afternoon before the hackney carriage they had taken from the General Post Office in St Martin's-le-Grand dropped Lucy and Amy at the door, only to find the Duchess of Aylsham's smart town carriage drawn up outside and the lady herself, almost seven months pregnant, descending the front steps with some care.

'There you are! Your landlady said you had gone out of town—and never a word to me, or any of the others. I was beginning to think you had eloped!' Verity smiled as Amy bobbed a curtsy. 'Good afternoon, Pringle.'

'Eloped?' Lucy felt a sudden urge to laugh hysteri-cally. 'Hardly. It was...a commission. In Dorset.'

'*Dorset?* You have only just got back?'

'On the Mail, Your Grace,' Amy said when Lucy merely shrugged.

'Why—? Oh, never mind that now. What am I thinking of, keeping you out here talking when you look exhausted? Come back with me and be looked after for a day or two, and catch up on all the news. The others are all in town, too.'

'I—' Suddenly it was too much effort to resist. She was home and the practical business of travel was done with. Now what was there to keep her from simply sinking down and being miserable? Besides, she and her four friends, Verity, Melissa, Jane and Prue, had always told each other everything and the others' tales of woe caused by men had been equally as shocking as hers—they were hardly likely to be appalled by her story.

'Thank you. I would like that.' She emerged from Verity's embrace to find the footman had already loaded their few bags into the carriage—clearly he knew his mistress too well to doubt that her sugges-tion would be taken as definite.

Having got her way, Verity was too considerate to demand answers on the short drive to Grosvenor Square. She swept Lucy inside, calling for the house-keeper. 'Mrs Blagden, here is Miss Lambert come to stay. She has been jolted all day on the Mail, so what she needs is a lovely hot bath for a soak and then a quiet rest. The Blue Bedchamber, I think. Are you hungry, Lucy? No? Tea and a little bread and butter then, Mrs

Blagden, and please tell Cook, dinner for Miss Lambert in her room.'

She waited until the staff had left before taking Lucy's arm and guiding her up the stairs. 'I will send to the others to come tomorrow morning after breakfast. You don't want to be talking now, I can see. But something is wrong. We'll put it right between us, don't worry.'

Lucy had every intention of taking her bath, lying down for an hour and then going down to take dinner with Verity and Will in a civilised manner. Instead, as she explained at breakfast, she fell fast asleep and not even the arrival of the dinner tray woke her.

'You obviously needed the rest,' Verity observed, sifting through the little pile of post and notes the butler brought in 'Excellent—all the others will be here at ten. Will, you must make yourself scarce, this is a convocation of ladies.'

'Yes, my love,' the Duke said mildly, then winked at Lucy. The Duke of Aylsham had been known as the Perfect Duke, but that was before Verity's influence had done its work on him.

Lucy smiled, recalling Verity's tale of how they had first met when the Duke had plunged down the side of an excavation she was conducting, only to be bitten on the posterior by an ancient skull. After that the poor man had found his life turned upside down by an unconventional lady who was the exact opposite of the wife he had intended to wed.

They lingered over the breakfast table after Will had left muttering about Tatts, boots and Christie's auction house.

'Which sounds expensive,' Lucy observed. She was feeling rather better, but only in the way one feels when a dentist appointment has been made and one's nagging toothache will be dealt with.

'How many pairs of boots can one man require? When I tease him about it he points to my milliners' bills, but surely boots cannot be a matter of fashion like a bonnet? As to Tattersall's, we do need a new pair of carriage horses. But I dread to think what he might find in Christie's—he has conceived a passion for Dutch Old Masters.'

The door knocker was heard at half past nine, heralding Melissa Taverner's arrival. She was always early for anything she was interested in—and late for things she was not.

'Darling! You look ghastly, what have you been doing? Oh, yes. Tea, please. And I have found a house in Half Moon Street, isn't that bold of me? I have left home now I am in possession of Great Aunt Melly's fortune and intend to be an independent lady author. You see how convenient it will be for harassing Mr Murray, the publisher in Albemarle Street? But never mind me, that can wait until the others come and we have put things to rights for you, Lucy.'

'Thank you,' Lucy said, feeling somewhat as though she had been run over by an over-enthusiastic youth in a pedestrian curricle, the usual result of an encounter with Melissa.

The others arrived shortly afterwards and they retreated to Verity's sitting room where they could kick off their shoes and curl up on the especially comfortable sofas.

'Now,' Verity said. 'Tell us what happened, what is wrong and how we can help.'

Lucy described Lady Sophia's trick to escape to the house party and Max's plan to discover who his sister fancied herself in love with. The others nodded understanding and agreement that, of course, a commission paying such an excellent fee would be irresistible at this precarious early stage of Lucy's business.

'So, what is he like, the Earl of Burnham?' Prue asked. 'I have seen him at a distance, but never met him. Very good-looking, I thought.'

Jane, as Lucy had suspected, did not agree. 'Too perfect, therefore not interesting,' she pronounced. 'And he seems completely without emotion. He would be a nightmare as the subject of a portrait.'

'He is not lacking in emotion,' Lucy said. 'But he is skilled at hiding it.'

'So what happened then?' Melissa demanded.

Lucy took a deep breath and told them everything. Everything except what Max had revealed about his tragic first love. That had been told in confidence. She simply explained that something in his past had convinced him that 'unsuitable' marriages were doomed from the start. The others could be trusted not to betray Sophia's secrets, so she did not hold anything back about the unfortunate Reverend West.

There was silence when she reached the end of her tale. Then Prue, ever practical, frowned. 'I do hope this will not have any repercussions for your new business, although you said from the start that you thought you would get most custom from the middle-class households, and they are not going to hear any gossip from Lady Hopewell's house guests.'

'You changed your name and nobody there knew you could play the piano, except Lord Burnham,' Jane mused. 'I am sure you would be safe.'

'Yes, I think so,' Lucy agreed. 'And I have some appointments for next month when families are returning to London at the end of the summer—City addresses, not West End ones.'

'That is important, of course,' Verity agreed. 'But surely what is making you so miserable is the fact that you are in love with the man.'

'In love? With Max? I mean, with Lord Burnham? But that is ridiculous, I do not like him, even,' she protested, knowing as she said it that it was untrue.

'Poppycock,' Melissa said. 'I thought from the start that was what we were here to discuss, not pianoforte lessons. I mean, I can understand you wanting to kiss him once, just out of curiosity, and the situation must have been most…provocative. But a second time? A third? I intend to take a lover as part of my plan to be a fully independent woman, but I cannot imagine you risking as much as a lingering glance or a mild flirtation with anyone you were not deeply attached to.'

The others, having heard Melissa's purely theoretical views on free love and female independence many times, did not turn a hair at her declaration, but nodded in unison.

'You are, you know,' Jane said. 'It is perfectly possible to love a man while wishing him at the devil, believe me. That is why you are so miserable and you will be until you reconcile whatever it is that infuriates you about him with the other feelings you have.'

'How?' Lucy demanded.

'He may change or you may find you are mistaken

in him. Some things you will disregard as unimportant when the major obstacles are overcome.'

'Such as?' Melissa asked.

'Never you mind,' Jane retorted, blushing.

'This is all beside the point,' Lucy said, trying to be firm and not be distracted. 'Even if I did love him, he is an earl and I am a perfect nobody and a crippled one, to boot.'

'You are not crippled,' Verity said. 'Your hands are getting better. I noticed at breakfast how much easier you were at managing cutlery, how you have stopped lifting a cup as though you expected to drop it at any moment.'

'I still cannot play.'

'But you can do everything else,' Jane pointed out. 'And yours is a perfectly respectable gentry family. Look at me—that is precisely my background, too, and I married an earl. Prue a marquis. Verity's papa is a bishop, to be true, but even so, I cannot imagine he expected her to marry a duke.'

'None of you is estranged from your families.'

'None of us has a father who would slam a keyboard lid down on our hands because they disapproved of us playing on a Sunday.' Melissa, never overly sensitive, could be counted on to mention the one thing everyone in the room was avoiding.

'I do not believe he intended to injure me. I was so shocked at their early return from church when I was engrossed in a new piece of music that I froze, just for a second.'

'And then, instead of being appalled at his own actions, he blames you, says it is a judgement on you for breaking the Sabbath,' Melissa retorted. 'I can understand that no man is actually going to *welcome* Mr Lambert as a father-in-law, but if he loves you, he will set that aside.'

'But Max *doesn't* love me. He offered to marry me because I had been compromised, so he felt honour-bound. He seemed to enjoy kissing me for some reason, although I cannot think why—'

'Men enjoy kissing. Frankly, they are fairly undiscriminating about it,' Jane said sagely.

'There, you see? He would have kissed anyone foolish enough to offer and he proposed out of simple gallantry. And I refused him because I do not love him.'

'No, you didn't,' Prue contradicted. 'You refused him because you have too much pride and honour to accept a proposal made for that reason.'

'Oh, you are exasperating, all of you,' Lucy said. She just wanted to go and sulk somewhere, away from overbearing aristocrats and well-meaning friends who thought they knew her better than she did herself.

'He knows where you live?' Melissa asked.

'Yes. And I am not moving just to avoid him. Besides, I cannot stop advertising. I will not go into hiding. If he has any sense, he will take the very strong hint that I want nothing to do with him and stay away.'

'Hah!' Jane snorted inelegantly. 'I'll wager you a guinea that he is on your doorstep within seven days.'

'Done,' Lucy said. 'I will take your wager. Lord Burnham has too much pride to persist once he has been rejected.'

Chapter Sixteen

Max arrived back in London three days after Lucy's flight. By an effort of will he had restrained himself from haring off immediately and had successfully chilled the atmosphere of Dorothea's house party by scrupulous civility to everyone, until Lady Moss was driven to apologise for her *misunderstanding* of his actions and motives.

Lucy would have been safe on the Mail, he told himself. She had her maid with her and he was not so inexperienced with women as to expect to turn up on her doorstep hours after she returned home and receive a warm, or even a lukewarm, welcome. She needed a day or so to recover and think things through logically. She was intelligent—she would see the necessity of doing as he said, surely? A woman's honour was so easily lost and there was no way back from a wrong decision, as Julia had found to her cost.

Something nagged at him, an awareness of a contradiction, and he teased it out on the long journey back. Julia had ruined herself in the hope of a marriage for love. Lucy was quite clearly *not* in love, with him or anyone else, it seemed—so why was she risking everything and throwing away a brilliant match, security and reputation? It was deeply puzzling and he had an uneasy suspicion that her motives, too, had something to do with that treacherous emotion.

His secretary, Paul Bentley, received him with his usual efficient calm. 'Not being apprised of the date of your return, my lord, I thought it prudent to offer provisional regrets to those invitations where your absence would cause little or no inconvenience. Naturally, I sent apologies to all invitations to dine. There are three invitations for this evening. Lady Fellowes's dinner I have declined. I declined in respect of Lady Twistelton's musicale and, as for Lady Devonham's ball, I said that I thought it unlikely that Your Lordship would be able to attend.'

Lady Twistelton's musicales were to be avoided at all costs and Bentley knew that, just as he knew Emilia Devonham always provided the best of entertainment. 'Thank you, Bentley. Please send a note to Lady Devonham to say that I will be delighted to attend.'

It would be pleasant to be in company that did not regard him as either an unprincipled seducer or a cynical rake.

That optimism lasted just past the end of the receiving line at Devonham House. A few steps into the already crowded ballroom, he encountered the Duchess of Aylsham, her pregnant form elegantly draped in ice-blue silk, the Marchioness of Cranford and the Countess of Kendall.

Max bowed. Three pairs of eyes narrowed, three mouths pursed and, for a stunned second, Max thought he was about to receive the cut direct from the three of them. At which point he recalled that it was the Duchess who had recommended Lucy to Sophia as a pianoforte teacher.

'Lord Burnham. How...convenient. I was just wishing that I could have a word with you.' Between the Duchess's smile—a shark would have been envious—and the sweetness of her tone, any sensible man would have quailed.

Max had moved from being sensible to downright stubborn at some point in the past few days. He returned her smile. 'Convenient indeed. I would welcome your advice on a problem I have.'

The Countess's inelegant snort was only partly muffled by her fan. The sweet-faced Marchioness, an unlikely match for the privateering Marquis, gave him a look of deep reproach.

The Duchess took his arm. 'I find myself in need of some fresh air. Shall we take a turn on the terrace?'

Bishop's daughter, knowledgeable antiquarian, the unconventional lady who had humanised the Perfect Duke: this was a woman to be wary of if you were a man with something on your conscience.

'I assume this is about a certain mutual acquaintance of ours,' Max said as soon as they were alone outside. This early in the evening the temperature in the ballroom had not reached the point where dancers were driven outside and the crush was not so great that young people could escape chaperons to enjoy a flirtation in the shadows.

'Indeed. You owe the lady in question a not inconsiderable sum for an agreed service.'

'This is about debt collecting?' he asked, incredulous.

'Certainly. I believe you have received a clear answer to your… I suppose I could call it a proposal.'

'You do not think I should persist?'

The Duchess tapped her closed fan to her lips. 'Why should you need to?' she asked. She sounded surprised.

'Because I compromised the lady, of course.' Max felt mystified. Why wasn't the Duchess insisting he marry her friend, or protégée or whatever Lucy was?

'She does not appear to feel compromised and her identity is not known.'

'I am having some difficulty in understanding why she does not wish to marry me,' Max said between gritted teeth.

'Why on earth should she marry a man whose only motivation for offering for her is his pride and his honour?'

'Because I am an earl?'

'I am beginning to understand her point of view very clearly, Lord Burnham. It appears to have escaped your notice that women are also possessed both of pride and of honour.'

'Yet you married after being stranded with the Duke on an island, I believe.' That went well beyond good manners, but this was a lady who had wed a man whose rank was eclipsed only by the royal family.

'Yes, indeed. Was it not fortunate that we were in love with each other?' the Duchess observed sweetly. 'I am certain the lady in question will be delighted to receive the sum owing. It would be best delivered by messenger, don't you think?'

She smiled and this time, as she turned and the light from the ballroom caught her face, he believed it was genuine emotion that warmed the lovely brown eyes. 'Lucy has three friends who married for love. She knows it is possible. Do not expect her to wed for less and at the cost of her conscience.'

Then she was gone with a swish of silk across the flagstones.

Love? What is the matter with everyone? Sophia pining for her confounded Vicar, a duchess lecturing me on the subject, Lucy turning down wealth and status for lack of it?

Were they all suffering from an excess of sensibility? Because they were certainly all lacking in sense. He'd read that novel and the point was clear: sense won over an excess of feeling.

Max went back into the ballroom, scanned the room and identified at least a dozen young ladies of good birth, excellent connections and most respectable fortune. He could work his way around all of those in one evening, he was sure. It was about time he married and found a wife who could deal with Sophia and her emotions, because he was damned if he could.

'Lady Mortain, good evening. Lady Catherine. Might I beg the honour of a dance?'

Yes, this was exactly the kind of girl he should be looking for: pretty, flatteringly pleased at his request, poised and, he was certain, brought up by her mama to be an excellent match for a man of standing. He could not help recognising the calculation behind the expression of sweet attention to his every word. Just as it should be, so why did it send a shiver down his spine?

After two nights with Verity, Lucy returned home the next morning to deal with her correspondence. She matched the encouraging number of enquiries about her services with her diary and did her best not to jump up every time the door knocker was heard. That, given that this was a lodging house with three other ladies in residence on the various floors, plus Mrs Todd, the landlady in the basement, was a frequent occurrence.

She was only alert because she wished to be perfectly poised and cool when Max arrived, as she was quite sure he would, despite her rash wager with Jane. He was stubborn, used to getting his own way and he owed her money.

Or perhaps she would simply tell Amy to accept the payment from him and inform His Lordship that Miss Lambert was not at home. That might be safer after her friends had talked such nonsense about her feelings for Max. Why on earth was she in love with the man? There was nothing lovable about him.

Except for his care for his stepsister, she supposed. And his distress over the girl Julia's tragic mistake. He'd been very brave over being shot, of course, and the way he looked on a horse was certainly productive of a particular...stirring. And, if she was to think of stirrings, there were his kisses and the way she had felt when he danced with her—

And that was most definitely enough of that. His character had some well-hidden good points and she found him physically attractive. That could not amount to love. Her friends were besotted with their own husbands and, being warm and generous women, wished all their acquaintance to be as happy as they were. It would be a mistake to think they possessed some special insight into other people's feelings.

Max had restored her music to her through dance, though. That was a debt she owed him, but love was not founded on debts owed. She wondered when she would dance again. Perhaps if she told the others who had been present at Lady Hopewell's house party they could invite her to their own dances when none of those people would be present.

Her fingers cramped on her pen and she sat back and began her stretching exercises. Her hands were definitely improved, she thought. Less painful, less stiff. She still could not span as widely as she had before and the missing fingertip was still sensitive. Her hands were never going to be perfect again.

And I should stop sitting here brooding. There's the rent due today.

She counted out the money and went downstairs, encountering Amy in the hallway.

'Did you lock the door, Miss Lambert? I was just about to bring up the fresh linen.'

'No, it is open,' Lucy said as the door knocker thumped.

'I'll get that,' Amy said brightly, dumping the sheets unceremoniously in Lucy's arms. 'Millie downstairs is up to her elbows in washing. It'll be the post at this hour, I expect.'

She flung the front door open with a cheerful, 'Morning, Mr Potts. Oh. Oh, my lord. Er... Miss Marsh—I mean, Miss Lambert isn't At Home, my lord.'

'She appears to have miraculously materialised behind you in the guise of a chambermaid,' Max observed. 'Good morning, Pringle.'

'Good morning to you, my lord. And she might be in, but she isn't receiving.' Amy's ears were red, but she was as stubborn as a little bull terrier, standing squarely in the doorway.

'In that case, could you convey to your mistress that I will be seated out here in my carriage until such time as she is ready to receive me.' He resumed his hat, turned and took his leisurely way down the well-scrubbed steps, across the pavement and into a smart town carriage.

'Look at them horses, miss. Really raises the tone of the street, doesn't it?' Amy was still transfixed in the open doorway.

'*Those* horses and please close the door, Amy. Gawping at the traffic does *not* raise the tone.'

'Yes, miss, sorry, miss. I did right, telling him you weren't receiving, didn't I?'

'You did. Now, what am I going to do? Go out of the back door every time I want to leave the house?'

'He won't stop there for ever, surely, Miss Lambert?' Amy was wide-eyed.

'I would not put it past him to have his butler deliver meals. To resort to hiding is undignified and impractical. I suppose I must get it over with.' A wicked idea occurred to her. 'I know how to make him really uncomfortable. I'll ask Mrs Todd if I may use her parlour and if she will act as chaperon.'

Her landlady was almost overcome at the thought of an earl in her front parlour, a chamber of the utmost respectability and solid discomfort, but she came to the immediate conclusion that the nobleman in question was a cunning seducer, out to ruin a genteel young working woman. 'He'll get no chance to work his rakish wiles in my house,' she declared stoutly.

Lucy left her ramming extra pins into her already severe coiffure and ran upstairs to tame her own escaping locks into a bun that would have done credit to a workhouse matron.

'Let His Lordship in,' she told Amy as she made her way downstairs to settle on the overstuffed horsehair sofa.

'Lord Burnham,' Amy announced after a few minutes.

'Mrs Todd, may I present Lord Burnham? My lord, Mrs Todd is the householder here.'

Max was looking at his most aloof. 'Ma'am. Miss Lambert, I had hoped to speak to you alone.'

'Not under my roof. This is a respectable house and Miss Lambert is a respectable young lady.'

'Both are clearly apparent, ma'am. However, the conversation I wish to have is of a private nature.' The grey eyes intent on her face were dark with some emotion she could not read. Anger? Desire? *Surely not.*

Even while feeling so inwardly flustered, Lucy was aware of a considerable respect for her landlady. Most people would have quailed in the face of a rigidly controlled, and clearly deeply displeased, aristocrat.

'I should explain, Mrs Todd,' she said meekly. 'Lord Burnham has proposed marriage and I do not wish to accept, but he persists.'

'You don't?' For a second the landlady's facade of gentility dropped, then she recovered herself. 'Then that's that, my lord. No more to be said, although, naturally, I will be honoured to receive you on any future occasion should you call. Pringle will show you out.'

Lucy could only admire Max's dignity. He rose, bowed to Mrs Todd and to her, took his hat from Amy and strode out of the door without further comment.

'Thank you, Mrs Todd. I appreciate your assistance.'

'Well, I can't say I understand you, Miss Lambert, for he's a fine-looking gentleman, never mind the title. But I expect you are right: no good comes of marrying far above, or far below, I always say.'

She was halfway up to the hall when she realised that Amy was talking to Max and stopped, her head just below the level of the floor.

'...as well as the money you owe Miss Lambert. There's the hire of the gig and the Mail coach fare and the tips. I wrote that down. Here it is. And then there's the guinea she wagered with Lady Kendall that you'd be too proud to turn up on her doorstep.'

'Have you considered a career as a clerk, Pringle?'

'No, my lord. They don't employ women in jobs like that, more's the pity.' There was a rustle of paper. 'Thank you, my lord. I'll find you some change.'

'Keep it for yourself, Pringle. You have earned it.'

When the front door closed she climbed the rest of the way. 'Amy, you are wonderful—you got the money?'

'To be fair, miss, he'd got it all ready. And he must have estimated the fare and so forth coming back. And it's almost ten pounds too much, even allowing for Lady Kendall's guinea.' She clutched the banknotes tight as they tried to roll back up again. 'Wasn't Mrs Todd clever? He'll not come back and risk being greeted by her again.'

'Very clever.' Lucy bit her lip as she looked at the closed front door. 'But Lord Burnham's not a man to give in to threats and he's used to getting what he wants. I wonder what he will do now?'

Lucy was right: he did have too much pride to beg. Max ordered his driver to take him to the bottom of St James's Street. He got out, walked through Cleveland Row past the front of the Palace and out into Green Park.

He wanted to ride hard, gallop off the anger and the frustration, but London parks in the late morning were no places for furious riding. Instead, he would walk off the edge of his temper through the Park, then walk along Piccadilly to Old Bond Street and Gentleman Jackson's Salon. There would be someone willing to strip off and fight, or Jackson himself might condescend to give him a bout. It wouldn't do his healing arm any good, but to hell with that.

Confound the woman. He slashed at an innocent clump of dog daisies with his cane. There was no denying Lucy's intelligence—setting her landlady on him was a stroke of genius. He should give up now. She was clearly not being coy. He had paid his debt to her—his monetary debt, that is—so logic insisted that he walk away, stop thinking about her and get on with his life.

And keep well away from that coven of friends she possesses, he added as he reached the south-east corner of the reservoir. Aristocratic ladies advocating marrying for love? That was dangerous, almost heretical, thinking.

* * *

He encountered Trevor Atkinson, an old friend, on the doorstep.

'Max, my dear fellow! What have I done to offend you? That expression could kill a nest full of wasps at ten paces.'

'Not a thing, Trevor.' Max managed an apologetic smile. 'Just thinking through a problem—a difficult employee. Fancy a round or two?'

'If you promise not to take my head off—and no black eyes, I'm off courting this afternoon, I'll have you know.' Atkinson held the door for him.

'What, heading for parson's mousetrap? Who is the lucky lady?'

His friend lowered his voice. 'Eugenia White. No, don't raise that devilish eyebrow, I know her father's a liability and her brother's a hell-born babe. But it's love, you know. I must have her, even if it means towing her family out of the River Tick.'

'I seem to be hearing a lot about marriages for love recently,' Max said as they went through to the changing room and began to strip off down to their shirt sleeves.

'It's the devil, believe me, old man. I tried to be sensible.' Atkinson began to unwind his elaborate neckcloth. 'But I was just too miserable. My valet threatened to leave me because I threw my boots at him, my sister said she'd not have my escort anywhere and I quarrelled with Lawson.'

'What, Sidney Lawson?' Max looked up from the bench where he was tugging off his boots. 'That's impossible, surely?'

'Almost,' Trevor said gloomily. 'Anyway, I realised

after that I had to do something and the only thing that works is surrender. I love her, I think she loves me and, if she accepts me today, I'll be the happiest man alive.'

'Let me see if I can knock some sense into you,' Max said, rolling up his sleeves. 'I'll do my best not to spoil your beauty while I'm at it.'

Chapter Seventeen

'I promise, none of the guests who encountered you and Lord Burnham at Lady Hopewell's will be there. I was talking to Mrs Plaistow only this morning when we met in Berkeley Square where she was deciding on the ice-cream order from Gunter's. It will be a delightful small dance—not even big enough to be called a ball. Her two nieces are coming out next Season and she wants to give them a little polish beforehand. Nice girls, both of them, but rather shy.' Jane poured Lucy a fresh cup of tea. 'I asked her if I might bring a friend and she was delighted. Do say you'll come.'

'Well, I suppose I could,' Lucy said cautiously. 'It would be very pleasant and I have no students this afternoon, which means that I can prepare. So, thank you, I will.'

'I think it is quite safe, you know. I mean—Burnham has stopped calling, hasn't he?'

'It is almost a week, yes. I think Mrs Todd would be enough to rout the Regent, frankly. Max—Lord Burnham, I mean, has paid me, I sent him a receipt and that is that.'

'You do not look very happy about it.'

'Of course I am,' Lucy protested. If she said it often enough, she might come to believe it.

'Yes, I suppose it is for the best now. You might love him—' Jane waved one hand holding a biscuit when Lucy began to protest '—no, don't argue with me, I know best. You might love him, but the beast clearly does not love you or he would find some way to be with you.'

'Absolutely. Not that I am in love with him,' she lied. She might tell herself she didn't, but she knew she was only deceiving herself. 'I mean, even if he did love me, which is impossible, he is far too sensible to persist. I will put him behind me. I already have,' she added hastily.

'Of course you have,' Jane said briskly. 'It will be painful, I know, but better that than finding yourself married to such a proud, unyielding man. Now, tell me, how is your business prospering? Do you have many wealthy cits clamouring to employ you to teach their daughters?'

Lucy pushed away the inexplicable feeling of disappointment at the change of subject and conjured up a smile. 'Yes. I had expected a slow start, but it only took Mrs Grisholm, a banker's wife, to tell all her friends for me to receive a positive flood of enquiries and I now have ten regular pupils and several more appointments to call and discuss terms.'

'That is good news,' Jane said warmly. 'Oh, I almost forgot. You know that new rose-coloured gown I had from Madame Mirabelle? I haven't even worn it and I was showing it to Ivo in his study and he stood up and knocked his inkwell to the floor and it soaked the ruffle around the hem. My maid cut it off, but now it is far too short for me, but it would be the perfect length for you.'

'She could sew on a new ruffle, surely?'

Jane wrinkled her nose. 'She could, but we will never get a match—Madame said it was the last of a batch of French lace. And I think it actually looks better plain because it draws more attention to the lace at the bodice and on the sleeves. And that is ornate enough for you to need nothing more than your pearl ear drops. I think it was *meant*.'

'But you've had no wear from it. And Madame Mirabelle is not cheap. I couldn't—'

'Yes, you could. And I have had full value from it, believe me. Darling Ivo was so remorseful about the accident. He had to help me out of it before the ink stained my petticoats and so forth and then he felt he had to make it up to me...'

So Lucy went home with a new evening gown, the prospect of being able to dance again and a warm glow at the kindness of her friends. She only wished she could do something to help them in return.

Jane collected her in her carriage and Lucy was glad of the interior gloom to hide her blushes when Lord Kendall—*Darling Ivo*—greeted her. He and Jane were so much in love, she thought, firmly refusing to consider what memories the gown she was wearing might evoke in him. Jane came from exactly the same background as she did, the respectable squirearchy and country gentry, and here she was, happily married to an earl.

Who loves her, she reminded herself.

She also realised, as the carriage drew to a halt, that Jane's idea of what constituted a 'small dance' had changed a great deal since they were unmarried girls. There was a strip of red carpet from kerbside to the front steps, the footmen wore powdered wigs and Mrs Plaistow's modest ballroom hummed with conversation, laughter and the sounds of a good-sized string ensemble tuning up.

An anxious scan of the room revealed no familiar faces. Because of the presence of a number of very young ladies there were to be no waltzes, Jane told her and, as there also appeared to be a number of rather young male guests as well, the punch was much milder than the norm.

'Catering to the infantry,' said Ivo, grimacing at his first sip. 'And there are no card rooms.'

'Do your duty and charm the young ladies,' Jane told him.

'I shall begin by asking Lucy to dance,' Ivo said and promptly led her out for the first set.

He was a good dancer and Lucy enjoyed herself, felt the thrill of moving with the music and the newly discovered pleasure of moving in harmony with a partner. It seemed to amplify the impact. Ivo was not Max, of course.

Even as she thought it she and Ivo reached the head of the line and turned and she saw Max. She was standing still, otherwise she thought she would have tripped.

Lucy blinked. Yes, he was there, not watching the dancers but in conversation with a red-headed man. Then he turned and she saw him full face and almost missed Ivo reaching for her to promenade down the double row of dancers.

'Ivo, that was Max.' She had no doubt that her married friends took their husbands into their confidence. 'His arm was in a sling again and his face… Did he have a black eye?'

'I saw. He's been fighting by the look of it. The bruising has turned yellow, so it wasn't in the last day or so.' Ivo appeared to find that amusing.

'But what can have happened? Footpads, do you think?'

'Doubt it. Probably a bout at one of the boxing salons.'

'Surely not when his arm cannot have been healed.'

Ivo managed to turn her under arm and shrug at the same time.

'Men are so peculiar,' Lucy said, anxious and baffled.

When they came off the floor she found Jane and pulled her to one side. 'You told me that no one from the house party would be here.'

'No, I didn't. I said that none of the guests who were there with you and Burnham would be present. I didn't say he wouldn't.'

'You… You… Words fail me.'

'Good, because Lady Playfair is giving us a very peculiar look.'

'And the wretched man is hurt—his arm is in a sling, his face is bruised.'

'It cannot be serious if he is here, can it?'

'He's a man. They do any number of ill-advised, ridiculous things,' Lucy retorted and stalked off.

She found Max still in conversation with his red-headed acquaintance. He saw her and murmured something to his friend who bowed to her and walked away.

Max was sporting a fading black eye and a healing split on his cheekbone and his arm was supported in a black silk sling.

'Have you been fighting?' Lucy demanded.

'And good evening to you, Miss Lambert. I have been boxing, since you ask.'

'With stiches in your arm? Presumably you burst them.'

He grimaced. 'It was worth it.'

'And I suppose I should see the other fellow and marvel at your superior skill in making even more of a mess of him.'

'Actually, no. It was Trevor Atkinson to whom I was talking when you arrived to lecture me. I promised not to mark his face because he was going courting that afternoon.'

'Idiots, the pair of you.'

'But we felt much better for it,' Max assured her.

'How could you? You would have had to have your wound re-stitched and your eye must have been closed, never mind all the bruises I can't see.'

'Spiritually, I can assure you, we were greatly uplifted. Trevor worked off his pre-proposal nerves and I recovered my temper.'

'So what are you doing here?' she demanded.

'Not following you about, I can assure you, Miss Lambert. I am enjoying the company of my friends, assuring Trevor I will support him at the altar and regretting the absence of card tables. Naturally, I would ask you to dance, but as you can see, I am not equipped with sufficient functioning limbs.'

'And I would refuse in any case,' she said, then caught herself. 'No. That was rude of me, I beg your pardon. You are a very good dancer and I would, of course, accept.'

'But without pleasure?'

'With pleasure in the dance and irritation at your company,' Lucy confessed.

'But why? I am no longer pressing you to marry me. Why else should you be annoyed with me?'

'Because... I find you unsettling,' she admitted without thinking.

Max smiled enigmatically. 'How very flattering.'

'Oh! You are impossible.'

She turned to walk away and found herself face to face with his stepsister.

'Lady Sophia. Good evening. Um...what a delightful gown.' She sounded gauche, she knew, but she was so shocked by the other woman's looks that she found herself burbling. 'I am here with my friends Lord and Lady Kendall. Perhaps you know them?'

'No, I have not had the pleasure.' Sophia was as beautifully dressed and turned out as ever, but there were dark shadows under her eyes that powder could not conceal and she had lost weight in the short time since Lucy had last seen her. Her voice sounded artificially light and her smile was forced.

'Oh. Well, I must get back. How lovely to see you again.'

'That was Lucy Marsh,' Sophia said when she reached Max.

'Yes. I spoke to her.'

I unsettle her...

'She looked nice, I thought. A lovely gown.' Her voice was flat.

'Sophia, are you feeling unwell?' He had hardly seen her for the past few days and this evening, when they were ready to go out to the carriage, she had the hood of her cloak pulled up. Now he realised that he had not noticed her because she had been unusually quiet. She looked as though she had not slept for nights.

'I am perfectly well, thank you, Max.' That was definitely a brave smile.

'You look tired.' It was a test question—normally any suggestion that she was not looking her best, or that she might wish to leave an entertainment early, would be met with cries of protest.

'Perhaps, a little. But I would not wish to drag you away. After all, you asked specifically if I would like to come this evening. I had not realised we had been invited.'

They had not until the last minute. Mrs Plaistow had sent a note with the invitation, apologising because she had not thought he would be entertained by such a small affair, but her dear friend Lady Kendall had wondered if Lady Sophia would be there.

Lady Kendall was one of the coven, of course, and that made him wary, but curious. She was matchmaking, it seemed, because she had certainly not been acting at Lucy's request. Most peculiar...

But now he was worried about Sophia. 'Come, we will go home. My arm is aching,' he added, although it wasn't. Not, at least, as much as his head.

Max spent a thoroughly unsettled week. It was inexplicable and peculiar. He wasn't sleeping well—and he always slept well except when the nightmares struck. His concentration was all to pieces and he was restless. He waved away the invitations that Bentley gave him every day because nothing appealed and when he came back from his morning ride and was changing, Hobson startled him by announcing that, 'If Your Lordship is on a reducing regime, then perhaps it would be best if I were to cancel the preliminary fitting for your new evening suit.'

'I am doing no such thing,' Max protested as he shrugged on his waistcoat. 'I have no need to, I would hope.'

'So I would have said, my lord. Your Lordship has a fine figure: enough to give any valet great satisfaction in the finished effect, if I may be so bold. But, if you will excuse me—' Hobson hooked one finger in the waistband of Max's breeches that he had just fastened and tugged gently. 'An inch too loose, my lord.' He cleared his throat. 'I would not wish to presume, but perhaps it might be as well to consult Your Lordship's physician.'

He wasn't ill, surely? He was certainly not, unlike that mountebank Byron, on some ghastly diet involving soda water and dry biscuits. But Max realised he didn't seem to be hungry. In fact, he had found himself missing luncheon and waving away desserts.

Perhaps he should consult Dr Finnegan. He would mention it that afternoon when the man came to remove the stitches he had replaced with much tutting and disapproval after Max's bout with Atkinson. Perhaps he had caught whatever was ailing Sophia.

He went down to luncheon, for which he had no appetite, just to see how she was. The answer was decidedly wan. She picked at her food, but answered his attempts at conversation brightly enough and with a smile.

Max knew his stepsister. She was putting on a brave face. Not sulking—no one could miss Sophia sulking. No, this was different—she was miserable, but pretending not to be.

'What is wrong, Sophia?' He pushed away his plate and looked at hers, almost identical, with hardly anything eaten.

'Nothing that you can do anything about, Max.' She set her knife and fork down on her plate, her concentration apparently fixed on aligning them exactly.

'Are you unwell?'

'No. Just not… Just not sleeping, that is all.'

'Or eating. Or smiling unless you think someone is looking at you.'

She kept looking down at her plate.

'Sophia, what is wrong?'

'My heart is broken,' she said with a calm that made him catch his breath at the pain in it. Sophia raised her gaze to look at him. 'There is nothing to be done, I see that now. Anthony will not accept my money and he will not marry me because he cannot support me in the way he believes he should on his income as a clergyman. I expect I will become used to it in time and it will hurt less, but for now I find it impossible to sleep and I do not have much appetite. I am sorry if I am a blight on your spirits—I have noticed that you seem very unlike your usual self lately.'

'There is nothing wrong and you are not blighting my spirits.' *Except that I should have realised earlier how unhappy you were.* 'Is there anything—?'

'No.' Her smile was more genuine this time. 'Eat your luncheon, Max.' She got up and went out.

What *could* he do? Not go back in time and make West's father marry his mother, that was certain. He could hardly get the man elevated to a high position in a few months. Even if he had that kind of influence on church quarters, West had admitted himself he had no great vocation for the life, just the ability to make a reasonable country parson. If he would not take Sophia's money, or his father's, then he certainly would not accept Max's.

What was needed was buried treasure or a legacy from some distant relative, but he had no belief in fairy stories or any confidence that something would just happen to heal Sophia's broken heart. She was in love, he had to accept that. For her it was real and for the first time in his adult life Max felt powerless in the face of something that he did not understand and he had no ability to make right.

'Doctor Finnegan is here, my lord.'

Startled, Max looked at the clock. Two-thirty. He had been sitting here chasing a mangled piece of cold beef around his plate and brooding on Sophia's lover for almost an hour.

'Send him to my bedchamber. I will be with him directly.'

He submitted to having the stiches removed and to another lecture on the inadvisability of extreme physical exertion with half-healed wounds.

'There is no infection?'

'No, none.' Finnegan began packing away his instruments. 'A very clean healing process. Are you experiencing any discomfort?'

Max recounted his lack of appetite and loss of weight, restlessness, difficulty sleeping.

After prolonged prodding and probing and a series of highly intrusive questions, the doctor sat back. 'It is, I believe, all in your mind, my lord. You are worrying about something, I should imagine. I would not like to suggest that you have anything on your conscience. That just leaves us with the possibility that you are in love.' He chuckled. 'I jest, of course, my lord.'

'Of course,' Max agreed and managed a hollow laugh. It had been a difficult few weeks, disrupted and aggravating. That was all that was wrong and he was not going to let some sawbones' foolish quip get under his skin. He had, somehow, to make things right for Sophia.

Chapter Eighteen

Strangely, being exceedingly busy with teaching, meeting with prospective students and keeping her accounts did not prevent Lucy's brain from filling with inappropriate daydreams about Max Fenton. He would arrive on her doorstep, braving Mrs Todd and drop to one knee before declaring his undying love for her, a love that overcame every scruple about their inequality of status. He would send her letters revealing the torment in his heart because she refused him. Slim volumes of tender verse would arrive by every post...

'Oh, for goodness sake, stop this nonsense,' she said aloud and realised she had been sitting with her pen in mid-air while a large blot of ink fell on to her account book.

If her friends were right and she had fallen in love with Max, then there was nothing she could do about it. Thank goodness the thought had not occurred to her when he was asking her to marry him or she might have weakened to such an extent that she agreed.

People fell hopelessly in love all the time—look at poor Lady Sophia and Mr West—and they just had to learn to live with it. Not that she was absolutely convinced that she did love Max, she thought, confused.

If she did, wouldn't she think him perfect in every way? Wouldn't she forget his more aggravating habits and his cool perfection? This was doubtless some kind of foolish infatuation, probably an after-effect of her injury, the upset of leaving home, the disruption of her new life.

But she might be able to do something about Sophia. If Mr West did not want to be a clergyman, then perhaps he was suited to some other occupation that would pay him more. Normally, she knew, young men found such positions due to the influence of their fathers' friends, but Anthony West would never have dreamt of asking his father for help, whoever he was. But perhaps she could consult an influential man herself and see what his advice would be. And they did not come with much more influence than the Duke of Aylsham.

Lucy was on the point of handing a coin to the hackney carriage driver when the door of the familiar house in Grosvenor Square opened behind her. Goodness, but the staff were efficient.

'Thank you.' She smiled up at the driver and turned, feeling the smile freeze on her lips. Not a highly trained footman, on the alert. *'You.'*

'Me,' Max agreed. His smile looked as convincing as hers felt.

'What are you doing here?'

'Calling on the Duke. Have you any objection?' Max appeared to have recovered himself because he came slowly down the steps, drawing on his gloves.

She could hardly demand to know why he was here.

Perhaps they were friends. Perhaps they had business together.

'The Duchess is not at home, by the way,' Max said helpfully. 'Apparently she is visiting an elderly relative in Hampstead.'

'Yes, I know, she goes every fortnight.' Lucy found that she was walking away from the house, her hand tucked firmly into the crook of Max's elbow. How had that happened?

'So you were visiting the Duke yourself? He was not expecting you, I think.'

'No, he was not, but I hardly need an appointment to call upon a friend.'

Max turned into Charles Street.

'Where are we going? And why?'

'Berkeley Square. I feel the need to buy you an ice at Gunter's. You seem a little flushed and it may cool you down.'

'I am flushed because I am being kidnapped in broad daylight!'

'But not at all. If you do not wish for an ice, tell me where you would like to go?'

'Back to see the Duke, of course.'

'He was on his way out, hot on my heels, I imagine. He was good enough to spare me ten minutes, but he had an appointment at the Home Office.'

'Botheration. I particularly wanted his advice.'

'Can I help?'

'Hardly,' Lucy retorted. 'You are the problem.' Then she realised what she had said. 'I mean, not you, only—'

'I had believed that when I stopped asking you to marry me I had ceased to be a thorn in your side,' Max said, and she glanced up at him sharply. It was difficult to tell, what with the brim of her bonnet and the fact that he was looking straight ahead, but there had been something in his voice that caused a little stab, just under her heart.

'I think I would like that ice cream after all,' she said. 'They do a wonderful one with black cherries, Verity tells me. You would enjoy it.'

The fashionable confectioner's shop was as busy at that hour as it ever was, but Max found a table in a far corner. When the waiter came with his menu on a board he ordered the cherry ice cream for them both with *langue du chat* biscuits and coffee. 'Although I recall your predilection for more exotic ices.'

She waved that away. 'What is wrong?' Lucy asked as soon as the man had gone back to the counter. 'You called to see Will without him expecting you, it is urgent enough for him to have to squeeze you in to a spare ten minutes—and it would have only been ten, because Will, being perfect, is never late for anything. And you look—' She studied him, trying to read what was different behind that mask of composure. 'Unhappy.'

He would not tell her, of course. Lucy braced herself for the snub.

'It is Sophia. I am concerned about her. It seems she truly does care deeply for her highly unsuitable clergyman. What they need, if they are ever to overcome his very correct scruples and marry, is for him to find some better paid occupation, one where his birth may not be a hindrance. I have no influence in the Church, let alone in government circles, and I thought the Duke might be able to advise me.'

'But that is wonderful—it is precisely why I was calling on Will. He is just the person. Sophia must have told you what she confided to me and I am so happy that she felt able to do so.'

'What, exactly, did my stepsister tell you?' That darkness was back behind his eyes again, and Lucy felt she had blundered.

'It wasn't a confidence as such,' Lucy hastened to tell him. 'Just that Anthony never wanted to be a clergyman, but, without any other options or sponsors than Lady Hopewell, that was his only choice of respectable occupation. He cannot take chances with his career, you see, not with his mother to support. But Sophia told me that his education was very good—it was the one thing they would accept from his father—so I thought that Will might know of an opening for someone intelligent and honest. He is very hard-working and conscientious, you know. Even though he does not feel a calling to the church, he is doing his very best for his parishioners. And you know that he is honourable.'

'Yes, I do. And I knew about his education and character from Dorothea Hopewell, who knows about the circumstances of his birth. She could not break confidences, of course, but it is clear the entire blame lay with his father. Aylsham seems to have some ideas of how to advance West and has promised to get back to me when he has made enquiries.'

The waiter came with their ices and coffee. Lucy picked up her spoon, tasted and gave a little moan of pleasure. 'This is so good.' She licked her lips, reluctant to lose the slightest taste, and watched as Max sampled his.

He closed his eyes and she indulged herself with the sight of his thick black lashes, then looked away quickly when he opened his eyes.

'Did you know that the Reverend Sydney Smith said that a friend of his thought that heaven would be like eating *pâté de foie gras* to the sound of trumpets? I think he was wrong. I believe it may be eating black cherry ice cream and watching you lick it from your bottom lip with the very tip of your tongue.' He apparently ignored her gasp. 'I have to tell you, it is one of the most erotic sights I have seen.'

'*Max.*' Lucy swallowed. 'We are in the middle of Gunter's, for goodness sake.'

'Nobody can hear us. Your ice is beginning to melt.' He sounded quite cheerful, all of a sudden.

'I am not surprised! I hardly dare take another spoonful.'

'Please, eat. I promise not to make another shocking remark.'

They ate in silence. Lucy had no idea what Max was thinking, other than, apparently, quite shocking things, but she made herself focus on the tart sweet taste on her tongue and tried to shepherd her stampeding thoughts into some sort of order.

Finally, as she crunched the last of the little biscuits, she realised what it was. Max desired her. Why, when the world was full of far more desirable women, goodness knew, but he had enjoyed kissing her and wanted to do so again. That was all it was. And perhaps her stubborn refusal to marry him added piquancy to his feelings.

Max industriously scraped every last trace of ice from his bowl, for all the world like a schoolboy with a treat.

'Walk with me,' he said, putting down his spoon at last.

'Why?'

'Because I wish to test a theory. Because we have not been on good terms and I would like to change that. Because the sun is shining.'

He poured coffee and sat sipping his while Lucy stared fixedly at the top button of his waistcoat and tried to think.

Yes, she was in love with the man, she could not deny it now, not after the way her heart had skipped a beat when she had seen him on those steps, not after the way her pulse still fluttered. But what did he want of her? Kisses, it seemed, but something more? He wouldn't try to seduce her, would he? He was too honourable, she told herself.

'Where shall we walk?'

'It is not far to Green Park. We could stroll down to the reservoir, find a seat in the shade and watch small children feed the ducks.'

That seemed safe enough and excited toddlers, swarms of nursemaids and quacking ducks were hardly the sort of company a wicked seducer would choose.

'Very well, I would like that.' It would be a mixed pleasure and pain, she thought sadly as Max paid the waiter. He said something to the man, who looked startled, but he came back after a moment with a small parcel tied with a loop of string as a handle.

Gentlemen did not normally stroll along the streets of Mayfair carrying brown paper parcels, but Max seemed oblivious to the stares as they made their way southwards to the park.

They found a bench at the western end of the reservoir, a safe distance from shrieks, splashing and quacking. Max dusted the seat off for her, sat down and began to untie the string to reveal a mass of bread crusts and what looked like stale cake. 'I thought you might like to feed the ducks.'

'You are the Earl of Burnham and you walk through the street carrying a package of scraps and want to feed the ducks?'

'I haven't since I was about six years old,' he said. A flock of sharp-eyed sparrows had already gathered around their feet, followed by the inevitable pigeons. Ducks, alert to any likelihood of food, were already swimming towards them like a flotilla of ships of the line going into battle.

'I imagine there are any number of things you haven't done since you were six,' Lucy said. She threw a piece of cake to a particularly scruffy sparrow. 'Why have you changed your mind about helping Sophia? You were so convinced about the perils of unequal marriages.'

'She has changed,' Max said slowly, apparently intent on lobbing bread to a duck whose parentage appeared to include a variety of farmyard fowl. 'I expected tears, sulks, tantrums and slammed doors. My stepsister is not self-centred, precisely, but she is heedless, lacking in introspection, endlessly optimistic that everything will work out just as she wants it.

'Now Sophia is quiet, sad but controlled. It is as though something inside her has died, or has been so crushed it has changed out of all recognition. When I finally got her to talk she acknowledges that it is hopeless, that West's sense of honour will not allow him to make this match. She says her heart is broken.'

He took some more bread from the brown paper and seemed intent on seeing how far he could send the sparrows with a wide scatter of crumbs. Lucy waited: there was more to be said, she was certain.

'I believe her,' Max said abruptly. 'I thought that sort of thing was nonsense. But you know what affected me most? She said she would get used to it in time and it would hurt less. And she apologised for blighting my spirits. This is Sophia—if I held up a notice to say my left foot had dropped off and I was bleeding on the carpet, then she would be all attention, all concern, but otherwise she might not notice. Yet now, when she is truly miserable, she notices that my spirits are low.'

Lucy shifted on the bench so that she could see Max better. Were his spirits low? Other than worrying about his stepsister, what had he to depress his mood? He had escaped an unsuitable marriage, after all.

'Hearts cannot break, or we die,' she said, conversationally. 'But *something* breaks when a person or a thing that is truly essential to us is with us no more. And it changes us profoundly. Your heart broke when Julia died. Mine broke when my fa—when I injured my hands and could no longer play. I can see now that before I was so wrapped up in my music that I was careless of my friends, hardly noticed the world around me. Finding that world was all I had now and knowing I had not been as good a friend as I should have been if I had been paying attention, that hurt. It made me cross and prickly.'

'I noticed,' Max said with a little huff of laughter. 'Go on.'

'You were still a youth when Julia died, I imagine you were full of daydreams and idealism, not ready to be an adult yet. But you found yourself dealing with tragedy and loss and having to take responsibility for her funeral because her parents would not. I imagine you grew up very fast.'

'Too fast,' Max said, his gaze resting, unfocused, on the melee of squabbling waterfowl.

For a moment Lucy thought he was going to say more, then he reached out and took her left hand in his. 'What happened to your hands?'

He needed to change the subject and she could understand that. 'I told you—an accident with the keyboard cover falling unexpectedly.'

'It was not an accident, was it?' He was as implacable as a prosecuting attorney. 'A falling cover might break a finger, cause bruises or cuts, but not so much damage, not unless it was slammed down with force. Who did it, Lucy? Your father?'

She had not spoken of it since she had fled to London and had stammered out the whole story to her friends, almost incoherent through anger and misery and pain. But she trusted Max.

I love him, she acknowledged, finally facing the truth. *What change is this heartbreak going to make in me, I wonder?*

'Yes, my father. My parents, you see, are country gentry. Respectability is their watchword. They are also deeply observant of every dictate of the church, far beyond what most parishioners are, even the most devout of them. There is a little coterie of them, all, it seems to me, striving to outdo each other in holiness.'

'And they have not joined one of the more rigorous Protestant sects?' Max asked.

'Dissenters are not *respectable*,' Lucy said. 'The Church of England is. They were beside themselves with joy when I became friends with Verity Wingate whose father is a retired bishop. They never questioned what I was doing there at the Bishop's Palace and what I *was* doing was playing. Verity was pursuing her antiquarian interests, Melissa was writing, Jane painting and Prue studying the Classics. At home I was only allowed to play hymns and uplifting music.

'Sundays, of course, was for attending church twice. That day I had some new sheet music that Verity had ordered for me. I pretended to have a hacking cough—I made my throat sore with it—and, of course, nothing could be allowed to disrupt the service, so I was allowed to stay at home. The Vicar broke his leg falling down the pulpit steps and the service broke up. I was so lost in the music that I didn't hear my parents come in and Papa slammed down the keyboard lid. I wasn't fast enough, I was taken so by surprise…'

Max said something under her breath that Lucy was glad she could not make out. 'I suppose it was all your fault?'

'Of course. I brought it on myself by lying to avoid church; I was playing scandalous music; I was disobedient. The list goes on. Fortunately I had a small inheritance that they could not control so, when I was well enough, I said I was leaving home and coming to London. When they tried to stop me I threatened to tell everyone in the parish what had happened. Goodness knows what *respectable* tale they've come up with to explain my disappearance.'

'I know what I would like to do about their so-called respectability,' Max said grimly. He looked down at her hand, still in his. 'You know, I think you are using your hands more freely. Are they getting better?'

Lucy looked down and spread her free hand. 'I think you are right, this one is a little improved.'

Max opened his own hand, gently parting the fingers and taking hers with them. 'And this, too, I think. Which doctor are you seeing?'

'None now. The doctor at home said they would never get better, but gave me some exercises to help the stiffness.'

'I know a doctor who has been helping a friend of mine who was wounded at Waterloo. He lost a finger and his thumb on one hand. I can give you his name if they don't continue to improve.'

'They will never be perfect,' she said sadly, looking down. 'There is the missing fingertip and those fingers will never be quite straight.'

'Lucy.' She looked up and found Max was watching her intently. 'Do you insist that everything and everyone is perfect?'

Chapter Nineteen

'Do I insist on perfection?' Lucy repeated, puzzled. 'No, of course not. Only in my music. No one is perfect.'

'I wondered, that is all,' Max said. 'Was your music perfect before? Were you the very best pianist in the world?'

'Of course not. I was good, I believe, but never perfect. I could always improve and, if nothing had happened to my hands, I would have become better. But not faultless, I know that.'

'So what is stopping you playing now? The pain? The fear of failing?' Max was back to being the prosecutor again. 'Does this hurt?' He spread his fingers a little wider, hers still enmeshed with them.

'Hurt? No. But they are stiff. I could never be perfect…' Her voice trailed away as she realised where he had led her. 'But I never was perfect, was I?'

'And at some time in the past you had to begin, to learn. It would be like going back many stages and I should imagine you would have to modify your technique, but couldn't you accept that?'

'I don't know whether the magic would be there,' she admitted, shaken. Why had she never thought of learning to play again? Because she had been so unconsciously arrogant about how good she had been before?

'It is there when we dance. I suspect it may be there when we kiss,' Max said, his voice low and warm. He shifted on the bench, his broad shoulders shielding her from the group of chattering nursemaids farther along the bank of the reservoir. 'Shall we see?'

She should say, *No.* Or at least, *Why?* But Lucy knew neither word was going to cross her lips. She loved Max, he wanted to kiss her and it would be the last time.

So she lifted her face to him and sighed into his mouth as their lips met. She felt warm and safe, protected by his body, even though they were right out in the open where anyone might see. Oh, and the magic was there, coursing through her veins, hot and dangerous and fizzing with need and energy. It reached all those forbidden places, it made her breasts ache for his hands, it filled her limbs with the need to twine around his and her hands with the desire to rip off his clothes, her clothes.

Something—not amorous hands—tugged at her hem and Lucy jumped, opened her eyes and met Max's gaze. He looked like a man who had taken a blow to the head.

'Max—ouch!' She looked down. Ducks crowded around their feet and a goose was attacking her skirts where the remains of the brown paper parcel was squashed.

Max took one corner and shook it hard, sending bread and cake crumbs flying. The birds chased after them in a noisy, wing-flapping mass, leaving them looking out at the reservoir and, at least on Lucy's part, attempting to gather both wits and breath.

She brushed down her skirts. 'I should be going home. I have a lesson to prepare for this afternoon.' Yes, her legs would support her when she stood. A firm hand with her bonnet, which was decidedly askew, and she would be able to hail a hackney carriage without causing passers-by to stare.

Max rose, too, of course. All he had to do was put his hat back on to look perfectly respectable, although he was still holding the sheet of wrapping paper in front of him. Lucy held out her hand. 'If you give me that, I will fold it up and put it in my reticule.'

'In a moment.' He took a deep breath and began to fold the paper, making rather a long business of it. 'I will walk you home,' he said when he eventually handed her the neat square.

'I will hail a hackney carriage. I really should get back.' *I really should not spend any more time with you. Ever.* She began to walk the short distance to the nearest gate out on to Piccadilly.

Max caught up with her. 'Thank you.'

'For a goodbye kiss?'

'Is that what it was? I meant for your help and advice about Sophia.'

'Yes, it was goodbye. I do hope Will finds some way to help the Reverend West. I expect we may see each other again in the street or at social events. I do not think it would be a good idea to acknowledge that we know each other, do you?'

They walked through the gate just as a hackney carriage drew up and a portly gentleman got out. Lucy waved at the driver who touched his whip to his hat brim. 'Little Windmill Street, if you please. Goodbye, my lord.'

She did not look out of the window as they drove off and she managed to get inside her own door and take off her bonnet before she gave way to misery and dissolved in tears.

Aylsham, the Perfect Duke, lived up to his name. Four days later he called on Max with a proposal for Anthony West's new career.

'Is he competent at languages?' he asked after he had accepted a cup of coffee and settled himself in a chair in Max's study.

'I have no idea. He has a university education, but beyond that I cannot say. Why do you ask?'

'You are aware, naturally, that Brazil is a Portuguese possession? And, of course, Portugal is our oldest ally. There are enormous opportunities for trade—exports from Britain and imports that this country would benefit from. Trade does exist now, but it is not as well developed as it might be. A delegation will sail next month to take the new British consul and a number of, shall we say, trade experts, to assess the possibilities and to cement good relations. An organised and competent secretary is required. The opportunity to impress a number of influential people is considerable.'

'I imagine that various government departments can provide a number of suitably qualified men.'

Will smiled. 'But not anyone for whom I am the patron. I suggest that you make the proposition to Mr West immediately. It cannot be guaranteed, of course, and if his language skills are so poor that he cannot learn functional Portuguese in the length of the ocean voyage, we will have to think again. But the sooner I speak to him, the better.'

The letter was sent and Anthony West was on Max's doorstep two days later, leaving his curate in charge. No, he did not speak Portuguese, but he did speak Spanish, French and Italian and he was confident he could master it. The prospect of the Duke's patronage seemed to dazzle him, but he had no hesitation in saying that he wanted to try for the position.

'My birth will not affect this?' he asked abruptly.

'With the favour of a duke and your betrothal to the daughter of an earl? No, I think that may conveniently slip people's minds.'

West's mouth opened, but no words came out.

'If you still want to marry the chit, that is,' Max had drawled. 'It is up to you, of course, but I suggest that some arrangement is made that you draw on an equivalent sum from her fortune to match your salary and the balance is held in trust for the children.'

Max said nothing to Sophia until West returned the next day, dizzy with his good news. Max called her down to the drawing room, closed the door on them and ignored the long silence that followed her shrieks of delight. He thought he could trust the Vicar-turned-diplomat not to anticipate the wedding night.

Sophia's happiness was the one bright light in Max's life. He could see clearly now that he was in love with Lucy and equally clearly that she did not love him. The more he brooded on her words in the park, the more he came to recognise what had happened to him after Julia's death and the desperate words in her letter. He had grown up with a jolt, that was true, but like any very young man he had fixed some very black-and-white theories in his head and had not let them go.

Theories about his duty, theories about marriage and utterly unfounded ideas about love and its dangers were like those strange creatures turned to rock that scientists were beginning to say were not from Noah's flood, but the relics of some immeasurably distant past.

They had acted like a bulwark against loneliness and hurt and had long since served their turn. Now they only stifled him. But worse, they had stopped him recognising what he felt about Lucy, about seeing, right from the start, that something in her attracted him and that it was more than simple physical attraction.

Now what was he to do, when the person who seemed to give him the best advice was the last one that he could ask?

Lucy stood and eyed the piano in the Duchess of Aylsham's music room. It had taken her a week to work up the courage to come and ask Verity if she could use it and her friend had simply waved a hand towards the instrument, said, 'Whenever you want, Lucy dear', and had left her alone.

Now her skimpy reserves of courage seemed to have run out and the one person who had given her enough to have even got here was impossible to ask for support.

She sat down, adjusted the stool, opened the lid. Max had faith in her or he would not have suggested she try to play, so she would. She peeled off her gloves and folded them carefully, then did her finger-stretching exercises. She adjusted the stool once more.

Then Lucy closed her eyes, thought of Max and laid her hands on the keys.

She was uncomfortable and clumsy. The wrong notes, the lack of subtlety, the impossibility of playing with one finger slightly shorter than it had been—the result was awful. Dreadful. A travesty.

Without opening her eyes, she reached out and closed the lid over the keys again before her tears fell on the ivory.

But Max had reminded her that once she had not been able to play at all. She'd had to learn. Lucy opened her eyes, lifted the lid again and studied her hands. What if she thought of them as belonging to a pupil? How would she advise that person? She just had to forget that she was the one who was leaning to play all over again.

Adjust the position of her hands to accommodate the shorter finger, of course. Work with the finger-span that the pupil had. Do not expect too much from digits that were unpractised and stiff. Be patient.

She tried again. It felt awkward still, there was no magic yet, but if she took it slowly…

She did not have to be perfect, he was right. 'Thank you, Max,' Lucy breathed. She could not have him, but now she would always have this.

Ten days later she sat and massaged her aching fingers and marvelled at how much progress she had made. She had rented the pianoforte owned by Mrs Todd, who kept it more for appearances than anything, and she hired labourers to move it upstairs and a tuner to repair the neglect of years.

The new hand position had become automatic, the

span of her fingering had increased and slowly, slowly, the result was becoming less about technique and more about pure music.

It gave her pleasure and satisfaction, joy, even, but the old all-consuming magic was not happening. Perhaps that was because she was so much more aware of the world around her, of other pleasures.

There was the satisfaction of working with her pupils, the constant interest of the city around her, the company of her friends whose own lives had widened to more than they had ever been. Yes, perhaps it was that and not the endless ache, the hollowness in her chest, the absence of Max and the pain of loving him.

It might be that the magic would never return, she thought sometimes when she lay awake in the small hours of the morning and the satisfaction of her playing was hours away and the distractions of London were silent and still.

But now she ran her hand lightly over the black and white keys and smiled. There was a lesson in the afternoon with Master James Cricklewood, aged eight, one of her few male pupils. Master James was wildly enthusiastic, very naughty and a pleasure to be with. She had found a wonderfully thumping march that he would enjoy and she was looking—

The door knocker thudded. Really, she had to stop that ridiculous habit of stopping, listening, every time a knocker sounded. It wouldn't be Max, it would *never* be Max.

But there were feet climbing the stairs. Several pairs of feet. Some of her friends, perhaps, unless they were going upstairs. No, they had stopped on her landing.

Lucy went across, opened the door and stepped back abruptly.

'Mother?'

'There, I knew it would be a lovely surprise for her,' her mother said to Mrs Todd. The landlady nodded and went back downstairs, leaving Mr and Mrs Lambert on the threshold, their fixed smiles fading along with the sound of the landlady's feet.

Lucy's lunge at the door handle was too late and they were inside the room, the door closed behind them.

'What are you doing here?' she demanded.

'How could we not come when we heard what you had been doing, you wicked girl?' her mother said. She placed her bonnet on the table and sat down on one of the upright chairs, her husband behind her, one hand on her shoulder, for all the world like a portrait of rectitude.

'Your flouting of the Sabbath, your lies, your frivolous music—those were bad enough, but to learn that you have disgraced the family name by becoming a...' She flushed, her throat and cheeks flaming.

'Trollop,' Lucy's father stated. 'A nobleman's plaything. A harlot.'

'I am no such thing,' Lucy said hotly. 'I am a respectable pianoforte teacher. Where have you got those lies from?'

'Did you think you could come back to Dorset, to virtually our doorstep, and flaunt your paramour without word reaching us? How can we hold our heads up in the parish after this?'

'Who has been lying about me?' Somehow word of her presence at Lady Hopewell's house had got back, but how?

'The third parlourmaid is Jenny Hawkins and the Hawkinses—'

'The Hawkinses have that smallholding with all the chickens on the edge of the village,' Lucy said wearily. She should have thought of that—a big house drew in servants from miles around.

'And she came home on her monthly day off and told her sister Annie who works at the inn and after that it was all over the village.' Her mother shook her head, the picture of righteous sorrow. 'You arrive alone in a closed carriage with a man, you cause an uproar, then you flee the house. How could you, Lucy?'

'As all you have heard is unfounded gossip, you are very quick to judge, Mama. I was employed by the gentleman in question to help him with a family problem which, thanks to that intervention, has been solved. Because of necessary discretion some people got the wrong idea and I felt it prudent to leave. I am not that man's mistress. I am nobody's mistress and, if your sole reason for visiting me was to lecture me on the subject, then I suggest you leave. Now.'

'No, it is not the sole reason, as you should know. You have been compromised, now you will marry that man.'

'I will do no such thing.' Lucy fought the instinct to retreat into her bedchamber and push a chair under the door handle. 'You cannot make me.'

'We can make him,' her father said grimly.

'As you do not know who he is—'

'The Earl of Burnham.'

Behind her parents the door opened and Max walked in. 'Did someone say my name?'

Lucy sat down on the pianoforte stool.

'I was about to knock.' He looked around the room from her doubtless white face to the two middle-aged people in their Sunday best and his face took on the expression of icy control that Lucy hated.

'You are Burnham?' her father demanded.

'I am the Earl of Burnham, yes. You would appear to have the advantage of me.'

'I am Frederick Lambert and this is my wife. We are Lucy's parents. Now, what do you have to say to *that*, my lord?'

'Good morning.' When her father merely glowered at him, Max raised one eyebrow. 'What would you have me say?'

'You compromised my daughter!'

'I can assure you, madam, I have done no such thing.' Max looked across at Lucy. 'Unless, of course, Miss Lambert says I did.'

'*No.* I have not and I *will* say no such thing. Ignore them. They have heard gossip and rumour and lies and have seen an opportunity.'

'Wicked girl! We have seen our duty and that is to ensure this man makes good the damage he has done and marries you.'

'Mother, I do not wish to marry Lord Burnham. He most certainly does not wish to marry me. There is no reason why he should.'

'He should know his duty!'

'Which is to follow Miss Lambert's wishes. Not yours. Not society's. Your daughter does not wish to marry me and she has made that abundantly clear.'

Her father ignored Max, or pretended to, and spoke directly to her. 'I have no doubt,' he said, 'that you would not have strayed so far from your upbringing as to have wantonly given yourself to this man without the assurance of marriage. If he does not marry you, then we will have recourse to a suit for breach of promise.'

'Blackmail does not appear to be a very promising beginning to a happy marriage,' Max said with deceptive mildness. 'We are all aware, I think, of the effect of such a suit, successful or unsuccessful, on a lady's reputation.'

'What reputation?' lamented her mother. 'We will have to leave the parish, move far away where we are not known. I cannot bear the humiliation.'

'Your humiliation?' Lucy sprang to her feet and began to pace. 'Never mind mine! You listen to lies about me and do not defend me, you try to force me into marriage to save your own face—and because you would love to gloat about *My daughter the Countess.*'

'How dare you speak to your mother like that.'

Her father took a step towards her and Max moved, like a fencer going in to attack, and stood between them.

'You, sir, are the person responsible for the damage to Miss Lambert's hands, I believe.' The sound of an invisible rapier being drawn was almost audible.

'It was an accident. She should not have been playing on a Sunday. I merely closed the lid.'

Max seized the older man by the arm, jerked him towards the piano, pushed him down on to the stool and held his hand flat over the keys and took hold of the keyboard lid. 'I will *merely close it*, shall I, and we will see what effect that has.'

Lucy froze as her father, no weakling, struggled against the implacable grip. Max's hand tightened on the lid… Then he shut it, just as though he was doing so after playing. It rested lightly on her struggling father's knuckles. 'What a very strong man you must be, Mr Lambert.' He released her father and stepped away, still keeping between her and her parents. 'We can only be grateful that you did not slam the lid down in a fit of temper.'

She would not hide behind him. Lucy side-stepped and looked at her shaken mother and father. 'I think you should go now.'

Have you ever loved me? she wondered. Or, if they had, when had it stopped, when had she become simply a projection of their own vision of themselves—virtuous, godly, upstanding figures who were very large fish indeed in their tiny country pond? 'You can go back ho—go back to Dorset and tell everyone that you have cast me off. They will be impressed that you have done the right thing.'

'I will not leave you with that man.' Her mother was on her feet, trembling but defiant.

'I can assure you, ma'am, I will be right behind you,' Max said. 'We are all unwelcome intruders here.'

He did not look at Lucy as he opened the door and followed her parents out on to the landing. She stood listening as footsteps descended the stairs, two hurried pairs, one more measured, heavy, almost.

Then the front door closed and she ran to the window and looked down. Her parents had hailed a hackney carriage and she saw only the top of Max's tall hat as he stood watching them drive off. Then he turned and walked away towards Mayfair. He did not look back, he did not look up. He turned left across the road, into a side street and was gone.

Chapter Twenty

It was not until Lucy had fled the house and gone for a long walk around St James's Park that she felt calm enough to think about what had just happened. As she was growing up she had sometimes wondered whether those tales about fairies changing babies over, just to cause chaos in the human world, did not have some grain of truth. Perhaps somewhere there was a staid, obedient young woman who had grown up in a house full of cheerfulness and music.

She should feel sorry for her mother and father, she knew. They never seemed happy. Why had they married? Perhaps, thirty years ago, another set of parents had arranged a *suitable* marriage and the two of them had been forced together and whatever joy they had in their lives had curdled so that only appearance and respectability were left to them.

Anger and resentment would curdle her spirits, too, she suspected, if she slammed the door on them and left those feelings to fester. Perhaps, in a day or so, she could find it in herself to write to them, tell them about her life, send them news. But not yet. She was too sore to do it now.

And there was Max to think about, to feel sore over. Worn out with her angry striding, and with a blister on her heel, Lucy sat down wearily on the nearest bench and contemplated a pair of pelicans perched on a log at the edge of the lake.

They seemed wildly exotic in the middle of London, but Prue had told her that the original ones were a gift from the Russian ambassador to Charles II. She tried to imagine the man transporting the creatures all the way from Russia—in the diplomatic bag?—terrified they would expire before he could deliver them and having his fingers snapped at. As she thought it, a pigeon strayed too close and one lunged at it. The pigeon escaped, much to Lucy's relief.

Max had been furious with her father, she recalled with a shiver. His expression as he had held the older man's hand flat on the keyboard had shown emotions Lucy had never seen in him. He had moved, so protectively, to stand between her and her parents and he had refused to bow to threats and do something he thought she did not want.

But why had he been there at all? He could not have known her parents would descend on her like that. It could not have been to give her news of Mr West and Sophia, because Sophia had written to her to tell her that she was to be married the day before Anthony sailed and that she had every intention of sailing with him. Although, she had added, she had not told Max this. Lucy would receive an invitation, of course, but as the wedding was to be in the port of Falmouth, Sophia said she quite understood if it was too far for her to travel. Lucy wondered whether Anthony West was also aware that his bride intended joining him and decided it was none of her business to interfere.

Limping slightly from the blister, she began to walk slowly back home, giving the pelicans a wide berth. It made her think of that kiss beside the Green Park reservoir and the squabbling ducks around their feet. Probably she would not even have noticed a pelican attacking her skirts if Max had carried on kissing her like that.

She let herself in with her latch key and climbed the stairs to her floor. It was gloomy now and the curtain on the landing window was still closed. As she reached out to draw it back her foot disturbed something and she bent to pick it up: a little bouquet of rosebuds in all shades of pink, tightly bound with a trailing ribbon.

It had been right under the window next to her door, as though kicked there by a careless foot or tossed away. Someone carrying it upstairs could not have dropped it there. Yet it was quite fresh, only a trifle dusty, and one bud had a bent stem.

She unlocked her door and carried it inside, puzzling over it.

'Oh, what lovely flowers, miss.' Amy got up from her seat at the table where she had been darning stockings.

'Yes, and quite a mystery. I found them on the floor under the landing window just now, as though someone had dropped them.'

'Did you have any callers while I was out, miss?' Amy asked as she went into the bedchamber. She came back with a large flat package. 'I got ever such a nice material to make a new underskirt for that blue gown.'

'My parents,' Lucy said, opening the parcel.

'Oh, gawd, miss.'

'It was not amusing,' Lucy admitted. She saw no reason to tell her maid that Max had also called. 'Yes, this is very nice, you have such a good eye for these things, Amy.'

The maid began to repack the fabric. 'I...er... I suppose someone might have called with the flowers and heard...um...raised voices and went away again.'

'Yes, perhaps. Where are you going?'

'Just to check there isn't anything else, Miss Lambert.'

Amy reappeared a moment later. 'There was this card, right in the corner, and it's got your name on it.'

Lucy. Nothing else. No message, no signature. She did not recognise the handwriting.

'It's a man, don't you think?' Amy was craning to see.

'Rather hard to tell from four letters,' Lucy said, turning it over. She lifted it to her nose and sniffed. Dust—and just the very faintest hint of...spice?

One thing was certain, her parents would certainly not be bringing her flowers. But Max had been her only other caller, unless someone else had come and, as Amy said, heard the raised voices and went away without knocking. But why throw down the flowers?

But if it had been Max who brought them, if he had been on the point of knocking and had then walked in because of what he heard—then, yes, he might well have either dropped them, unheeded, or tossed them away because he would not wish to appear in the middle of an argument like a suitor at her door.

Which was the only reason she could think of why a man would turn up with an exquisite little bouquet, complete with trailing pink ribbons.

Lucy sat down with an inelegant thump.

'Miss?'

'I have such a painful blister on my heel. I walked a long way in these shoes and they are still too new and stiff for that.'

'I will get a dressing for it,' Amy said. 'And I'll put these in water.'

If Max was bringing her flowers, what did that mean? Was it possible that he had feelings for her after all? That he wanted to make a fresh start? Or was he simply another man who thought that if a woman allowed kisses she might permit far more?

No. This was Max and she loved him and she would not believe that of him. But how to ask him? It would be ghastly if the flowers were not from him. He might think she was angling for him to marry her after all.

'Save the ribbon!' Lucy called to Amy. She had an idea.

'Oh, yes, miss. It's a lovely colour, isn't it?' She came back in with the roses in the white china vase from Lucy's dressing table in one hand, the ribbon around her neck and some soft cloth in her hand. 'If I cut a pad of this and you slip it inside your stocking and put on some older shoes, that should make you more comfortable.'

'Amy, can you make a rosette with that ribbon? Something I could pin to my gown like a corsage?'

Amy looked up from snipping the cloth. 'Oh, yes,

that's easy to do.' She handed Lucy the little pad for her heel. 'I'll just get my sewing box.'

An hour later Lucy came out on to the street wearing a soft brown walking dress with a cream spencer decorated by an elaborate knot of pink ribbon over her heart, hailed a passing hackney carriage and gave him an address in Cavendish Square. She felt hollow inside with nerves, but she told herself that this was too important to allow terror to get in her way. This was the rest of her life, the difference between true happiness and making the best of things.

She had it all worked out. She would tell Max that she had called to thank him for defending her in front of her parents and to apologise for the embarrassment it must have caused him. She would say nothing about her own feelings, nothing about rosebuds. Then she would see what happened when he saw the rosette of pink ribbon.

After all, what have I got to lose but my pride if I make a fool of myself? she thought, gazing out of the window.

Then, as the carriage rounded the first corner, she saw a familiar figure on the pavement ahead.

The driver pulled up with an oath as she flung the door open. 'Wait till I've stopped, won't you, you stupid woman!'

'Sorry.' She half fell out into the road, scrabbled in her reticule and tossed him a coin. 'Max!'

Like most of the passers-by he had stopped and turned at the cabby's shout. He strode towards her and almost towed her on to the pavement out of the way of a coal wagon. 'Are you trying to get yourself killed?'

Lucy grabbed hold of his lapels to steady herself. He was clearly furious and she felt her dream of a calm meeting where their true feelings might become clear vanishing like a faint mist in the morning sun. Then she realised that he was far too angry for mere irritation at her carelessness. This was the anger of someone who cared.

'I was coming to see you,' she said. She kept hold of his lapels and he still held her wrist. Surely he must feel her pulse hammering under his fingers?

Max lifted his free hand and touched the ribbon. 'That is…pretty.'

'It is from a bunch of rosebuds someone brought me this morning. They dropped it outside my door.'

She was half aware of other pedestrians, of people staring at them as they passed. Max seemed totally oblivious to the fact they were not alone.

'Have you any idea who it was?'

'I think so. I hope I am right.'

His expression was no longer controlled, there was no icy calm now. A nerve twitched at the corner of his eye and she could see the tension in his jaw. 'Why do you hope that?'

'Because I would like it very much if that person brought me roses. Or if they came to see me bringing nothing at all.'

The world had gone still and quiet around her. There was only Max staring down at her, her reflection in his eyes looking back, the way his lips parted as though he was about to speak. Or—

'For Gawd's sake, guv'nor, kiss the wench or move out the way!'

Max's gaze did not even flicker as a burly porter

shouldered his way past them. 'Ah,' he murmured. 'The voice of common sense.' And he lowered his mouth to hers.

The now familiar magic was there, but something new, something better. Max was not kissing her because it was a pleasurable thing to do, he was kissing her because he had to, because he was compelled, just as she was compelled to ignore the fact they were in the midst of a crowd, on a public street. This was Max and she loved him and she was filled with hope that he loved her, too.

It was the near silence as much as anything that broke the spell. Lucy opened her eyes, blinked up at Max as he lifted his head. Around them there was a collective sigh.

'We have an audience,' he murmured and smiled.

'Go on then, miss. Say *yes*,' a female voice urged and was seconded by a chorus.

Lucy looked, blinked. They were surrounded. There were two women hefting a load of laundry between them, an errand boy with his mouth open, a porter with a parcel on his shoulder, Miss Wilkins, who lived in the apartment above her, a trio of giggling maidservants with laden baskets from the nearby market and the looming figure of the parish constable.

'Move along there, now, you're causing an obstruction and I'm not sure as that ain't indecent behaviour.'

''Ere, Albert Prewitt, they can't do that, not until she's said *yes*,' one of the washerwomen protested.

'I haven't asked her yet, ma'am,' Max said, making the woman blush and simper.

'Well, go on then! Better than that serial story

they're reading out loud every week down at the Fox and Geese, this is.'

'The middle of the street was not quite where I had planned to do this, but will you do me the honour of becoming my wife, Miss Lambert?'

Lucy swallowed. It was what she wanted and she was terrified. He was an earl. Her parents were a nightmare. They had already caused a small scandal. It was impossible.

'Yes,' she said firmly. 'Yes, Lord Burnham, I will marry you.'

There was a ripple of applause and a whistle from the messenger boy.

Max grinned and looked around. 'Hey! Cabbie!'

He bundled her into the hackney carriage and they sank back against the lumpy upholstery, side by side and silent.

'Did I just do that?' Max asked after a moment. 'Kiss you and then propose in the street?'

'Yes.'

'That's a relief. I thought I was dreaming.' His hand found hers, but they still did not look at each other.

'So did I,' Lucy confessed. She gripped his hand tightly. 'But I think it is true.' The nasty insidious worm of doubt squirmed, intent on crushing her happiness. 'I know why I said yes, but Max, why did you ask me?'

He turned then, twisting on the seat so that he could look at her. 'Because I love you.'

'Oh. Thank goodness, because I love you so much and I think I knew it even as I was on the Mail coming back to London. But I couldn't tell you, not when you kept proposing out of honour.'

They sat and smiled at each other with no need to

speak. Lucy remembered the number of times she had watched her friends and their husbands exchange long, lingering looks tinged with a smile and an edge of something that sent shivers to her toe-tips and made her feel like an intruder. But now she and Max were the insiders, this was *their* lingering look and the smile and the shivers were for her.

'Make love to me, Max.'

'Oh, yes.' It sounded like a vow. 'But not here. I have been on the point of making love to you under a bed, on a terrace and on a bench in Green Park and I have no intention of actually doing so in a hackney carriage. I told the driver to take us home.'

'Home.' Home with Max. She held his hand tighter and the nasty worm of uncertainty gave a final, desperate wriggle. 'Max, my parents—'

'I told myself that they are more to be pitied than anything. What a very joyless life they seem to lead. I told myself to wonder what had made them like that, on the grounds that to understand all is to forgive all, but I'm afraid that, unless I ever do understand, then I am never going to forgive them for making you unhappy, for taking your music from you.' He let go of her hand only to put his arm around her and pull her close. 'Perhaps grandchildren will soften them.'

'Children? Max, we haven't discussed children.'

'We have never discussed anything except my stepsister and your music.' The carriage lurched to a stop. 'We're here. Home.'

'One of them,' she said faintly as he handed her out. 'How many houses do you own?'

'To live in as opposed to those with tenants? Just the four. This one, Knight's Acre, my country seat in

Shropshire; the hunting lodge in Northamptonshire and a villa on the south coast that I bought last year. Is that enough?'

Max teasing her was new and unsettling. Almost as unsettling as the reality that she had agreed to marry an earl.

The front door swung open. 'Good afternoon, my lord.' The butler was surprisingly young to Lucy's eyes.

'Miss Lambert, this is Pomfret. Pomfret, Miss Lambert has just agreed to marry me. I do not expect that information to move beyond these walls at present.'

'Certainly, my lord, and congratulations. Ma'am, I am honoured.'

'Thank you, Pomfret.'

'Miss Lambert and I have a great deal to discuss. See that we are not disturbed.'

'My lord. Dinner, my lord? Lady Sophia is dining at Lady Henderson's with the Reverend West.'

'Lady Henderson is her other godmother,' Max said to Lucy. He glanced at the long-case clock. 'At eight, Pomfret.'

'Max,' Lucy whispered as he guided her towards the stairs. 'We are going *upstairs*.'

'My study is upstairs,' Max said. 'Where better place to discuss the details of our marriage.'

She did not know whether to be relieved or sorry. She had thought Max was bringing her home to make love to her. And then she had realised, the moment she saw the butler, that if he took her upstairs the entire household would know what was happening. So, if the study was up there, too, this was much less embarrassing and she was still with Max.

There is nothing to be disappointed about. She

scolded herself for wanting so much when, already, her dream had come true. He loved her. They would marry. She could wait.

Max opened a door at the head of the stairs and she went in to his study. Then he locked the door and went across to open a door in the far corner. 'This is rather more comfortable.'

It was his bedchamber. Max turned the key in what must be the door on to the landing, then another she supposed was his dressing room.

'And now, Lucy my love, we are alone with only the truth between us.'

Chapter Twenty-One

Now she was nervous. 'Max, why *did* you come to my rooms this morning?'

'To propose,' he said as he shrugged out of his coat, sat down and began to take off his shoes. 'It took me a while to realise just why I was feeling so very out of sorts, you see. I ended up needing to fight someone or pack up and drive to the other end of the country— and at the same time I hated the idea of leaving London. I couldn't concentrate, I lost my appetite, nothing gave me any pleasure. It took me far too long to realise that I was missing you and it was not until I looked at Sophia that I understood that I was in love with you.'

'But you went away again. You threw away the roses.'

Max untied his neckcloth and tossed it aside. 'What would you have thought if I had offered to marry you this morning?'

'That my parents had forced it on you,' she admitted. 'I would not have believed anything else you told me.'

'So I went away, almost convinced that you truly did not want me and that it was hopeless.'

'Almost?' Lucy put her bonnet on the dresser and began to unbutton her pelisse with fingers that had not fumbled so badly since before she had left home. She peeled off her gloves and did not look at her hands.

'Almost.' Max smiled, his eyes that she had always thought so hard speaking to her gently of love. 'I brooded and paced and snapped at Hobson and kicked the furniture and then told myself I was being a coward, that I should go back and tell you, from my heart, what I felt. Not ask you to marry me yet, but ask you if you could love me.' He stood and took her in his arms.

They kissed as he undressed her down to her shift, then broke apart for her to pull his shirt over his head. Max fought his way out of his breeches, she kicked off her shoes and snagged her stockings wrenching them off. Then they stood, just looking at each other.

She ought to feel shy. Max was naked—not that she dared drop her gaze below the middle of his chest—and she was, almost. Lucy realised that she was not embarrassed, but she was uncertain.

'I'm not pretty,' she said abruptly. 'I'm skinny and I've not got much bosom and my hands—'

'Aren't you pretty? I hadn't noticed.' Max stepped close, ran his thumbs over her cheekbones, teased one finger down her nose, traced the line of her lips. 'Perhaps a little pampering and being happy will put more flesh on your bones, but I am very fond of them, just as they are.' His hands gently cupped the small swells of her breasts. 'And these—' He dipped his head and ran the tip of his tongue over first one nipple, then the other through the fine lawn. 'These are delicious.

'And as for your hands, these are the fading battle scars of a courageous fight. Nobody is perfect, Lucy.

No one needs to be. I am certainly not and yet you say you love me.'

She tugged at the shift, pulled it over her head and then, shy at last, stepped close and curled one arm around his neck. 'I think you are *almost* perfect. You can be colder than an ice house in winter when you are annoyed and you are far too handsome.'

Max snorted.

Lucy ran her finger down the faint depression in his chin. 'But I even love your dimple.'

'I do *not* have a dimple.'

They landed on the bed, more by luck than judgement, she thought, and then stopped thinking, only feeling.

A man's body was a fascinating collection of different sensations and she found she was rubbing herself against Max as though she was a cat. There was the friction of hairy legs entwined with hers, the surprising softness of his hair at his nape, the smoothness of his upper arms with the hard muscle beneath that shifted under her roving fingers. His hands strayed lightly over her body as she explored his, caressing, not demanding, sending shivers and tingles through her.

His chest was even more fascinating. A dusting of hair that narrowed down, nipples that hardened and puckered to her touch and more of those impressive muscles. He was such a different shape, so powerful.

Then she leaned forward and touched her tongue-tip to his right nipple, and Max growled, rolled over, and she found herself between a very soft mattress and a very hard man. Her legs seemed to know what to do, curling around his hips, opening her to the urgent pressure. He moved his hips, rubbing against her until she began to pant and squirm. Vaguely, she realised that the soft pleading gasps were her own, begging for more, needing it all.

There was more pressure, fullness, an alarming moment when this seemed impossible, painful, not right and then they both shifted, stilled and they were one and it was...

'Perfect,' she whispered against Max's cheek.

Slowly, he began to move and the magic began, better than dancing, better than music. This was both of them, in harmony, giving and taking pleasure, making something that was only for them, building and building to a crescendo she could not imagine.

'Come with me,' Max said, and Lucy let go and soared.

'Lucy?'

'Mmm?' She was not certain where she was, but it was a very pleasant place to be when her body was as limp as a half-filled feather pillow and little lightning flashes of delicious sensation kept darting through her body. She let her eyes open and found she was lying with her head on Max's chest, his heart beating reassuringly under her ear. His arm was around her and his breath whispered in her hair and she knew she was home.

'Speak to me.' He sounded almost as stunned as she felt.

'I love you.' She felt rather than heard his sigh. 'And that was magical and mysterious and the most perfect thing that has ever happened to me.'

'You leave me no words because you have taken them from my lips.' She felt him shift and press a kiss to the top of her head. 'You know, when you first described how playing had made you feel, I thought about making love. That was the closest I had ever been to that feeling. And now I have felt it, too.'

The warm body she was resting on was so still that Lucy wondered if he had fallen asleep. Then Max said, 'We had better get married soon.'

'Very soon, if we are going to do this often.' Lucy found the strength to sit up. 'You look like a very superior cat who has stolen the cream and has eaten so much of it he cannot move.'

Max levered himself up against the pillows and smiled that slow, secret smile.

Perhaps after all I am not so very exhausted...

'Where?' he asked. 'St George's would be the obvious choice. The chapel at Knight's Acre is another. Your parish church here in London. Or your parish church at home in Dorset?'

'That is not my home any longer. Home is where you are.' She thought about it. 'Knight's Acre, I think, if that is what you would like.'

'It is. And my mother will be happy. She has severe arthritis and finds travel difficult. Will a month give you long enough for whatever preparations brides have to make?'

'It will be with my friends helping. I imagine that if a duchess, a marchioness, a countess and one very determined spinster cannot extract a trousseau for the bride of the Earl of Burnham from London's best modistes, then there is something very wrong with the city's shopkeepers.'

'Open accounts with whomever you need to and have them send the bills to me,' he said. He looked more alert now, more the everyday Max, not the new, sensual, heavy-lidded lover. 'No, don't poker up. I know by the time your friends have finished with you the total will be beyond your means.'

Lucy nodded. He was right and she was not going to stand on her pride and look less than a suitable bride for an earl. He had enough to contend with marrying someone from an obscure county parish with thoroughly awkward parents.

'And we will invite your parents,' Max said, as though reading her mind. 'It will be interesting to see if they accept. If they do, it may be the beginning of a reconciliation.'

'Soft words turn away wrath,' Lucy said. 'You see—I did attend church most of the time and listen, too. You are right, I would hate our children to be estranged from two of their grandparents, and they say that anger corrodes the soul.'

A clock struck, seven thin, silver notes.

'Shall I ring for hot water? I expect you would like a bath.' Max got off the bed and picked up a heavy silk robe from a chair. 'Put this on and take your clothes.' He opened the door on to the corridor and looked out. 'Quite clear. Second door on the left is a guest room. I'll send a maid and everything you'll need.' He turned. 'What is it?'

'I was simply admiring you. I haven't seen you all over at the same time before,' she admitted, considering fanning herself. Not that Max's self-esteem appeared to suffer from neglect—he stood there perfectly assured, without a stitch on. It was she who was blushing.

But when she reached him at the door and looked up into his face, Lucy realised this was not the composed, controlled man she thought she had come to know. There was warmth in his gaze and questions in his eyes, and an air of openness and vulnerability that she could never have imagined Max Fenton revealing.

'I love you,' she said and kissed him. 'I loved you before and now I love you even more.'

He took her in his arms and she felt the last of the ice shatter.

Lucy was lolling in the bath, trying to ignore the rapidly cooling water because she was so happy lying there remembering and looking forward and generally being happy.

There was a tap on the door and Amy peeped in. 'Oh, miss! His Lordship sent a note to say how you was staying for dinner and he'd see you home after and I wasn't to worry. But I thought, I can't have my lady eating dinner with an earl in her walking dress, now, can I?' She came right in, revealing a sheet-wrapped bundle in her arms. 'So I've brought an evening gown and the right slippers.' She gazed around her. 'Lovely room, miss. I s'pose you'll live here when you're married and a countess.'

'How did you guess I am going to be married?'

Amy just rolled her eyes.

'Yes, I suppose I will live here. Could you pass me the towel? Thank you.' She looked at the maid. 'What's wrong, Amy?'

'Nothing, miss. I expect you'll give me a decent character when I leave, won't you? Only I like being a lady's maid.'

'Of course I would—if you were leaving. But why?'

Lucy climbed out of the bath and snuggled into a vast length of very soft linen.

'Well, you'll be a countess, won't you? You'll need one of those starched-up dressers, not a girl from a village who can't do your hair properly.'

'You will learn how to do my hair—I'm sure you can get lessons—and then you'll learn how to be starched-up, too, I expect. I hope you'll stay, Amy—I'm going to need all the help I can get to learn how to do this.'

Lucy found Max in what Pomfret described as, 'The Small Dining Room, Miss Lambert.'

It was still large enough to hold a table that, with all the leaves out, could seat eight, but the two places were set together, one at the head and the other next to it on the right, and there were no servants. Lucy felt her shoulders drop a little. She had imagined sitting at one end of a long board with Max at the other and making polite conversation while a small regiment of footmen lurked around the room. Even her friends' dining rooms were like that unless they all gathered together for an informal supper.

'Come in. Do you mind if we serve ourselves?' Max caught her hand. 'It is all on the sideboard—or shall I serve you?'

He is talking too much. He is nervous. Max, nervous?

She felt better still and returned the pressure of his fingers. 'Show me what there is. It smells delicious.'

But Max was frowning, looking down into her face. 'What is wrong?' He traced a fingertip under her eyes. 'You have been crying.'

'Amy thought I would dismiss her and employ a

starched-up dresser because I will be a countess. And I promised her I wanted her to stay with me and she burst into tears and so did I. We have been having a happy weep.' She leant against his shoulder, just for the pleasure of feeling him, solid and strong.

'I suppose, when I am married to one, I may come to understand women better,' Max said solemnly. But there was a smile in his voice. 'Tell me about happy weeping when you have tried the pea soup.'

They talked about weeping and happiness, about how good the soup was and whether Lucy would like to redecorate the whole London house from top to toe. They talked about Max's mother and whether Max was absolutely certain she would be happy to move to the Dower House. Lucy complimented him on his carving of the roast guinea fowl and he wanted to know which type of pianoforte she wanted to be installed in each house.

It seemed to Lucy that they spoke of everything and nothing and it was all a miracle. Then Max put down the delicate silver spoon with which he had been eating the lemon posset.

'I may be hell to live with, you know. I am used to having my own way since I was eighteen and left home.' He frowned at her. 'You'll want to leave me after a week, I'm sure of it.'

'If you are difficult, then I will tell you,' Lucy said firmly. 'I'll be just as bad, you know. I have been getting my own way by subterfuge for years, sneaking off to play at the Bishop's Palace. And then when I was thwarted I left.' She picked up her spoon, eyed the posset and put it down again. Rich food, happiness and

lovemaking were quite enough for one evening without adding sweets.

'Will we have arguments?' Max asked.

'Terrible ones, I expect,' she said and laughed. 'Then
we can make it up afterwards.'

'Perhaps we could pretend we have just had the
most terrible, blazing row,' he suggested as he pushed
her untouched dessert to one side, leaned across and
kissed her.

Max tasted of lemons and sugar and wine and himself, an intoxicating mixture. He stood up, drawing her
with him, then, to her surprise, kicked her chair out at
an angle to the table and sat her down again as he went
to his knees before her.

'The door…'

'Is locked. And, yes, I know you do not wish to
appear to the staff later all rumpled.' His hands were
sliding her skirts up to her knees. 'I have no intention
of rumpling you. None whatsoever.' Irresistible pressure spread her thighs apart as the skirt rode higher
and Max leaned in.

'Max? Max!'

It was indecent, improper, outrageous and… Lucy
ran out of words. She should stop him. This couldn't
be right. She would push him away. Yes, that was what
she would do. In a moment when his clever tongue
paused, then she would… She would…

Lucy's hands closed on Max's bent head and clung
until she had to lift them away to stifle her own cries.

At last he sat back on his heels and grinned at her.
'See? Not rumpled at all.'

'Oh, you *wicked* man.' She swooped forward and
kissed him. Lemon and wine and Max and… Oh, good-

ness, that must be her that she was tasting on his lips. *Wicked, wicked man.*

'I do love you so,' she said and burst into tears.

More happy tears, Max diagnosed, as he got to his feet, scooped Lucy into his arms and went to sit on the sofa. He was glad she had told him about that, because otherwise he'd have been shaken. *More* shaken.

He couldn't claim to be inexperienced. He'd had his share of mistresses, he thought he was reasonably well practised in the arts of love and what his partners felt had always been important. But he had never loved anyone before, never felt this shattering responsibility, as though he held something very fragile, very precious, cupped in his hands. Making love to Lucy had been a revelation and the responsibility had almost brought him to his knees.

Had brought him there, he thought, and enjoyed a brief flicker of masculine smugness. Lucy's reaction from shock and outrage to melting, squirming, delirious female had been delicious. Exploring lovemaking together was going to be a wonder.

But that did not explain the way he felt about her. She was not a beauty, she had no figure to speak of, she was lacking in sophisticated conversation and society graces—and none of that mattered because she was simply Lucy and he loved her. Honest, prickly, brave, talented. Lucy. Somehow he knew that the nightmares that had haunted him had fled.

He found a handkerchief by dint of some determined wriggling and managed to apply it to her face before his shoulder was completely soaked.

She snuffled inelegantly, which made him smile,

and blew her nose with even less elegance and eventually emerged damply and smiled. 'Sorry.'

'Was it that awful?' Max asked, managing to keep a straight face.

'It was *dreadful*. Can I do the same thing to you?'

Chapter Twenty-Two

One month later—Knight's Acre, Shropshire

The chapel was all dark polished panelling and dully gleaming marble. Light streamed in through the high windows, painting the floor and the guests with rich reds and blues, striking gold off the candlesticks on the altar and saturating the masses of flowers with even richer colours.

Max studied the altar frontal in forensic detail. Counting the embroidered flowers was doing little for his nerves.

Beside him his best man, Trevor Atkinson, nudged him in the ribs. 'You all right, old fellow? You've gone awfully white. It'll be fine, just you wait and see.'

Trevor had married his Eugenia three weeks before and was radiating the smugness of a newly married man who did not have to experience this ordeal again.

It was all very well for Trevor to talk. Even if Eugenia hadn't loved him, her father and brother, unable to believe their good fortune, would have marched her up the aisle and into his arms. They were learning now that Trevor was not the amiable soft touch they had thought he was.

But Lucy had every reason for not marrying him. She was independent. She had her music again now. He knew he could be arrogant and icy and difficult to live with. She wasn't used to vast houses and numerous servants and—

The organist, who had been producing soft, twiddling music, opened up all the stops, or whatever it was they did, and the organ trumpeted, bringing the congregation to its feet.

Max swung round. *There you are. My love.*

Lucy was a very slender column of cream and white lace on her father's arm: repentance on his part, forgiveness on hers, Max thought. A fragile miracle that might last beyond this day.

Then, halfway towards him, she threw back her veil and smiled, slid her fingers from her father's arm and walked alone to Max, both hands held out.

It seemed as though trumpets had joined the organ as she reached his side.

'Have I told you I love you, Lady Burnham?'

'Not for the past ten minutes.' Lucy side-stepped into an alcove away from the mass of chattering, laughing guests and leaned against Max for a moment. 'And I love you, too. I thought I would hate this—all these people—but it is going so well, don't you think? Not that I can recall half the names, but it doesn't seem to matter. Oh, look, your mother is talking to mine. Do you think that's safe?'

'They've been in conversation for at least ten minutes, so I think so. Although it is mainly my mother telling yours that *of course* she doesn't mind being the Dowager Countess now, given that my wife is *such* a charming girl. Which means that your mother has to tell her what I paragon I am and as a result they are in perfect harmony.'

'And the Bishop was congratulating my father on my upbringing, which has utterly dumbfounded him. Oh, look, there's Melissa waving at me from the door to the little sitting room. I'll just go and sit with her for ten minutes and get my breath back.'

It took five minutes to work her way across to the room and when she did finally reach it Melissa promptly closed the door behind her and turned the key in the lock. All four of her friends were in the room and no one else. They sat in their wedding day gowns and beamed at her.

'We thought you needed a rest,' Jane said. 'We've got tea and we promised Will to make Verity put her feet up for half an hour.'

Verity, eight months pregnant now, rolled her eyes, but her feet were obediently propped on a stool.

'Oh, bliss.' Lucy flopped into the nearest chair, and Melissa handed her a cup. 'I didn't realise how much I need this.'

'It is a lovely wedding,' Prue said. 'I cried all through the service and even Ross had to blow his nose and clear his throat and pretend he wasn't welling up.'

As her husband, Ross, the Marquis of Cranford, was a tough, scarred ex-privateer, this was, indeed, something.

'And when you threw back your veil and I saw Max's face— Oh, here I go again.' Jane produced a crumpled handkerchief.

'Put your feet up, too.' Melissa pushed a footstool across. 'You need to be well rested for your wedding night.'

'Oh, yes,' Lucy agreed.

'Your face! You smug thing, you've already been to bed with him.' Melissa was never the reticent one.

'Of course.' *Just once, although I'm not telling them any more. And now I can't wait...*

'Where are you going on your honeymoon?' Verity asked. 'Last time you said it was still a secret.'

'Max realised that he had to tell me so I had the right clothes. We're going to the new villa he has recently bought on the coast and he is going to teach me to ride and to swim.'

'Very energetic,' Melissa said with a grin.

'Don't smirk,' Verity chided. 'You, Melissa, are the last of us unmarried, so our efforts must be focused on finding you the right man and then we will all have gorgeous husbands.'

'Not me.' Melissa poured herself another cup of tea and lifted it in a toast. 'Here's to freedom. I am coming to London. Papa is letting me have the little house he has just inherited and I will write and find myself interesting and handsome lovers and be an outrageous bluestocking spinster.'

'Melissa says she is going to be an outrageous bluestocking spinster and live in London.' Lucy curled up against the bedhead and waited for Max who, clad in his dressing gown and little else, was rummaging in a cupboard. 'What are you doing?'

'I knew there was one in here somewhere.' He produced a blanket. 'Come on, it is a lovely night.'

'For what?' Lucy slid off the bed and found her slippers. She was disappointed—she had waited a long time, it seemed, for them to be alone—but she was also intrigued.

'Star watching.' He turned back. 'Perhaps two blankets.'

They crept down the winding stairs from his dressing room like a pair of eloping lovers and then ran across the lawn down to the edge of the little lake. Max spread out one of the blankets and they sat side by side, hands linked.

There was no breeze, the air was heavy with the day's heat and somewhere, distantly, a fox barked. A fish jumped out on the lake with a splash and above them the stars were sharp and bright in the sky.

'I am happy,' Max said. 'It isn't something one thinks about, is it? You know when you are *un*happy or afraid or bored or having fun, but being aware of simple, plain happiness is rare. There is nothing to worry about. We are safely married, tomorrow we will slip away and go south and it will be someone else's problem to worry about our guests. When we arrive at the villa there will be nothing to do but make love and enjoy ourselves and get to know each other even better.'

He lay down, pulling her with him so they lay side by side. 'Look up. There is the music of the spheres, the celestial harmonies playing for us. And down here, on earth, we can make our own music, even though I cannot play a note.'

Lucy lay and watched the stars as Max shrugged off his robe and then parted hers, baring her skin to the soft night air. He began to kiss his way down her body, his own silvered by the moonlight, making her sigh and then cry out as he found her nipples, caressed her breasts until she was shifting, writhing, the scent of crushed grass rising around them.

'Now, Max. *Now.*'

His body was warm over hers, his weight both a prison and a liberation as she rose to meet his thrust, took him in, arched to match his rhythm, stared up blindly at the cold arch of the skies above them as the magic and the music took them both.

'I love you.'

Who said that? She did not know, only that it was true and a miracle and, like Max, she was utterly, purely happy.

She came to herself to find Max wrapping her in his robe, then both of them in the second blanket.

'I am going to make love to you for as long as my strength lasts and, one day, when I am too old and decrepit to do more than remember, I will still be making love to you in my mind and my soul,' Max said.

And Lucy laid her head on his chest and heard his heart beat under her cheek, and knew it was true.

* * * * *

*If you enjoyed this story, be sure to read
the first three books in Louise Allen's
Liberated Ladies miniseries*

Least Likely to Marry a Duke
The Earl's Marriage Bargain
A Marquis in Want of a Wife

*And look out for the next story in the miniseries,
coming soon!*